THE VOYAGE

BY ROBERT MACNEIL

NONFICTION

The People Machine:
The Influence of Television on American Politics

The Right Place at the Right Time

The Story of English
(with Robert McCrum and William Cran)

Wordstruck

FICTION

Burden of Desire

The Voyage

NAN A. TALESE

DOUBLEDAY
New York   London
Toronto   Sydney
Auckland

THE VOYAGE

ROBERT MACNEIL

PUBLISHED BY NAN A. TALESE

an imprint of Doubleday
a division of Bantam Doubleday Dell Publishing Group, Inc.
1540 Broadway, New York, New York 10036

Published simultaneously in Canada by Doubleday Canada Limited
105 Bond Street, Toronto, Ontario, Canada M5B 143

DOUBLEDAY is a trademark of Doubleday, a division of
Bantam Doubleday Dell Publishing Group, Inc.

This novel is a work of fiction. Any references to historical events; to
real people, living or dead; or to real locales are intended only to
give the fiction a setting in historical reality. Other names, characters, places, and incidents either are the product of the author's
imagination or are used fictitiously, and their resemblance, if any, to
real-life counterparts is entirely coincidental.

Book design by Gretchen Achilles

Library of Congress Cataloging-in-Publication Data

MacNeil, Robert, 1931–
    The voyage / Robert MacNeil. — 1st ed.
        p.   cm.
    I. Title.
PR9199.3.M3363V69   1995
813'.54—dc20   95-22795
                                                            CIP

Canadian Cataloging-in-Publication Data applied for

ISBN 0-385-46952-7 (U.S. edition)
ISBN 0-385-25559-4 (Canadian edition)
Copyright © 1995 by Neely Productions, Inc.
All Rights Reserved
Printed in the United States of America
October 1995
FIRST EDITION

10   9   8   7   6   5   4   3   2   1

FOR JIM

AUTHOR'S NOTE

Two former Canadian prime ministers, Pierre Trudeau and Brian Mulroney, appear in this novel. While their actual deeds and policies in office are rendered factually, the episodes in which they and their subordinates interact with my characters are entirely fictional. Their actions and dialogue are imagined.

One morning we set off, our brains full of passion,
Hearts swollen with rancor and with bitter desires,
And we go, following the rhythm of the waves,
Rocking our infinity on the finite seas:

Some, glad to leave an abhorrent homeland;
Others, the horror of their cradles; and some,
Astrologers drowned in the eyes of a woman,
Tyrannical Circe with the dangerous perfumes.

To avoid being changed into beasts, they get drunk
On space and light and fiery skies;
The ice that bites them, the suns that bronze them,
Slowly efface the traces of kisses.

But the only true travelers are those who leave
For the sake of leaving; with hearts light as balloons,
They never deviate from their destiny,
And, not knowing why, they always say, Let's go!

—from "THE VOYAGE"
by Charles Baudelaire

ONE

NEW YORK

ADVENTURE DIES IN domesticity; every man knows this eventually, and David Lyon was no exception.

Yet he seemed a man settled in himself, the last person likely to be tempted into behavior that might embarrass him or the foreign service. In any case, Canada's Department of External Affairs wasn't the place to look for scandal. In all the government excesses of the eighties—forced resignations, corruption, conflicts of interest—when almost every department had a minister in some disgrace, External Affairs appeared uncorrupted and old-fashioned, adhering to values fast vanishing in Ottawa. Its diplomats were known internationally for their intelligence and sound positions, even a kind of boyish enthusiasm for the task of world building.

David was proud to be part of this service, proud of its traditions and of his own achievements. As a young foreign service officer, he'd sometimes been mistaken for a more senior diplomat.

His height contributed—most people were forced to look up to him, at six foot one—but it was more his manner, reserved and faintly amused, that suggested a man of mature judgment. Now, with his hair receding, his emphatic brows and searching blue eyes added to this commanding demeanor.

Professionally he had grown into his looks. At fifty-two he was consul general in New York, one of the most senior career postings. And he'd "got his five," as they said, the top civil service pay scale EX-5. He had reason to feel pleased with himself.

And yet . . . all day he had felt vaguely dissatisfied. He'd awakened with the feeling and it had distracted him through all the meetings and calls of the morning. He felt it now while making conversation at lunch across the mahogany table in the consulate residence on Park Avenue.

His guest was from the National Gallery in Ottawa, an intelligent, sympathetic man a few years younger than David.

"I'm in New York on a buying mission. Confidentially—in the strictest confidence—I'm negotiating for a Rothko."

His wife, Marilyn, had invited this fellow to lunch. He was assistant director of the gallery; a useful contact if she wanted a curatorial job when she finished her degree. Marilyn was in Ottawa because her father had suffered a stroke.

"This is really Marilyn's field. I'm sorry she can't be here. She'd be fascinated to hear how you're going about it."

"Very carefully. The process can take years."

David said, "It must be quite an art in itself, knowing not only what to buy for the gallery, but how to buy it."

The director smiled and sipped his wine.

"Choosing an important painting and buying it isn't as hard for us as dealing with the reaction in Canada. When we bought Newman's "Voice of Fire," all hell broke loose, a storm in the media, outrage in Parliament, talk of a cabinet inquiry . . ."

"I do vaguely remember."

". . . why were we spending millions of dollars to buy American art and not Canadian . . . ?"

"Millions literally?"

"Well, one point five million U.S. for the Newman. Less than two million I hope for the Rothko. They started by asking five and I've gradually whittled them down."

The butler came in to clear the first-course plates.

"That was delicious."

"We're fortunate to have a terrific cook. The residence comes with the job, so Ottawa likes us to use it. You were saying about the Newman . . ."

"Oh, it tied us up for months. Work at the gallery practically stopped, and it'll probably happen all over again if I get the Rothko."

"Well, just to play devil's advocate, when public money is so tight, why are you spending millions to buy American paintings?"

"Remember, building the Canadian collection is still our first commitment, and that doesn't suffer when we buy internationally. It's a different fund. But we feel it's important to collect artists who changed the direction of painting. After World War Two, they were in New York. If we're to be part of the larger world of ideas . . ."

David listened, uncomfortable to find himself in any way out of touch with the temper of his country. His unease was vague, unspecific . . . like the discontent of a young man.

In a few hours the prime minister was coming to New York, and he would have to dance attendance.

The director caught his boredom, so David said, "Part of our job is to drum up interest in Canadian art, but I sometimes wonder where to draw the line: promote something because it's Canadian, or because in the larger sense it is good . . ."

He politely held up his end of the conversation until the director said, "I wonder if it would interest you to come and see the Rothko with me? I'm having another look this afternoon."

"I really wish I could, but I'm afraid I have too much on. The PM's coming in, so there's a lot to do. Can I drop you?"

"Thanks, but I'll enjoy the walk."

David would have far preferred the Rothko to his next appointment, as he would have preferred to walk himself, but he needed to hurry, and his driver was waiting.

The larger world of ideas. As the car turned down Park Avenue, he knew the director had hit a nerve. He felt chronically out of touch with the arts, books, music—anything he might have chosen to think about himself—because work constantly overflowed his time and filled his mind.

Objectively, he had every reason to be content. His three years as consul general had been highly successful, or so Ottawa kept telling him. Just this evening he'd assembled a prestigious Wall Street audience at short notice to hear the prime minister. His friends in Ottawa kept assuring him he was still destined for higher things.

And yet . . . his private hopes of becoming under secretary had recently evaporated with the appointment of an old rival, and there'd been no hints of another posting. The big ambassadorial plums—Washington, London, Paris—were all political, rarely given to career diplomats. New York might be the end of the road. Still, he'd known that uncertainty for months; it shouldn't have provoked this feeling of wanting more professionally and personally.

Personally, David considered himself happy. He and Marilyn had salvaged their marriage from the wreckage he had caused ten years ago. More than salvaged. Rebuilt. Their two daughters appeared to be setting out promisingly in life. New York was as stimulating a city as any they'd been posted in before, London, Paris . . . and yet . . .

Something was bothering him; it had been nagging him all day and he didn't know clearly what, although it wasn't the first time he'd felt this way.

4

TWO

FINLAND

FRANCESCA LOCKED THE door of the old Saab, hoisted the kit bag on her shoulder, then immediately put the bag down to zip up her anorak. It was cold on the coast after hours in the warm car, driving from Helsinki. She could hear the wind slapping and jingling halyards on masts in the yacht basin. The familiar sound gave her an ominous thrill, but she felt wonderfully clear-minded, almost amused, as she headed towards the shop.

The warm building packed with nautical gear muted the sound of the wind, although through the windows she could still see masts shifting restlessly. A man with sleepy features, the Swedish type of Finn, looked up from a catalogue and quickly registered the sexual curiosity she was used to, even now. Mechanically, her demeanor automatically frosting, she turned it off.

"*Goddag.*"

"*Goddag.* Do you speak English?"

5

"Oh, yes."

"My name is D'Anielli. I believe you have a boat ready?"

"Of course. It is ready." He lifted a file from the counter. "I know because we have nothing else to do. We have no other business this week."

He opened the file. "So. Baltic Thirty-five. The name is *Havsflickan*."

She laughed. "Sea Girl?"

He looked up, surprised. "It is funny in English?"

"In a way. It's not important."

"Everything is on board. Fresh water tanks full. Diesel, full. You have paid in advance. We have the check. We did not put ice yet. You tell me how much and I will bring it down. Then I go over the boat with you to check everything. Then you must come back and sign these papers. The other person with you, the man is it, has to come and sign too, for the insurance."

"He hasn't arrived yet. He's coming separately."

"So! When he arrives, he should come and sign."

"All right."

"Also he must give his qualifications to sail such a boat. He did not fill out the form."

"I put down my experience. I thought that was enough."

"Yes, yes. I see. Very good. You were crew on a charter boat. I see that. It was a big boat?"

"Sixty-foot ketch, Sparkman and Stevens."

"Yes, yes. But it was many years ago. And now the man who is coming, he will be the captain, so the responsible person, for the insurance."

She hesitated, flaring up, masking it with a smile. "I see. When he arrives, I will get him to come in. He's had a lot of experience."

"He is coming today?"

"No—tomorrow morning. He couldn't get away today. I came to get everything ready."

"Of course, to buy food and provisions. You can do that in our shop right here. We have liquor, beer, wine. Everything here."

"I saw some shops in town as I came through. I think I'll go there."

She didn't want him watching what she bought.

"I think you also need alcohol for the heater. It will be cold on the boat tonight."

Another significant look, which she withered away with a glance.

"If you'll show me the boat, I'll drop my things and then go and do the shopping."

In a few minutes he completed the check-out on the foredeck of *Havsflickan*.

"Spinnaker halyard and guys on the mast here, but there is no spinnaker on these charters. You don't need it with the big foresail. One-ten Genoa. Lot of wind this time of year."

The wind kept whipping her short hair into her eyes. She needed a scarf or hat.

"CQR anchor in this locker. Twenty meters chain, fifty meters nylon. Spare anchor in locker in the stern. Now we look below."

She was impatient for him to leave. He filled the cabin and lingered over the inventory, finding excuses to squeeze past her, some sardonic interest aroused by her obvious knowledge of boats.

"Extra life jackets up here. Wet suit in case of emergencies, because the seawater is cold now. Propane stove. Tank in the cockpit. You must turn the tap there before you can cook."

"I know."

"Volvo diesel under the companionway. You lift this step. Check oil here every day. Instructions in the desk there."

"Where are the charts?"

He laughed. "So, you are navigator also?"

"Yes."

"There. A full set, Aaland Islands, coast of Finland. Coast of Sweden. Rolled in this rack."

"Please show me how to use the heater."

The sweetish odor of wood alcohol filled the cabin as he lit the circular wick and replaced the perforated aluminum cover.

"You must be careful. Keep the hatch open a little bit for air. It uses up oxygen. You can suffocate. Better put it out before you go to sleep."

"Leave it on now. It's quite chilly in here."

"If you are too cold, you could come to sleep tonight at my house." He smiled. "My wife is there."

"Thanks, I'll be fine here. Would you start the engine just to make sure it's running?"

"Oh, it's running. Today we ran it for one hour, to charge batteries. You must do that every day, one hour minimum, and change the battery switch. Charge on position three, here, start engine on position five. Like this."

He hiked up into the cockpit, pushed the starter, and diesel rumble filled the cabin. Her heart quickened. The throbbing engine brought the boat to life and made her plan ominously real.

The manager swung his legs over the lifelines, then paused on the dock. "I think you know the boat quite well. Did you come here before to charter?"

"Yes, I did. But that was years ago."

"Ah-ha. The name D'Anielli . . . is from Italy?"

"My husband came from Italy."

His lazy eyes flickered to her empty ring finger. "Ah-ha. Well, good luck. I see you tomorrow when your husband comes here. *God afton. Lycka till.*"

"*Tack sa mycket. God afton.*"

She gave him a friendlier smile and a wave. Stupidly transparent —like many men. Years ago she might have teased more—just for the kick, for the daring of it.

She noted that the afternoon shadows were longer. Time to go shopping.

She was growing more excited with each stage completed, and

8

had to fight indifference to buy enough food. In a clothing store she found a warmer jersey, a woolen cap, and long underwear intended for cross-country skiers.

She put her packages in the back seat, because the heavy bag she had brought from Helsinki filled the trunk. It was growing dark as she drove back to the yacht basin, and she felt the chill of the surrounding water when she climbed down into the cabin. Still in her anorak, she relit the alcohol stove and stowed her coffee, soup, bread, salami, cheese, fruit, aquavit, and wine.

When the cabin felt warmer, she closed the sliding curtains on the advancing night and stripped down to pull on long underwear and dress again in warm socks, jeans, and the new jersey.

One task was more urgent than eating. Ignoring the roll of charts in the rack, she pulled out of her bag the two folded charts she had carried with her. In her Helsinki apartment she had studied them carefully and drawn in a course. Nervousness dictated one more look. She opened a bottle of red wine and poured a glass, then, feeling daring, lit a cigarette. She hadn't smoked for a long time, but in the shop she had impulsively bought the Marlboros.

With the chart table light on, she perched on the navigator's stool and studied intently.

A deep channel separated the yacht basin from the next island. It was almost straight, marked by flashing green and red buoys a quarter of a mile away, where it opened into clear water. A right turn then to a red flashing buoy three miles off. She opened the dividers and measured again, three miles at 115 degrees. At the red flashing light, steer 220 on a wide thoroughfare between the islands. By daylight she would be gone.

The difficult bit would be getting out of the slip and into the channel. She remembered how carefully the men she had sailed with had planned maneuvers like this.

It was not her nature to plan so meticulously, but, remembering their habits, she found the binoculars and climbed on deck. Yes, the red and green lights at the end of the channel were winking brightly. It made her nervous but elated to be so close to doing it. To study the way out, she walked to the end of the dock on the channel, where larger yachts tied up to fuel. There was a fresher smell of the sea.

Below again, she forced herself to light the stove and heat a tin of mushroom soup. She ate it with fresh bread and cheese and another glass of wine, then washed the dishes and stowed them.

The floating slips and connecting dock were deserted, the lights out in the office on shore. She walked up the dock to find the luggage cart she had noticed and pulled it over to her car. It took all her strength just to heave up the bag containing the inflatable dinghy and let it fall into the cart. She found it harder still to lift it from the dock to the boat's deck level. Perspiring, she finally squeezed it between the lifelines, into the cockpit, then flopped it down the companionway. As she wheeled the cart back to the shop, the air was crisp. Beyond the horizon of fir trees, the stars blazed cold and distant.

She had trouble going to sleep. She had set her small alarm for three A.M., turned out the heater, and got into her bunk fully dressed, with all the blankets she could find. Her head was cold and she got up to put on the woolen cap. As she lay there with the lights out, *Havsflickan* became alive, lifting and shifting with little movements not obvious when she was standing. The mooring lines creaked as the boat strained against them, then eased. Tiny waves made small chuckles and gurgles under the stern. Her mind was as restless as the boat.

If only others could see what she was doing, a forty-year-old woman, totally in command of her life. She had laughed with and thrown away so many silly men . . . always reaching farther . . . always sure there was more . . . men's eyes devouring her in the aisles of aircraft . . . the airline insisted they wear girdles to discourage pinching . . . such weird days . . . the eyes of older wealthy men who came to the fashion shows in which she modeled . . . looking right at them, provocatively, swiveling on the turns to show them more thigh . . . hot men, cold men . . . panting men, pleading men . . . none who satisfied the ache for something deeper, more settled . . . none with whom to be content watching the snow fall softly on a winter afternoon . . . as she often had with Kaarina . . . listening to music . . . reading . . . no man except David . . . who never stayed long enough to make it work . . . because she always found ways to push him away.

She turned on the reading lamp and got out of the bunk to rummage in her bag. In a small purse she found the bracelet, rows of tiny gold beads separating larger balls, showing holes in the thin gold from constant wearing. She had twice had it restrung. She put it on her wrist, got back into the bunk, and turned out the light. He'd given it to her seventeen or eighteen years ago . . . she couldn't remember years . . . before she was pregnant with Colin, the name Frederico hated but she'd insisted on . . . the Italians couldn't pronounce it . . . or with Samantha . . . she must have been seven or eight months when she met David in Brussels . . . up the caged lift in the Métropole . . . lying on his bed on the rainy afternoon . . . wanting him despite her huge tummy . . . If only it had been his child . . .

THREE

NEW YORK

IN THE PRIVATE dining room of the Metropolitan Club, the prime minister rose to speak. The clitter of coffee cups subsided as two dozen senior Wall Street types settled, in polite skepticism, to be massaged by Brian Mulroney.

The PM went strangely out of his way in responding to David's introduction.

". . . just add that David Lyon is one of Canada's top career diplomats, a man of wide experience, seasoned in many important assignments—Washington, London, Paris, Geneva, Africa, Helsinki . . . he played an important part in negotiating the Helsinki Accords . . ."

Excessive—and unusual, David felt. Someone in Ottawa must have dipped into his file.

"That we choose to put one of our foremost diplomatic talents as consul general in New York, in addition to our ambassadors in

Washington and at the United Nations, indicates the great importance we place on this city. Whatever else, in communications, national news media, arts, and culture, but above all in finance, Canadians know that the heart of your great nation still beats here in New York City!"

They almost applauded. David could feel the innocent compliments generating a little ripple of pleasure, even among these shrewd professionals.

The PM needed their good will. His government was in debt up to the eyeballs, and these men—from Solomon Brothers, Kidder Peabody, Goldman Sachs, First Boston, Merrill Lynch, and the like —marketed the bonds that financed the debt. Uncertainty over Quebec's threat to secede from Canada, plus the high rate of government borrowing, had been making the market jittery. The prime minister wanted to calm it, and David had arranged the dinner for that purpose.

". . . so Canada feels . . . if we can make it in New York, we can make it anywhere!"

They all laughed.

By any nation's measure, Mulroney was skilled, nimble, and worldly, but tonight David thought he seemed provincial. Perhaps his clothes fitted too well, the perfectly cut suit, shirt cuffs showing a precise inch. Even if there were no old New York money present, the setting made the PM seem a little parvenu.

And there was the elusive interplay of a salesman's bravado and self-abasement.

He was doing it now . . . stressing his loyal support for President Bush in the Gulf War . . . the American press so often ignored Canada's role . . . extolling Bush's masterful leadership, adding, mock ruefully, he only wished he could borrow a little of the president's soaring popularity.

Six months after Desert Storm, George Bush, the most untalented politician of his time, still glowed with an incandescent popularity, approval ratings in the 90s. Yet none of it rubbed off on

Mulroney. Indeed, his coziness with Bush was probably one of the factors making him so unpopular at home. His poll ratings had recently dropped to 12 percent.

Perfectly bilingual, swift on his feet, Mulroney ran circles around Bush at their awkward joint news conferences—the parts the U.S. networks rarely showed. But tonight the PM seemed to be selling too hard.

It wasn't just the too-ingratiating personality. It was the unseemly posture he put Canada in—the suppliant, fawning, sucking up. Canadians wanted a PM on good terms with the U.S., not constantly kissing Uncle Sam's ass.

Mulroney had reached his principal theme, defending his fiscal and economic policies . . . he had *made* the difficult choices . . . he was *cutting* the deficit . . . the standard defense. No one listened to it now in Canada, and no one believed it on Wall Street. The markets thought the deficits too high, the ratio of federal and provincial debt to GDP alarming. There was a whisper that Canadian bond ratings might drop.

The PM was winding up, his rich voice vibrant and confident. He was either an amazing actor or incredibly self-deceiving. Only the crestfallen eyes showed anxiety.

He was delighted with the warm response and commended David for the stellar guest list, as they strolled around the block on Fifth Avenue to the Pierre Hotel. Indeed, he treated David like a close friend, very solicitous about Marilyn's father.

"I'll go out to see them in the next few days," the PM said.

And then the bombshell—taking David absolutely by surprise. When they reached the Pierre entrance, the PM asked him to come up for a moment.

Settled comfortably, the expensively tailored suit jacket casually yet carefully dropped on a chair back, his tie loosened, he said, "So you're fifty-two, David."

"That's right, Prime Minister."

"Right. Well, so am I. Lots of time ahead for both of us, isn't there?"

David wondered what in hell was coming next in this velvet voice Mulroney used when it suited him.

"You've been just about everywhere, haven't you—Africa, Helsinki, London, Washington, Moscow—we had a good time with you and Marilyn in Moscow . . ."

"Washington was in the sixties, my first posting."

"I know, but you've been around a lot, and you've had senior jobs in Ottawa—assistant under secretary . . ." He began ticking them off. "What do you think the next step in your career should be?"

"Well, I don't know, actually. I haven't given it much thought."

The PM's scoop jaw and little purse-mouth wore the smile cartoonists were always satirizing.

"You must have given it some thought, David. Everyone does, especially at External. I've never seen such a nest of career calculators."

David laughed, intrigued.

"I've had my eye on you since we met in Moscow. I think you have potential far beyond what you've accomplished. So I have a proposition. There's no obvious job for you in External. We both know that. But what I propose can take you beyond all that in one leap—well, two leaps."

He leaned forward intimately. His voice had become a beguiling purr.

"I want you in Parliament, David. We'll find a suitable riding. Since you're Nova Scotian, it can be there. An older member can step aside—we can arrange a retirement, appointment to the Senate —call a by-election, and guarantee you a seat. Once you're in the House, I'll make you a minister, bring you into the cabinet. Something not too exposed at first, to season you a little, let you get your sea legs in the House, then, before the election, I'd make you Minister of External Affairs."

"My God! I certainly didn't expect that!" David said.

"No, no—hear me out. Times of change, David, are times of tremendous opportunity. Canada's role in the world, so difficult during the Cold War, so frustrating at times, can now grow phenomenally. Conditions are ripe to bring our values as a nation to bear on global problems that are just emerging . . ."

Growing orotund, making David feel part of an audience, not a conversation.

". . . I can see Canada playing a part on the world stage as great as in the forties and fifties—the golden years—when men like your father-in-law made our influence greater than our actual power. But I need at my right hand a man capable of seeing that brave future, a man of leadership."

He paused, and his voice slid into its most intimate register. "I think that man is David Lyon!"

Even before this peroration rolled to a stop, David had swiftly considered the key issues. Of course he could run the department. And the intellectual challenge—to shape foreign policy, not serve it —gave him no anxiety. Only the politics involved gave him pause. Besides, it was habit with him to express excitement with a modest demur.

"I'm really out of my depth in politics."

"Come on, David, don't give me that stuff! You guys live and breathe politics every fucking day. Your paper on the Trudeau years—"

A paper David had written six years ago for private circulation in the Policy Planning Group.

"I didn't know you'd seen that."

"Nothing in government's really private, David. That wasn't just a foreign policy analysis. It was a highly political document—which is why someone made sure I saw it. I want you to think about this seriously. Call me when you've decided. Not through channels. Call me personally. Take my private phone numbers."

David sat facing this man who was so much despised. The polls rained fury on him each week, yet he was still prime minister, still carried his cabinet and his majority in Parliament, could still raise taxes and pass laws. And he exuded confidence.

"I presume this means you're not serious about the UN job."

The PM laughed. "That's George Bush's little pipe dream, but it can't happen. The Africans have the Third World vote."

That sounded genuine.

"Besides, David, you know I can't leave Canada like this . . . Quebec and the constitution festering . . . the economy to turn around. I'm still prime minister. For two more years I'll have a working majority in the House, and I intend to use it. That's where I belong, David, and that's where you belong."

David left the hotel. The October night was clear and mild. He told his driver he'd walk the few blocks to the apartment at Park and Sixty-second.

Minister of External Affairs sounded terrific. So did Secretary of State for External Affairs, the snootier title from the days when External could look down its nose at the rest of government.

Of course, Mulroney could be turfed out by the voters. He had brought no particular vision or principles to the office of prime minister. He was essentially a deal-maker, always improvising.

But, what the hell! If the prime minister of Canada wanted him at the top, should he just dismiss it? What else could life offer as exciting?

FOUR

FINLAND

THE *PEEP-PEEP* of the little alarm found Francesca instantly and nervously awake, the darkness dense in the freezing cabin. She shrugged out of the warm cocoon of blankets, donned the anorak, and lit the stove for coffee. Necessity forced her to use the small head, its compartment even colder than the cabin.

The stars were still diamond bright when she pulled back the hatch cover, warm inside all the extra clothing, but shivering from nervousness. At least the air was still, no wind to make boat handling awkward.

She would wait until the last moment before starting the noisy engine, but switched the battery in case she forgot later. She loosened the spring lines from their cleats on deck, then jumped ashore to free them from the mooring posts. Coiling the lines wet with seawater numbed her hands, and the weight of the coils made her arms ache. She had forgotten how heavy the lines were. She tidied them into the cockpit locker as she remembered, leaving only one stern and bow line attached.

Below again, she made coffee and warmed her hands on the mug.

Almost ready.

She remembered the lock on the wheel, climbed up to unscrew it, and removed the chrome cover from the compass binnacle. But she couldn't see the compass card. Oh, there were so many things to remember! She went below to the electrical panel and flipped the instrument display switch. Climbing back to the cockpit, she found it had lit the depth sounder, log, and wind-speed indicator, but not the compass. Below again, warm now from the exercise, she found the navigation lights and flipped the switch, but that illuminated more than the compass; she found masthead, stern, and running lights all blazing conspicuously into the darkness. Below again to douse them. The compass wouldn't be needed until later. Once out of the docks and into the channel she could steer by the flashing buoys at the entrance.

Everything was ready. She could go. She let out a long breath. She needed a few minutes to calm down. It was only 3:45 and totally dark, no sign of anyone about. She made a second cup of coffee and lit a cigarette to calm her nerves.

At 3:55 she swallowed the last gulp of black coffee and heard the cigarette hiss out when she tossed it over the side.

Now!

When she sailed here with David, he would start the engine before letting go the last lines. Instead, she cast off both lines and quickly climbed aboard in case *Havsflickan* began to drift. But the yacht lay perfectly still against the floating dock, like a patient horse.

Finally, now or never. Shaking a little, she advanced the throttle and pressed the button. The cold engine revved loudly and barrenly. It made so much noise, she released the button, then held her breath, pushed again, and felt the immediate rumble and vibration. Quickly! She pulled the lever through neutral into reverse, and the boat began to move astern. When the bow looked clear of the dock, she spun the wheel all the way to the left and gave the engine a short hard kick with the throttle. The louder noise shattered the morning silence. As the stern began to swing, she reversed the wheel and nudged the lever to forward. There was a jolt and a heavy bump. Oh, God! She'd hit the other dock! No, the docks were too far away. She looked over the stern. She had forgotten the dinghy. Terrified, she hauled in the slack painter and made it fast. How stupid she would have looked, drifting helplessly, immobilized by a dinghy line fouling the propeller. She grabbed the wheel again as the yacht picked up forward speed.

She had done all this many times, but it was totally different without David or Geoffrey nearby to remind her of each move. She eased the throttle to quiet the engine as *Havsflickan* slipped quickly between the shadowy lines of moored boats. It seemed lighter on the water, and the main dock coming up was a sharp edge against the starlit water beyond. She turned left, giving the dock a wide berth, and felt the fresher air in the channel. Then panic. There was no sign of the flashing lights, nothing but the black silhouettes of fir trees menacing against the sky. She must have the wrong heading. Disoriented and breathless, she scrambled for the binoculars, aimed them, and found the lights past where she expected, winking brightly red and green.

Now she felt wonderful, except that her hands were freezing on the stainless steel wheel. No time to get the gloves from her bag. She put one cold hand in her anorak pocket and steered with the other.

The stars were glorious, shimmering in the still water ahead. The channel was too narrow for her to risk leaving the wheel for more coffee, so she waited, glancing astern. The yacht basin showed no sudden signs of life. As the diesel throbbed quietly underfoot, the flashing lights grew bigger, and at 4:12 she passed between them, the whole boat for a second bathed in red, then green.

She left the wheel to duck below, grab her gloves, and flick on the navigation lights, making the compass glow a cheery pink. Right turn to 115 degrees, past the ornate E for East. When she looked up, she caught the wink of the red flashing buoy three miles ahead, almost on the nose.

Tears filled her eyes.

"Don't be stupid!" she said aloud and then shouted at the sky, "Don't be stupid!"

She heard her voice echo back from the nearby shore.

"Fuck you!" she shouted and laughed, and the shore shouted back, "Fuck you!"

"Fuck you, *tout le monde* . . ."

But the echo had gone.

Relaxed now, she locked the wheel and went down to make more coffee. With that and another cigarette she came back up to watch the dawn.

It was true. Busy doing something risky and exciting, you couldn't think about anything else. Like sex—but more mind-filling than sex.

Havsflickan was tracking nicely, almost holding her course on the locked wheel. There was plenty of sea room. She went below again and rummaged in her kit bag, feeling for cassettes until she found what she wanted. She pushed it into the slot on the radio over the navigation table, and music filled the speakers in the cabin and outside in the cockpit.

She took the wheel again and listened.

Beethoven's Sonata Number 30 in A-flat, played by Alfred Brendel. She had heard it with David at Carnegie Hall during the week in New York that she had loved and he had hated. Later she had bought the cassette and carried it for years, replacing it when it wore out, like the gold bracelet.

The music seemed to fill the sky waiting for dawn to come over the Aaland Islands, over Finland and Sweden, over the Baltic, over the world. It filled her whole universe. Later she would play Sibelius for Kaarina. Who was all this really for—David or Kaarina? Kaarina who was dead; David who was dead for her.

FIVE

NEW YORK

EAGER AS HE was to talk with Marilyn the next morning, David could manage only a few quick words on the phone, because the car was waiting to take him to La Guardia with the PM.

"Hi, sweetie."

"How's your dad this morning?"

"He's still asleep. How was your big dinner? Tedious or fun?"

"You're not going to believe what he asked me after dinner."

"Ambassador in Washington?"

"Not bad! He asked me up to his suite at the Pierre for a chat afterwards."

"My, my! What did he say?"

"That if I'd quit External and enter Parliament, he'd make me a junior minister for a while, then Minister of External Affairs—"

"Oh, David!"

"—before the next election."

"Well, that's wonderful—in a way. But it's also—"

"I know, it's very dodgy."

"You know, if only it wasn't *this* government . . . *his* government."

"I know. I know. I've been thinking that all night. I wanted to call you, but I didn't want to wake the house up."

"Are you tempted?"

"Yes. And no. Back and forth. Look, I've got to run to take him to the airport. I'll call later so we can really talk about it. Probably this evening."

"Do you have to give him an answer right away?"

"No. We have a few days to think. Oh, he asked after your dad. He said he'd come out to see you."

"Well, that's very sweet. Just as well Daddy can't talk, considering how he feels about Mulroney."

"Bye. Got to go. Talk to you later."

As David shook hands at the airport, the PM murmured, "Since you're a few years shy of full pension, we can probably do something. Perhaps the party can help . . . a little trust fund perhaps."

That gave David even more to think of in the slow rush hour traffic back into Manhattan. A sniff of the little corruptions of political life. That was one of the problems with Mulroney: he'd done many things David considered sensible, yet managed to surround himself with an appearance of sleaze. Still, the career habit of being apolitical was very strong. Foreign service officers couldn't afford to be squeamish about the politicians the voters sent them.

But this would be entirely different. He would have to *make* policy with this prime minister, debate it in the cabinet, defend it in Parliament and with the public . . . share responsibility, be held accountable. He'd have to visit all his present colleagues in embassies around the world to sell the policy. And he knew how sardonic and derisive they could be in such briefings.

Something he'd forgotten to tell Marilyn: before making the big offer, the PM had said there was nothing obvious ahead for David at External. A very big point, and he'd pushed it aside.

He made it to the Exxon Building just in time for his executive committee at nine-thirty. The consulate general employed a hundred people, and administration alone took a lot of time. With phone calls to return, a lunch, and another meeting, it wasn't until midafternoon that David again had a few minutes to clear his mind and think.

Because of Marilyn's absence, they had canceled a small dinner, leaving him one brief engagement. Afterwards, he could have a quiet meal, call her up, and really discuss it.

At this moment, David found his doubts in retreat and the offer intoxicating. It was a crystalline October day. His mild attack of discontent had evaporated overnight. On a whim he went around his corner office on the sixteenth floor, opening all the vertical blinds on the long windows, then settled at the desk and gazed at the Manhattan skyline.

He should say yes to the PM. He would come back here as the minister, addressing the United Nations, taking the Security Council chair when it was Canada's turn, heading the delegation, not sitting behind passing memoranda, whispering advice.

His secretary opened the door and handed him a computer message from Ottawa.

Consul General, New York. Personal. Confidential.
Important call under secretary as soon as possible.
Dennison.

Michael Dennison, who had beaten David to the under secretary job. He'd probably heard of the PM's trip and wanted a little off-the-record gossip. But even the few words smacked of his petty delight in power, using COSICS, thus alerting everyone on the secure computer link that he had a confidential matter to discuss. Typical. Typical the way his secretary played phone rank.

"Is the consul general on the line? I'll wait till he's on. Is that you, Mr. Lyon? Very good. I'm connecting you with the under secretary now."

That tone would change fast if David became the minister. Even the Prime Minister's Office didn't give itself such airs.

"David!" The way Dennison said his name was full of overtones —the insolence of office.

"David. Sorry to disturb the work of high diplomacy—"

And sarcasm.

"A little awkwardness has come up. I thought it might smooth things a touch if I handled it personally and confidentially—in the first instance, at any rate."

Since his elevation to under secretary, Dennison sounded as though he'd been taking mandarin lessons from his betters in London, so perfectly could he pitch condescension, smugness, and concern. David would enjoy purging the department of its residual, postcolonial manners.

"Well, what is it, Michael?"

"Do you know a woman named Francesca D'Anielli?"

It struck David like an electric shock, then an ominous chord of music. No one had spoken her name in years.

Reluctantly, he said, "Well—I did once—yes . . ."

He felt irritation, mixed with a little dread. "It was quite a long time ago—why?"

"I've had a strange cable from the Helsinki embassy. Confidential. Something's happened to Miss—or is it Mrs.?—D'Anielli."

"Mrs.—it was."

"Something has happened to her and they've found an envelope with your name on it."

The pool of uneasiness deepened in David's stomach.

"What has happened to her?"

"Well, it's complicated. The police are not sure."

"Police?"

"Finnish police, in Helsinki. That's why I thought we should keep it to ourselves at present. The ambassador, Beaubien—you know Jean Luc—when he saw your name he messaged me personally—"

"But what's happened to her?"

"She's dead, David. Of course I'm very sorry, if it's a personal loss."

David didn't respond. He couldn't believe what he was hearing.

". . . That is, apparently dead, or presumed dead, but no body, so far. They say she'd chartered a yacht on the coast of Finland five days ago . . . last Friday . . . yesterday it was found abandoned out at sea. There was no one aboard, but her clothes were there."

Jesus! What was this all about? "What about the people she was with?"

"She wasn't. She told the charter owner she was going to cruise in the Aaland Islands with a friend. But no friend turned up. They think she took off by herself. Days later the boat was found miles away. The only clue is an envelope that says 'David Lyon, Canadian Embassy, Helsinki.' "

"What was in the envelope?"

"I'm told a few cryptic lines that didn't make obvious sense—and a gold bracelet. They've traced the boat back to the charterer. The police are getting a warrant to search her apartment in Helsinki. And that's all we know, probably till tomorrow. I'm sorry to be the one to break this to you."

"Yes."

"Apparently they don't know the connection with us. I mean, they know the name, but Beaubien is quick and he hasn't told the Finns that we know you—as yet, that is."

Beginning to sweat but trying to sound cool, David said, "You're suggesting he'll have to, sooner or later."

"Of course. But it gives us a little time to think. I haven't told the minister, but I must eventually . . . so he won't be caught unawares in the House, if it becomes public."

Now he began to understand Dennison's tone. *Schadenfreude,* sugar-frosted. He could see unlimited ugliness for himself, for Marilyn, the girls, her parents—the end of his suddenly accelerating career.

"In short, they're going to want to know what you know."

"Well, I don't know anything about this!"

"I should think at least they'll want you to explain the note she left . . . if you can."

There was turmoil in David's mind, but his voice was controlled.

"Well, it's years since I've heard anything of this woman."

"Of course. Take my number at home. I have a couple of receptions I must drop by this evening"—David could see him swanning through the diplomatic rituals, his little strutting walk—"but I'll be home later. Give me a call if you want to chat more about it."

As though he were a close friend.

"Thanks."

"Very good. Well, I must get on with things. Sorry to be the bearer of sad tidings." Dennison sounded quite pleased.

David put the phone down. How could she have drowned? He could see her swimming in the turquoise water in Barbados, lithe and fluent as an otter. Of course, she was older now and the waters of the Baltic were not the Caribbean. He saw her walking down the beach in Barbados, the golden wand of her body not hugged but lightly touched by the bikini, dangling the baby girl on one hip.

He looked at the notes he'd automatically scribbled during the phone conversation . . . *missing, presumed drowned.*

He'd often imagined accidents. She had seemed to court them; driving the motor scooter with such abandon in Paris, model's bag slung over her shoulder, legs bared to the thighs by the wind in her skirt . . . laughing, swearing at taxi drivers.

David stared at the darkening conglomeration of midtown Manhattan outside. Francesca dead? But why address an envelope to him—now? He didn't have time for this. He felt annoyed at the intrusion, yet prickly with apprehension. For the first time in years he felt the itch for a cigarette.

In her long fingers a cigarette made lovely shapes. Her fingers touching anything—a car door, a glass—gave that object some sexual poetry, the model ad agencies dream of.

Francesca dead. Bodies long in the water often lost their fingers to nibbling fish. Would they find her body in the cold Baltic tides? Why had she chartered so late in the season? Had she really been alone?

After ten years of silence suddenly to come alive for him—to announce she was dead? He felt irritation, not grief. Thank God, he'd escaped from grief and pain with her years ago. And the consequences with Marilyn. He hoped he wouldn't have to face that right away. She wouldn't need to know unless it became public. Just re-open terrible wounds.

He could not stop his mind saying, repetitively, like a police car light flashing, *Francesca is dead*.

His secretary opened the door. "They're wondering if you're coming to the meeting. It's after five."

"Oh, sorry. Tell them I'll see them tomorrow. Say something came up. I'll see them in the morning."

"You remember the Polish reception? Six-thirty, UN Delegates' Lounge?"

"Yes." He'd accepted as a favor because the UN ambassador was out of town. He could go and be out in fifteen minutes.

"How soon will you want the driver?"

"Let's say six-twenty."

"I'll tell him. Will you be all right for tomorrow's reception at the residence—with Mrs. Lyon away? I think everything's arranged."

A group of Canadian businessmen. Trade was now the dominant concern of diplomacy.

"No, I'll be fine."

"I ordered the flowers. If you like I'll go over and see they're nicely arranged." Ms. Tremblay was a motherly, efficient woman. In this generation she'd have been a foreign service officer herself. She was certainly smart enough.

"That would be very kind."

"Your invitation's for six-thirty."

"Yes, I'll remember. Thanks."

She closed the door. By habit she had turned his desk diary to tomorrow's page, and he looked at the engagements—breakfast discussion at the Americas Society on easing U.S.–Canadian trade frictions, meeting with the trade minister from Saskatchewan, remarks at the opening of a publishers' exhibition of Canadian books, the reception at the residence, Carnegie Hall for a performance by a Montreal violinist, dinner afterwards (optional) at the Russian Tea Room.

After three years he usually took such a schedule in his stride. Ken Taylor, consul general in the mid-eighties, had told him, "You can be almost totally your own boss. The ambasssador in Washington has to follow policy closely, but you can push the envelope here . . . go out and make a case for Canada in an aggressive way."

And David had done it well. Taylor had been lionized by America for sheltering their diplomats in Iran. Without that advantage, David had built up impressive contacts, leaders in New York media, cultural life, Wall Street, and their social intersections. He'd had less petty interference from bureaucrats in Ottawa than in any previous posting—until this call from Dennison. Now, suddenly, he felt the anxiety he hadn't known for years, the chronic apprehension of a foreign service officer that officials in Ottawa are discussing him . . . negatively.

He needed to get back to the implications of the PM's offer, but he couldn't push Francesca out of his thoughts. She was suddenly in every window, in every doorway of his mind.

He had an image of her on a languid morning in Trinidad cutting mangoes . . . their sweetness and tropical foreignness, like hers, overloading his pinched, northern senses. The curves of the mangoes nestled into his hands, like her breasts. The dark green blushing red and yellow were Gauguin and Cézanne and all the sensual hedonism bursting to get out of him then. She gave the mangoes an aura that intoxicated him, as she did.

It was getting dark. Five-thirty. After midnight in Helsinki, but Beaubien would understand. A feeling of caution made him avoid the MITNET line that connected Canadian government offices worldwide. He checked the code for Finland and dialed on his personal number.

"Jean Luc, it's David Lyon. I'm sorry to bother you so late."

"David, I was pretty sure you'd call. I'm sorry about all this. I would have called you direct but I thought I'd better go through channels. It makes Dennison feel important, as you know."

"That hasn't changed."

"It's good you called now. You know they found a note? I copied it down. Just a minute. I have to go to the study. Christine will hang up."

David knew they'd been discussing him from the way she came on the line. "Hello, David, this is Christine. How *are* you?"

"I'm fine."

"How is New York? I miss it so much."

"But now you have an embassy. Isn't that better?"

Her Quebec accent was stronger than her husband's. "Sure, if you like it cold and dark, and more snow than we have at home. But I have to admit it's gorgeous here now. Like Indian summer."

Jean Luc picked up the other phone, and Christine said, "David, I'm very sorry about this. I hope it is not something bad for you."

"Thanks, Christine. God bless."

"If you have to come here, you come and stay with us, eh?" She hung up. He envisioned Jean Luc, large and mustached, smoking in his pyjamas. He'd been one of David's favorite juniors.

"David—" Hearing Jean Luc blowing out smoke made David's craving stronger. "They let me copy it down. Some lines of poetry. I'll read it to you. *One morning we set off, our brains full of passion, / Hearts swollen with rancor and with bitter desires.*"

David didn't need to listen. He knew it well.

"Sounds familiar," Beaubien said.

"It's Baudelaire."

"Ah, yes. Doesn't make much sense to me in this context, but I didn't know the lady. I assume you did."

"Yes, I did. But it's years ago."

"Doesn't sound like a suicide note."

"Where did they find it?"

"Well, on the boat."

"I know, but where?"

"It was in a bag with her clothes. That's what's so suspicious. She left all her things on board."

"Where did they find the boat?"

"Swedish police found it, in Swedish waters, a kilometer or so off shore."

"Was it floundering around, or sailing?"

"They didn't tell me. Still, you know, I'm going to have to tell them we know who you are. Probably tomorrow morning . . . if they don't figure it out themselves. I suppose it hasn't occurred to them to look in the diplomatic records. I was just waiting for an OK from Ottawa. And when I tell them, it's going to be hard to keep it quiet. The press, I mean."

"What about the other person she was supposed to be with?"

"The police can't find anyone. They're checking her friends here. Apparently she's been living in Finland. But they said she's British."

"Well, she was."

"Name's Italian."

"D'Anielli's the married name."

"Not the Fiat people? The spelling's wrong."

"No. Different."

"Husband still in the picture?"

"No, divorced."

"So, David, it's a bit of a mess." Beaubien was ten years younger, yet his tone made David feel the junior. "Mysterious death, or mysterious disappearance because they haven't got a body. No sign of violence or struggle. And the only name they find is yours. It's a bitch." Jean Luc paused again to blow out smoke. "But how are you doing? This must have shaken you up a bit, eh?"

"I just found out. It hasn't had time to sink in."

"How's New York?"

"It's all right. How's Helsinki?"

"A bit slow, with no Cold War. A dead end, maybe. I don't know, David. I think the department's going to hell. Morale is bad. I think I'm out after this."

"A bit soon, isn't it? Could be lots of good postings ahead."

"The hints I get sound like dead-end stuff. Nothing important. You probably hear more than I do. You know where the good ones go."

The same notions David had been harboring himself—until the prime minister's bombshell. Well, this business could certainly kill that idea.

Beaubien was saying, "If you have to come over here, we could spend an evening. I'd like to pick your brains."

"I hope I don't have to."

"How's Marilyn?"

"She's fine. Working like hell at NYU."

"I thought she graduated."

"She got her MA in fine arts. Now she's going for the doctorate."

"That's serious stuff."

"Right now she's up in Ottawa because her father's had a stroke."

"Wallace Farquhar? Is it bad?"

"He's partly paralyzed and he can't really speak. Jean Luc, would you call me if you hear anything more? As a pal?"

"Sure, David. Better if Fuckface Dennison doesn't know I'm doing it, though."

Restless after putting down the phone, David was certain there were questions he should have asked. Rising dread over Francesca's death competed with rising anxiety about the prime minister knowing, about Marilyn.

He walked back to the deserted consulate library and opened the good atlas to stare at the Aaland Islands, reaching out from Finland towards Sweden . . . trying to picture it, his sense of horror rising as he began to imagine what she would have had to do.

It was sixteen years since they had sailed there together in 1975. It was the only perfect time in all those years of agony.

The water would be cold now . . . 50 degrees, perhaps. It was never very warm. In Nova Scotia he'd been under sailboats in water that cold to cut off a line fouling a propeller. It was absolutely numbing, but there was always a rubdown and a Scotch afterwards in the cabin.

He tried to imagine her slipping deliberately into the freezing water—for good, to end it. At night, in the dark, or in the bright, northern sunlight. She'd be cold on deck in the wind. She had hated being cold that December in New York. Would she have got drunk before going over? He remembered the bottle of cognac and the pills that last night in 1981.

It made him sick to imagine, yet he could not force his mind away.

Six-fifteen, and he had to leave. Across Sixth Avenue the buildings of Rockefeller Center showed blazing regiments of empty windows.

At the curb he found the black sedan with the diplomatic plates. "John, it's such a nice evening. I think I'll walk to the UN. Pick me up at the Delegates' Entrance at seven-fifteen."

The top of the Empire State Building was red, white, and blue: Leona Helmsley still cheering about the Gulf War, trying to ingratiate herself with a society about to jail her. Gulf superpatriotism the last refuge of the tax evader . . . the last refuge for everyone after a buck or a political lift . . . everything that made him squirm about Americans and Mulroney's coziness with them. That terrible cartoon showing the PM in front of the Stars and Stripes, his hand on his heart, as though pledging allegiance. Pierre Trudeau had continually annoyed Washington to no sound purpose. Mulroney had seemed to know just how to play it—until he went too far and began to look like George Bush's lap dog. To work with him, David would have to come to terms with his own ambivalence.

Waiting to cross Fifth Avenue, he felt the pleasure the city gave him on fall evenings like this, on fresh summer mornings, when the vast hive hummed with potential, the air spicy with possibilities. Forget the war hysteria, forget the jingoism, the poverty, all the contradictions. At moments like this—provoked by the pleasant odors of scorched pretzels or burned chestnuts—he loved being here as much as London or Paris . . .

A few feet away a man held out a paper cup as David waited for the light. A homeless Asian was rare. The man wore clean cotton pants and a polo shirt. Most homeless people's belongings burst out of shopping bags and overflowed grocery carts. This man's worldly goods were contained in cloth bundles tied with the precision of Chinese gifts, his two-wheeled cart packed like a work of art, as he might order his bedroom drawers, if he had a bedroom.

People averted their eyes. The first bill that came out of David's pocket was five dollars. He hesitated, embarrassed to change it for a smaller, then pushed it into the man's cup and hurried across Fifth, impatient taxis nudging pedestrians, angry horns behind them, a siren whooping in the distance, his moment of pleasure in New York dissolving into anger at a country hysterical with self-praise over the Gulf War, powerless to solve its own problems. A contrast Canada could be proud of, that Americans were beginning to notice. There were more press calls to the consulate for statistics on health care. A relief from questions about Quebec separatism. There were homeless in Toronto, but not on this scale.

He continued east on Forty-ninth Street.

How horrible to think of such a death. He had been obsessed with her for so long. Across First Avenue loomed the old Beekman Towers Hotel, where Francesca had stayed with him.

She had changed the carefully balanced chemistry of his daring and prudence. Like a car never driven faster than sixty, he had continually found himself doing eighty, ninety, a hundred—amazed at his own speed, aware that he was on the edge of control, yet suppressing the fear.

"Mr. Lyon. I am sorry to hear about your father-in-law." The elderly Norwegian ambassador had maneuvered skillfully through the crowded Delegates' Lounge. "I knew him years ago in the service. A distinguished diplomat who did your country much honor. I hope you will tell his wife that I asked."

"Of course I will. You are very kind."

"It was a stroke, I hear? Very debilitating?"

"It makes speech very difficult."

"Such a tragedy for a brilliant man. We had a card last Christmas. He said he was writing his memoirs."

"He had just about finished."

"That is good news, at any rate. Oh, by the way"—he put his head close to David's—"is your prime minister serious about the job of secretary general?"

"I haven't had an official briefing." David smiled.

"And unofficially?"

"Unofficially, he knows the votes aren't there."

"So does my prime minister. Well, well, my consolations to your wife and Mrs. Farquhar. We had many good times together in the past. Au revoir."

Silver-haired, erect, the Norwegian slid away, his glass untouched, his eye quick for the countless opportunities of his craft.

Marilyn's father, Wallace Farquhar, had shone in the formative years in External Affairs, emerging from the University of Toronto, a Rhodes Scholarship, then Harvard, with a bristly, arrogant manner. He had served with Norman Robertson and Mike Pearson through Ottawa's golden age of diplomacy, formation of the UN and NATO, when a quirky alignment of world powers exaggerated Canada's influence. He thought most politics cheap opportunism.

There was gossip years ago in External that David's plum first posting—third secretary in the Washington embassy—had been due to his father-in-law's influence. Quite untrue. He suspected Michael Dennison of starting it.

Nodding and smiling professionally, David edged towards his host. If the efficient network of diplomatic gossip knew within days about Marilyn's father, how soon would it pick up the Francesca story? And the newspapers: BEAUTIFUL MODEL DROWNS IN BALTIC. LEAVES NOTE FOR DIPLOMAT.

Guests were clustered thickly around the Polish ambassador, each attempting to register his *acte de présence* in the minimum time, as David awaited his chance.

Over the ambassador's shoulder, he noticed a young woman, slim and elegant, seated, talking vivaciously. Her shoe slipped off and her foot began to search for it. Something about the shape of her toes through the tip of her stocking gave him vivid recall of Francesca in a hotel room on Lexington Avenue, dressing for another departure. She had a peculiar way of putting on stockings . . . the young woman was leaning down to replace the shoe.

"Ah, Your Excellency. David Lyon, consul general of Canada."

"Mr. Lyon, it is so kind of you to honor us today. May I present my wife?"

"How do you do? I'm afraid my wife is out of town and couldn't have the pleasure of coming tonight."

"Perhaps we will meet her another time, Mr. Lyon. In Poland we have a very warm place in the heart for Canada. A great country."

"Thank you. Of course many fine Polish people now live in Canada, which helps to nourish the strong ties between us."

"Well, you are so kind to come."

"Not at all. It is a pleasure to see you."

David slipped away through the throng of African robes and Indian saris and the polyglot buzz, retrieved his coat, and found the driver outside. He needed to settle quietly to think.

He had not seen her or communicated with her in ten years; in fact, had gladly put her behind him. So why now so . . . *bouleversé*? That was the word . . . God, as a minister he'd have to respond in French as well as English in the House of Commons . . . at news conferences. Francesca's French had been so easy. She wore languages like clothes, lightly, casually, without studied effort. Her French was fluid compared to the stiff accuracy David had acquired when bilingualism became essential for senior civil servants. It was the same with Francesca's Italian, Finnish, Swedish . . . perhaps others. She'd probably never studied a verb. She picked it up, sliding from one language to another if she forgot a word, and the effect charmed everyone.

Marilyn's French had also become very fluent, as she had immersed herself more deeply in her art studies. Of course, she couldn't continue at NYU if he took the PM's offer.

At Sixty-second and Park the doorman hurried from the canopied entrance to open the door.

"Good evening, Mr. Lyon."

"Thank you."

The porter bowed him to the elevator to ascend to the pleasant fifteenth-floor apartment that came with the job. Hard to believe that when he'd descended this morning Francesca had been a speck of memory long buried. Now, memories of her were expanding to fill his mind.

He'd given the butler and the cook the night off. With Marilyn away, the rooms felt strange, the contemporary paintings she had collected making her seem oddly both more present and more absent.

He couldn't call her immediately to talk about the PM—still too unsettled. In the study, he poured some Scotch and sank into the comfortable armchair. As in Baudelaire's poem, he had "drowned in the eyes of a woman."

Francesca had had slightly more flesh at twenty. Later, when modeling, she was thinner, with a developed hollow under the cheekbones—very becoming to the camera, with the smart Sassoon haircut—and her pelvic bones, invisible the first year, later made two gentle points, obvious but in no way ugly. Later still, she was too thin from hard living. But at the beginning she had a tropical ripeness, and her breasts were never as full again, except when the children were born.

SIX

AALAND ISLANDS

BY MIDMORNING, SHE had threaded the nearest islands of the vast Aaland archipelago, slipping as planned to the northwest to avoid the route the big ferries ploughed between Finland and Sweden. There were so many small wooded islands and rocky skerries, with similar spiky or flat profiles, it took constant nervous glances at the chart folded on the cockpit seat to be sure she was following her course.

She wanted to sail instead of motoring as soon as she felt comfortable with the sea room between islands.

Remembering that it would be harder to leave the wheel under sail, she prepared food for the whole day and noticed she was hungrier than she had been in months. She made soup and coffee to fill the two thermoses provided, hard-boiled eggs, and a supply of cheese and salami sandwiches. All of this made her so ravenous that she ate the first installment immediately.

The day was going to be beautiful. A brilliant autumn sun was already warming her back and turning the birch leaves on passing islands into flashes of gold among the evergreens. But the day would be short at this latitude. The northern night would descend quickly, and she had to reach the protected cove well ahead of darkness.

She felt a strange excitement to be going to Kaarina's house. She had come to Finland because of David but had finally settled here for Kaarina—for feelings unlike any she had known with men or women. The sense of place she felt here in the quiet of Finland was tied to the calmness that had enveloped her with Kaarina, even when she was dying.

"Dear Francesca. Do something for me. Go to the island." She whispered it again the day she died, the birch trees outside the hospital window straight and silent.

It was time to make sail. Methodically, she took the ties off the mainsail, slacking off the main sheet so that the wind wouldn't catch the boat close-hauled. So far the wind was kind, a southerly breeze still light in the morning air. She slowed the engine to idling speed, turned the boat's head, and let her drift up into the wind. By the mast, she freed the halyard and hoisted until it got too heavy by hand, then put two turns on the winch, fitted a handle, and cranked. She had to lean all her weight on the last few turns, but the sail was well up, taut along the mast.

In the cockpit, she steered back to the course, let the wind carry the sail onto the port tack, and hardened up on the main sheet. Now the boat was heeling gently on a quarter reach. Panting from the exertion of hoisting the tall sail, she stopped the engine and gloried in the sweet silence, the soft hiss and swish of the sea under the bow, the whole boat feeling alive and airborne.

With a shock she recognized that she was happy. Humming with new confidence, she loosened the roller-furling line and let the huge genoa fill. Instantly the boat felt seized by powerful hands and thrust forward, while the hiss of the sea became a rush underfoot.

The water was calm between the islands, with no waves to impede the smooth acceleration.

On their long afternoons together Kaarina had read to her from the *Kalevala*: the girl who puts on her wedding dress and goes down to the sea, takes off the dress to go swimming, and drowns, becomes part of the animal kingdom, and is caught by the god. Pohjola's daughter, the Maid of the North, the story Sibelius had written music for. The girl snatched up and carried away in the flying sleigh, seduced in the furs, whirling away to the north. And the frustrated smith who forges a wife of gold that pleases him but frightens everyone else. She loved the stories, but perhaps she was mixing them all up. That was the difference between her reading and David's. He had remembered everything, or seemed to.

David said her body was a wand of gold. He could say a few words that would rouse her physically like kisses. She could scarcely remember a thing other men had said to her, but she did everything David had said. A wand of gold. She was always a golden color in those days. At first when she came to live in Europe she would go back to the Caribbean in winter to re-establish it. Now she was pale and it didn't matter.

Really, her body had never mattered as much to her as it had to others. She had been very careless with herself physically, especially in the modeling years, when she drank and smoked constantly and took pills to make her sleep or wake up, calm her nerves, cheer her up, knock her out. Despite all that abuse, and two children, and an abortion, little showed. Right now with a professional make-up and haircut, she could still carry off a fashion show.

She looked up at the contented curve of the wind-filled sail and breathed the clean tang of the sea air. She could have done this long ago, not waited for men to take her, going only because men went.

The genoa luffed, and she tweaked the winch handle to tighten the sheet. She didn't need a man to tell her. Strength was something else. But even for men they made boats easier all the time. Geoffrey's yacht had electric winches. You stepped on a rubber button to trim a sheet or raise the anchor. Strength became less and less important.

Of course men usually had the money to do things like this, the jobs that paid the kinds of money that let them have expensive toys, the sports cars, the ski chalets, the boats. What did successful women have? She thought of Kaarina's friends in Finland, where equal employment and equal pay were long the custom. They had nice apartments. They had sensible cars, lovely cottages on the lakes or by the sea, usually unpretentious, not competing for grandeur, not making statements. They had music and books and nice furniture. Beautiful Scandinavian table linen and crystal. Clean and unfussy. Quiet taste that made the houses feel as calm as the trees and the lakes that surrounded them.

Her mother's taste had been atrocious. Over-fussy outdated English white embroidered cloths—for Sunday lunch in the tropics at 90 degrees.

Her mother and father had never thought she would do anything, just supposed she would marry one of the young men in Guyana, or an Englishman, which her mother would have liked. When she announced she'd been hired as a stewardess by British West Indian Airways to fly to New York, her mother gave her one of her long addled looks and sighed. "Well, is that quite nice, Frances?"

"I don't want to be nice."

Her mother always looked exhausted by life, the heat, running a house with servants who had to be told everything and willfully forgot and had to be told again, until she couldn't be bothered. Her look meant, "You may be thrown in with the wrong kinds of people." And there was another meaning: "You're getting out—and I didn't."

She had such contempt for her mother then, not realizing how trapped she was, her listless teas with women who arrived crisp and left wilted after tea progressed to gin. They, too, looked at her with resentment in their eyes. She was not for one of their sons. She'd tried their Freddies and Adrians and they probably knew that too, and good riddance, their eyes seemed to say, as they fanned themselves with their bridge hands. Everyone knew everything there, probably who had poked her and who hadn't. That was obviously why they had sent her away to a girls' school in Switzerland.

The wind was freshening. Fifteen or sixteen knots on the dial. This boat sailed marvelously. So light, so responsive to the slightest touch on the wheel, she could steer with her fingertips.

SEVEN

GUYANA

THEY MET BECAUSE of Pierre Trudeau—or Trudeau's irritation with conventional wisdom. January 1971, two weeks before David's thirty-second birthday.

Just after New Year's he'd been called in by Ferguson, the Assistant Under Secretary for Hemisphere Affairs, who grumbled at him, "The Prime Minister's Office wants a young foreign service officer to do some work on Latin America. I don't know who's supposed to be running foreign affairs now, the PMO or us. Someone bright, they want, for Christ's sake. What do they think we have, a department full of cretins? Anyway, I thought you'd fit the bill. Go on over and find out what the hell they want."

David's heart leaped. Posted back from Washington the previous summer, he'd been finding Ottawa provincial and irrelevant after years of witnessing America explode over the Vietnam War. The only compensating pleasure was the brisk iconoclasm of Trudeau's new government. Even the External Affairs Department was in turmoil from policy shifts and reorganizations. Once the elite corps of the civil service, the department seethed like an ant's nest that has been repeatedly kicked.

The prime minister's disdain for External was palpable when David reported. He was seen by an assistant to Ivan Head, Trudeau's personal adviser on foreign affairs.

"So you're Lyon? Well, I'm glad they sent someone young. We can't get anything useful out of the stuffy old farts at External."

David smiled. It was a view he privately shared.

"You were at LSE?" He was obviously looking at the file.

"Yes."

"So was the PM, of course. And you made a good impression in Washington, I see."

The irritation David felt at being vetted by this youth was overridden by the thrill of feeling close to real power, to the prime minister who was giving Canadian life so much new confidence and zest.

"OK!" The official closed the file. "Look, the PM is going to make a trip, some Caribbean stops, maybe South America. It's not set yet. You're aware of the political noise that we're ignoring the region in the new policy?"

"Yes."

"Well, it's crap. Anyway, Guyana is one of the stops. We want someone to scope it out."

"But we have a high commission there," David said.

"What External has is some old fossil calling himself High Commissioner. The political reporting is from the dark ages. All Cold War rhetoric. Here's the assignment. Go down there for a week or two, try not to ruffle the High Commissioner's feathers, and give us some hard-edged stuff. We want an *independent* reading, not warmed-over External Affairs position papers."

Elated, if guilty about leaving Marilyn and two small kids in the Ottawa winter, David made his first trip to the tropics.

He walked on eggs around the High Commissioner, a retired army officer annoyed at being circumvented by a junior foreign service officer, but unable to complain because the authority came from the PMO.

"I gather you're Wallace Farquhar's son-in-law," he asked at the overformal dinner David was obliged to attend.

"Yes, that's right."

"Well, I knew him slightly years ago with . . ." He began an anecdote while David wondered whether this was another source of resentment or something to commend him. The snobbishness of the old External Affairs had left its tidal marks.

In ten days his work was virtually finished. On the second Saturday night in Guyana, he was sitting at the hotel with a young man from the British High Commission in Trinidad and a lawyer from the AFL–CIO in Washington. All they had in common was the anxiety of their governments about this rotting ex-colony, recently independent. Guyanians were divided politically—and sometimes violently—by their Indian and African origins. It seemed to David that big-power meddling had produced a comic upset worthy of an Evelyn Waugh novel. The new Guyanese government was certifiably noncommunist but as repressive politically and stultifying economically as the Marxists Washington and London wanted to suppress. The U.S. and Britain had jumped into bed with the wrong guy. This battle for freedom on the Caribbean rim was full of ironies Trudeau would appreciate.

David had drafted his report and planned to use the long flight home to refine it. This was his first evening to relax, and he was half-listening, bored by the stale argument, as they drank rum punches and tried to be cool in the sultry air.

The exotic feel of the night, the moon-silvered palm fronds brushing the low roof overlooking the pool, assaulted his senses. There was a sense of fecundity in the air that was heavy with sour-sweetness from the effluent of sugar cane mills and rum distilleries, lending a sickly spiciness to the night.

Beyond the neglected little Victorian town, Guyana's miles of coastal sugar cane and rice paddies rose to grassy savannah, then into rain forest crowned by mountains bordering Brazil and the Amazon basin. He imagined he could feel the primitive breath of that forest slipping down the northern shoulder of South America to the Caribbean Sea. The night seemed to breathe with the exhalations and contempt of that untamed jungle; the breath of darkness and mystery.

A steel band clattered into life for a weekend dance on the open verandah, a relief because it killed the political conversation.

The calypso music found its way past the defenses in his personality—automatically on guard against the primitive or the too popular. The intoxicating rhythm, the charming voice of the Caribbean, seduced the ear conditioned by Beethoven while, underneath, the darker pulse of Africa both unnerved and excited him.

A discontent crept over him, a conviction that he had lived too narrowly; had perhaps too hastily put on the appropriate harnesses —education, career, marriage, fatherhood—one dutifully after another. Now something told him that all this was not enough. In this mood he could foresee nothing ahead but years of frustration at External Affairs, where fresh ideas turned into bureaucratic dust, a factory for policy papers endlessly drafted and redrafted. No wonder the Prime Minister's Office was impatient. If he could be transferred there, where the real action was . . . if he could impress them with some bite in this report . . .

Across the pool on the open verandah the locals danced with easy nonchalance. The music, the thickness of the night, the moonlight shivering into the palms, all seemed to intensify the headiness of the rum. David had not realized until this moment that he was in any way unhappy.

The steel band went quiet. He could hear the *pleek-pleek* of tree frogs near and distant. There was a clatter by the pool, then giggling above, and a voice calling, "We dropped our key. Will you pick it up?"

Three young women were leaning over a balcony on the hotel roof, a blur of pretty faces between the palms. One voice more commanding: "Will you pick it up, please? The stairs are there!"

After a stilted moment, David retrieved the key, and all three men trooped upstairs to stand awkwardly until the prettiest of the young women said boldly, "We didn't drop the key. I threw it down to make you come up."

The others pretended to expire at her forwardness, but she added, "Since you've come up, you'd better have a drink."

She wore little make-up. Her dark hair set off a lightly tanned face and black eyes, with natural shadows at the outer corners that made her look wistful, ready to lose a tear, yet her lips, thin and sculpted, smiled invitingly. And his heart turned over.

Below them the steel band reignited, too loud for talk, so they danced and he gravitated to her. It was simple and inevitable. One of the other girls said afterwards, "It was love at first sight." Perhaps it was love before first sight; from the instant he had heard her laughter above him and her voice impelling him to go up.

From the first moments they were oblivious of the other four. When the music stopped at midnight it was obvious they would stay together. The night was still hot, and Francesca suggested a swim. She and the others lived in town but had come to the hotel dance and rented a room. She went to change and returned in a bikini revealing a figure so exquisite it took his breath away. The others disappeared, and she and David stayed by the pool, talking for hours.

Love sees essences. In the shy flicker of first glances that night Francesca and he must each have seen in the other some mysterious essence of the self, indefinable yet instantly recognized.

The hours evaporated. With no hesitation they began telling each other the stories of their lives, like medieval pilgrims meeting in a forest, stories the price of shelter from the dangers of the night.

They lay in lounge chairs or glided on their backs, looking beyond the black palm trees at the moon, its cold transit measuring their fate. It was a continuous conversation for three hours, softly spoken, sensitive to the windows of sleeping hotel guests.

"Are you married?"

"Yes."

"Happi-*lee*?" She pushed into dialect to be amusing and to cover her boldness.

"I suppose I have just been assuming I was happy. I haven't thought about it very much"—in the passing seconds, he could feel his life turning "—until now."

In the dense silence that followed, he was visited by an image of Marilyn—wholesome, loyal, dressing Jenny in a thick snowsuit—but the image seemed to come from another planet. And he talked, as though for years he had been waiting for someone to ask. He felt his soul unraveling.

"My name is not really Lyon. It should be Mackenzie."

He told her that his father had died in the war, a young officer in the navy, lost at sea, torpedoed off Newfoundland, when David was two and so had no memory of him. His mother had married again. And as he told it a sense of desolation for the small boy enveloped him, a strong emotion he almost recognized but could not remember feeling before, a great sadness. He had never told anyone about this. But the quality of Francesca's listening invited it. He was astonished by the emotion it awakened, and he knew she felt it.

"It doesn't matter what your name is," she said. "My name is really Frances. It sounded so boring I began calling myself Francesca. Does that sound stupid?"

David loved the candor. "It's much more dramatic."

"But do you *like* it?"

"I do."

"My father hates it, but I want to change it legally."

He liked the way her tongue lingered over the syllables, *lee-ga-lee*. Sometimes she deliberately broadened the West Indian intonations, and the lilting accent made words from her mouth as beguiling as her goofy perfume, Shocking de Schiaparelli. She believed it was sophisticated and international. And she acted the name: she loved to be shocking.

The perfume was unworldly, oversweet, but to David it suggested release and danger, the faintly sinister quality the tropics moved him to feel, like many from the north; the delicious ambivalence that drew Canadians to the Caribbean, fear and indulgence; the habit of self-discipline and the desire to abandon it.

She wanted to escape from that stifling little backwater of the British Empire, a town of louvered and shuttered houses built for colonial administrators and the more raffish British traders. Her ancestors had put down roots and become West Indians. Her father was in the sugar business, her relatives long settled throughout the British Caribbean. But she was restless to leave it.

Being with her made him swallow and feel breathless. It gave him an aching sweetness simply to be in her presence.

He had never thought someone as beautiful would be interested in him. He had never aspired to touch perfection like hers. She was like the fantasies he carried out of the movies, or the little grip of the heart at the sight of a model in a magazine, something unattainable.

A man gets used to settling for what he thinks is his due. That night and later David had moments of thinking, *She can't mean me.* And each time he realized that she did, a current went through him, like the effect of putting a finger in a small electric socket.

With Marilyn he had gradually grown into love. With Francesca a magic spell was cast the moment their eyes met. And he had fallen, crashed, plummeted—like a wild animal into a pit trap.

They did not go to bed that first night. The moon had passed through a long arc when they parted finally and arranged to meet the next evening.

Impulsively, he asked, "Will you have dinner with me?"

"I'd love to have dinner."

She breathed the words with such intensity that he heard them afterwards in his sleep.

THAT WAS HOW it happened. Remarkable to David now that, with no premeditation, no reason to be discontented with Marilyn, whom he loved, he was spellbound by Francesca and reckless. Georgetown, Guyana, was tiny, and word might easily have reached the crusty old High Commissioner, who would have loved dropping it into certain ears. But that was just the beginning of the risks David took, with his marriage and his career.

Until that evening he had been content with his lot, satisfied by his work, feeling reasonably fulfilled, convinced that life was giving him enough. And, with no warning, a field force had altered within him. As though he had jumped into another man's skin, feeling a new entitlement, that he was owed this, that this too was part of his portion, his take from life.

THE NEXT EVENING he found Francesca a little grave, her forwardness in dropping the keys retired behind a shy smile.

Her most intimate look was the same in private or public, a little smile, often while looking sideways, her thick cut hair falling over one eye, turning away as if even a touch of their eyes might burn, casting her eyes downward, still smiling.

In a dark restaurant, half open to the warm night, with candles flickering, they ate overcooked shish kebab and drank red wine. Their talk was reserved, strangers again despite the confidences by the pool under the moon.

"You didn't tell me last night what you're doing here."

"I'm doing a report on the political situation."

"Politics! You should talk to my father. He'd like to strangle the lot of them. Why are Canadians interested in our miserable politics?"

"Our prime minister may be coming here on a visit."

"And you're telling him what to expect?"

"Well, in a way."

"Very important! Your prime minister—you mean Trudeau?"

"Right."

"I think he's very sexy."

"A lot of Canadians agree with you."

"No, I mean exciting. Not like a politician at all."

"Or not like a Canadian?" He laughed. "That's what someone said when I was in Washington, 'Trudeau doesn't look like a Canadian!'"

"What is a Canadian supposed to look like?" Her smile enchanted him. "Like you?"

In the pause they gazed at each other, nervously but knowingly.

"There's nowhere to go really," she said.

"There's my hotel room."

"And everyone in town would know I went there? Anyway, everyone here goes to the drive-in."

They went in her small car to a stupid Hollywood comedy in which a car was driven into a swimming pool. She was delectable in the flickering movie light; expectation, like her perfume, filling the car, rising with each moment. When he kissed her, she responded with a sigh as if she had been holding her breath intolerably long. For David the kiss seemed to fulfill a long-postponed intention.

They did go to his room, he through the front lobby, she by a rear entrance. They closed the door and clung together, their bodies for the first time feeling each other fully.

"You mustn't make love to me, you know?"

They had moved to the bed, sitting, kissing.

"Why not?"

"Because . . . if I fall in love with you and you go away, I'll be miserable."

"I have fallen in love with you."

They sank back onto the narrow bed and the embrace became more passionate.

"But you will go away in two days and I will never see you again?"

"I have to go. But I will come back."

"You promise? You promise to come back?"

"I promise."

"But you still can't make love to me."

"Why not?"

"Because I have the curse."

"It doesn't matter."

Actually he felt both mild shock at the bluntness, and charm with the lack of coyness.

"It matters to *me* . . . the first time."

Charmed by that, too.

"You know, the local women believe a girl with the curse should not be seen by men at all. It is supposed to bring terrible misfortune. The Amerindians used to sling the girl up in a hammock so the evil spirit visiting her wouldn't touch the ground and spoil the crops."

She giggled in the dark. "I may be putting a curse on you, the evil spirit, right now."

"When will you remove it?"

"Tomorrow night . . . if you'll tell me a story."

Without knowing why, he told her about being in London when Kennedy was assassinated.

"I was studying at LSE—"

"What's that?"

She was less worldly in some ways than she acted in others.

"The London School of Economics. Everything stopped. Kennedy had been a student there briefly. I walked all the way to the American Embassy in Grosvenor Square and just stood there, like a lot of people, feeling a sadness I had never felt before. I'd just spent two years in Washington doing my MA in political science at Georgetown University. They used to let a few graduate students go to Kennedy's press conferences in the State Department auditorium. I had never seen anything like him. Intelligent, witty, totally in command—dazzling. I sometimes wished I were an American so that he could be *my* president. I was shattered by his death. Really depressed for a while."

"Is Trudeau another Kennedy?"

"No, but yes—in a sense. He gives Canadians a feeling of new possibilities."

He meant that Trudeau gave young Canadians an exciting license to think differently about everything. It was Trudeau as justice minister who had overturned traditional attitudes to divorce, rape, homosexuality, and now, as prime minister, to NATO, to defense, to the Cold War—challenging all the pieties.

Francesca nestled closer. "I'm dying to live in London, or New York, or Paris—and away from here!"

David found himself returning to the odd feeling he had discovered, that he might be living the wrong life.

"My mother married again, after the war, a man they'd known in the navy, an engineer, and he became my father. Once or twice when I was little my mother mentioned my real father wistfully, as a romantic. But until she gave me his papers, I never knew that he had been a writer, or had been trying to be a writer, before the war. That seemed to explain part of me to myself. I used to spend hours looking at photographs of John Mackenzie, who died at twenty-five."

"Did you dislike your mother's remarrying?"

"No. I was too young to know."

"But you could have felt it and resented it later."

Francesca had intuitively hit the target. That evening he had dismissed it, but now he remembered, twenty years later.

Marilyn was quite unlike his mother; much smarter, for one thing. And yet there was a wholesomeness about her that had made him realize there would never be any question of his mother's disapproving of her. Marilyn was as reassuring to his mother as she was to David himself. He could imagine what his mother saw in Marilyn:

reliable, well brought-up, well mannered in an easy way, comfortable, and pretty, not disturbingly beautiful, not flashy, not likely to give David any trouble, not some flibbertigibbet of a girl whose eyes would be flashing at other men. That is what his mother would have felt about Francesca. And David had felt the same. Perhaps that knowledge had prevented him from making the commitment to Francesca.

That night in Guyana, he had told Francesca, "I do wonder . . . if John Mackenzie had remained my father, how different would my life be. All the little decisions and assumptions that have gone into it might have been quite different. Now I have this feeling that I should be living out my father's fantasies."

"You mean, be a writer? Well, why don't you, if you feel it so strongly? Just do it!"

Being with her uncovered new feelings and made him talk more freely than he ever had, until, late at night, she said reluctantly she had to go. Her father was visiting a sugar estate and her mother worried.

"I can do what I like but it's easier not to make fusses."

At the door, she whispered, "Did you really say you've fallen in love with me?"

"Yes, I have."

"Really?" Nuzzling against him.

"Really."

"Well, I have with you. D'you hear? So, you'd better watch out!" She laughed and slipped out.

ALL THE NEXT day he felt inattentive and half faint with impatience for her that evening. He lingered at the pool, reading, hoping she might appear, then moved to his shaded room to work on his report. He did not think about Marilyn. He kept seeing images of Francesca, feeling stirrings of sexual anticipation.

When the night finally came and she slipped into his room, fresh and passionate, he was overwhelmed, his senses overloaded by her fully naked presence in the dim light, perfect and pliant, trembling and shy. In his eagerness, his erection wilted. Kissing it, caressing it, she easily recharged it, but not before he had a moment of anxiety at the letdown.

It was quickly forgotten in the relief and deliciousness of consummation, her tears of happiness. David felt his spirit transported to a sublime plane, as though thousands of years had fallen away and they were alone in Arcadia, the new children of Eros. They talked and made love again, fell asleep, and awakened with fresh desire.

Too soon it was morning. He was supposed to hop along the South American coast to French Guiana, inspect preparations for the French space program, then pick up the Air France flight north to Martinique and New York.

They said goodbye but couldn't part. She drove him to the airport and sat waiting for his flight, wan after a night of little sleep, her hair lank in the humidity, thinner in the face from lovemaking, he thought, a little shadow under her cheekbone. They were both in shock, very grave in their bubble of sound and time.

She said, "We could meet in Trinidad or Barbados. I sometimes go to see relatives, or I could say I was."

In Cayenne, he fretted in the tropical heat, long interviews and long meals with French officials. Dutifully under a scorching sun he listened and made notes at raw launching sites scoured out of the jungle and gleaming banks of high-tech instrumentation. The contrast was startling with the sleepy nineteenth-century colony, so undeveloped that even fresh lettuce had to be flown in from France.

"Undoubtedly," David noted, "residual guilt or sensitivity to world opinion, a desire to erase Guiana's reputation as a sadistic penal colony, is an added motive for the French Government in choosing to spend millions here for missile development. The geographic convenience, the long range for test firings, is obviously paramount, but public relations clearly plays a part. In any case the scale of the investment is enormous, a major statement of the

French presence in the Americas, far exceeding any British, American (or Canadian) enterprise in the region."

He noticed that he was inserting his opinions. It was new for him to stray beyond the coldly factual.

As long as he was actually working, Francesca idled in the shadows of his thoughts, but when he was alone in his airless hotel room, longing for her became a torment. Lying naked under an ineffectual ceiling fan, he relived every moment with her, every word they had spoken.

On the third morning, he was to catch the flight to Martinique. Impulsively, with no premeditation, he picked up the telephone and changed the flight. Instead of flying north, he booked on the local flight back to Guyana.

The piston-engined plane droned tediously over the forest canopy covering French Guiana, Surinam, and finally Guyana, giving his emotions hours to oscillate between guilt: he had never done anything so reckless—and anticipation: he had never approached anything so thrilling.

He telephoned from the airport.

"You are here?"

"I couldn't leave without seeing you again."

"How long can you stay?"

"Two nights." That's how it came out. He had intended one.

"Thank God. I've been going mad without you. Stay there. I'll come and get you."

Waiting, he buried his uneasiness about the days he was stealing from External Affairs and Marilyn. He'd think of some explanation —a crucial interview needed to complete his report—essential that he come back.

She drove up, got out of the car, and stood looking at him gravely, a sight that took his breath away.

"Did you *really* come back just to see me?"

"Yes."

"Not on business?"

"Just to see you."

"Then I'm very glad."

And she looked away for a moment in that shy-seeming gesture that he came to know as her sign of deep feeling. Then she kissed him quickly and said, "Come, let's go."

The hotel had no room made up so early and they went to the tropical public gardens. There were deep ditches with manatees— "sea cows," she called them—huge black creatures bovinely grazing under water.

They stayed there for hours on the soft lawn, shaded by the copious wealth of tropical greenery, in a glade utterly private, enclosed by fan palms, thick oleanders, and hibiscus, with little breaths of wind bringing occasional wisps of delectable frangipani, above them royal palms creaking and whispering.

No one came there, yet their bodies kept their distance until they could have certain privacy. Once she traced the outline of his lips with her fingertips and he touched the skin where her skirt was raised above the knee. He had never known a sexual attraction so strong.

"I told my grandmother about you?" Her statements ended like questions. "She asked if you are good to me?"

"What did you say?"

"I said, not bad so far!" She looked at David so possessively that he felt it to his toes. It was wonderful that she had confided in her grandmother.

But she suddenly chuckled. "My grandmother said, 'Is he poking you?' I said, 'Yes, but not enough, you know?' "

He wanted the humid tropics to melt the starch in his northern personality. He wanted to be looser, to be like her.

But it stayed with him, that taunting question from the grandmother: "Is he poking you?" Poking, pronounced humorously, po-*king*. Taunting. Mocking.

EIGHT

AALAND ISLANDS

BY NOON IT was warm enough to take off her anorak and cap and shake out her hair in the sun. Strange to think that she, who so loved the warmth of the Caribbean, had deliberately chosen Scandinavia as home. Perversely. And proudly. Proud of her independence.

In Guyana she had felt stifled and trapped; immensely freer in New York or London or Paris, but in the end freer only to be hunted, and oddly compelled to play at being hunted, the quarry without which there is no game. Now she could drop out, not playing anymore, and relax. It was not only that Scandinavian men were more complacent or matter-of-fact; she acted differently here. She did not invite the same attention she had elsewhere, no longer left the same spoor. She had discovered that a woman can exist outside the frame of a man's attention, can feel alive without the pleasant-unpleasant suspense of seduction, wanting it, not wanting it.

She should have married David when she had the chance . . . stupid to marry Federico simply because she was pregnant. He had spotted her at a show in Milan involving models and glossy sports cars. He asked her to pose with a red Ferrari, but all she agreed to do was to pose with a few fingers touching the door handle, looking away, as though expecting someone. Something in her diffidence, her slim black evening dress with bare shoulders, caught the fancy of the picture editors, because the photos were widely published. She thought her shoulders looked too bony.

"Better a little bony," Anthony had said. "It's the gaunt look they want, darling; better sculpting, better shadows, makes men think hungry and sexy."

Anthony had spoken to her on a flight from Port of Spain to New York and given her his card. At first impression he seemed a little sleazy, in his shiny suit, black oily hair combed straight back from a low forehead, and bad teeth, which showed because he smiled constantly. The sort of man her father called a gigolo. But Anthony had charmed her. When he said, in his slightly Cockney English, "A girl like you'd make a smashing model," she listened.

"Take my card, dear. If you're interested, look me up. It's my business, finding girls. I'm in New York when I'm not in London. I know the agencies."

Impulsively, she had written; then David saw the envelope. Instead of explaining, a little spurt of defiance kept her from denying it was a rival. Nothing about Anthony rivaled David, but she wouldn't say so. Another of her defensive flare-ups, a momentary flash of angry independence, which she regretted the moment the wrong impression registered. And that had blown it.

She called Anthony on the next trip to New York, going to the apartment where he kept a studio.

"I need a few pictures to show around, get them interested, whet their appetites, so to speak. No joy going in cold. They've got so many hungry girls pounding on their doors, they can't see them. I can show them how to look at you. I don't do actual fashion stuff anymore. Got bored with it. I just find girls and pass them on. If things work out, we do a little deal." He had a funny laugh, smiling and wheezing *hee-hee-hee* through his unpretty teeth.

"What sort of deal?"

"Oh, nothing like what I expect you're thinking. Finder's fee. Percentage. They pay it and charge you more commission. It's fair. Breaking in's very chancy. Millions of lovelies out there, but no one spots them."

There were pictures of a tall, gaunt model around the apartment.

"Her? Oh, that's old Belinda. My trouble."

"Trouble?"

"My trouble and strife, my wife. Lovely girl. Smashing looker, but a bit dim upstairs, if you get my drift. She's off in London on a shoot. Now, we'll need to find some better rags. Can't take your picture in that bloody uniform, though I've always been partial to fly girls, myself."

He disappeared into the bedroom and came back with several gowns. "Try one of these. Belinda's a touch taller, but no matter. You can change in there."

The bedroom was a mess, with clothes strewn about, as though his wife, if that's who she was, had left in a hurry; dressing table cluttered with make-up equipment in disarray, a lipstick left open, soiled tissues on the floor, in a corner a pile of Belinda's underwear waiting to be washed. There was nothing glamorous about her first encounter with the modeling trade.

That began the years when she became whatever the photographer, or magazine or designer or agency she was working for at the moment, wanted her to be. And that, she had believed, was independence: living nowhere, tied to nothing, spending whatever she made on haircuts, make-up, clothes, changing with the desired look of the moment, changing men like fashion accessories, a life so blurred now she could remember each episode no more precisely than she could the thousands of outfits she had put on, posed in, modeled, and removed. The only constant behind all the scrambling between cities, jobs, amusements, men, had been the fitful contacts with David.

If anyone looked at the messy drawer where she had thrown the thousands of photographs from those years, they would think, What a glorious life! In the pictures she always looked sparkling, seemingly having a good time at endless parties, dinners, receptions that followed the shoots or fashion shows in clubs, resorts, hotels, restaurants, yachts, castles, tropical beaches, St. Tropez, Davos, Aspen . . . every chic location the industry could dream up or rediscover to nourish fantasy in the minds of women who would buy the cheap knock-offs.

She had left in disgust several times, but came back because it was her only way to earn money. Sometimes fabulous money. The time she came back from the winter of crewing on Geoffrey's boat for the charter season, so tanned they said, "It doesn't fit this year's look," but she found another house that wanted the sporting, outdoor look.

She regretted Federico from the first weeks of their marriage. Lovely in bed, handsome, spoiled, he had expected Francesca to dote and cook like his mother, but the work offered him as favors by family friends in the car business paid fitfully—not a real career. The glossy borrowed Alpha or Ferrari or Lancia of the moment was parked outside a mean apartment. And when he zoomed off to rallies or shows around Europe, Francesca stewed angrily in the unwanted pregnancy. She should have gone to Sweden then for an abortion. She resumed modeling as soon as she could, and when she first saw David again she kicked herself for her stupid mistake.

Now she had had a long time to think about the nature of her happiness, of happiness for women, and to observe women who were happy. Somehow the clear light of the north made her vision clearer. What had she really wanted all these years? Just to be independent, to be her own boss, as the Americans said.

"Frances, if only you didn't have to be so headstrong and independent!" Her mother.

But it wasn't really true. She was always being caught in the net of her own seductiveness, her looks; caught on lures of her own devising, deluding herself that she was the fisherman making the catch, until it was too late and she was trapped; wriggling, squirming, thrashing until she spun free, the fish that got away, only to be caught again.

How typical that the first choices apparent to her had been stewardess and model, two professions dependent on appearance, professions almost designed to provoke male fantasies. David had encouraged her to go to college, to be something. He had spent most of his twenties in colleges, and once said he wished he had stayed in the academic life. Not interested then, in recent years she had flirted with it. She had visited Uppsala, the old university town north of Stockholm, its patina of centuries glowing on a golden autumn day of chrome yellow birch leaves and a cobalt blue sky warming the ancient pink brick. It had awakened a hunger to do something serious, to spend years concentrating on one thing, which she had never done. A day like today, blue and gold.

NINE

NEW YORK

IN THE STUDY David heard himself sigh, and was embarrassed to find himself wallowing in memories still erotic after twenty years.

His desire for Francesca had sprung from nowhere, a freak wave destroying his buoyancy and balance. He could not float above it. And yet it was in no sense a feeling of being pulled beneath the waves to suffocate, to be destroyed, but of drowning like one of the characters in the *Kalevala*, losing one life to enter another.

In those early encounters with Francesca he had felt exalted, suffused with joy, breathed into by deliciousness, buoyed up, borne aloft, soaring. And if he had drowned in the eyes of a woman, it was drowning in delight, in delirium, in magic and beauty.

Could Francesca have been as extraordinary as he thought then? Would he now agree with the David of twenty years ago?

The phone rang, and Marilyn's comradely voice startled him, as though he'd been caught deceiving her again.

"Hi. Where'd you go for dinner?"

"Oh, hi, sweetheart. I didn't. I went to the UN thing and then came home. I wasn't hungry."

"Here Mummy and I were eating boring scrambled eggs, imagining you somewhere having a scrumptious meal."

"When it came to it I just didn't feel like it. I'll open a can of soup or something later."

"You sound a bit down."

"No. No. How's your dad?"

"He's trying to speak a little more. Just a few words. But it's a terrible struggle. He looks furious."

"Well, he looked that anyway."

She laughed. "Now, now! I have to keep my voice down. You know—"

"Well, give him my love."

"I will."

"Can he understand you?"

"I think so. It's hard to say."

"Oh, the old Norwegian ambassador, what's his name, friend of your parents, distinguished-looking, silver-haired, Svenderling?"

"Svendenling."

"Svendenling—he'd heard about the stroke. I saw him at the UN thing. Wanted me to pass on his best to you and your mum."

"That's nice. You'd be amazed how many people have called or sent cards. Oh, and the Prime Minister's Office *did* call, asking when it would be convenient for him to come out. I think that's very sweet."

"Already? He's certainly trying to be friendly."

"What do you think of all that now?"

"I haven't had much time to think."

"Oh, don't be mean! You must have been chewing it over all day. At least you can share it with me."

"I've really been too busy to think about it much."

"Well, Mummy and I were talking about it a lot."

"You told her?"

"I couldn't keep it to myself! There's too much to think about."

A few hours ago he'd been dying to have this conversation with her. Now he wanted to turn it off.

"You don't sound as excited as you did this morning."

"I've been thinking of some of the difficulties."

"So have I. You know Daddy always said that Lester Pearson had succumbed to the power bug and cheapened himself by becoming a politician."

"Well, your father has a pretty monastic view of the service—purer than anyone else's."

"Still, I'll bet his advice would be good. I wish he were well enough to ask."

"He'd certainly give us all the arguments against it."

"Now be fair!"

"I forgot to tell you that the PM brought up that very negative paper I did on Trudeau years ago."

"What did he say?"

"That someone in External had leaked it to him and that what I'd written was a highly political document."

"Well, he's right about that."

"It makes me wonder why they dug it out . . . whether he's really interested in a minister with vision, or just someone with foreign policy credentials who can attack the Liberal Party record."

"I've been wondering whether he just wants to use your clean reputation to shore him up, and his cabinet. They're all so unpopular . . . and all those petty scandals."

Clean reputation. She could always find a phrase to touch the sensitive nerve.

"That's all a bit of ancient history now."

"I know, but is politics something we really want to get into? It's become so mean-spirited these days. And we've been sheltered from all that dirty stuff in the newspapers."

Again, as though she could read his mind.

"Anyway, do you like Brian Mulroney enough to work that closely with him?"

"It's hard to dislike a man who's just offered to make you Minister of External Affairs."

"You know what I mean—do you trust him?"

"I don't know. I'd certainly have some disagreements with him about policy. I'd have to make that clear right away."

"Mummy wondered what happens in a couple of years if the Tories are defeated and the Liberals get back in."

All the questions he'd been eager to raise with her but could barely listen to now.

"I'd still have my pension."

"But you don't get it in full till you're fifty-five."

"He talked about that. He said maybe they could help . . ."

"You're awfully quiet. Are you really uneasy about it?"

"No, no—just thinking."

"I know what just thinking sounds like. It sounds like real second thoughts."

"It doesn't hurt to be cautious. It's what I'm paid to do—first think of all the negatives."

"But have you cooled on the positives?"

"I'm trying to keep an objective mind about it. It's so easy to get swept away by something as heady as this."

She laughed. "Sweetie, nobody thinks of you as the swept-away type, except—well, we don't talk about that."

She had not mentioned Francesca for years. Jesus!

Marilyn said, "I'll tell you what I think. If you really wanted to do it, and really threw yourself into it, you'd be a terrific secretary of state. Who knows, you could even become prime minister. How's that for positive thinking?"

"Don't even think that."

"Well, why not? Pearson did."

"Pearson had a Nobel Prize and a whole different political situation."

"I know. I'm just trying to cheer you up. You sound so down. Did something happen today?"

"No, no. I'm just a bit weary."

"Well, go to bed early and get a good night's sleep. Put it out of your mind until the morning."

"You're probably right."

"You know, I'm sitting here stewing about it as well."

"I know you are."

"After all, it's my life too."

"I know. I've been wondering . . . how do you finish your degree if you're yanked away from New York?"

"I didn't want to bother you with that too, but I've been wondering. I've almost completed the course work. My adviser might let me do the rest on my own. He really likes me. I wouldn't have to be in New York to finish the thesis."

"Well, it's another reason to consider this very carefully."

"But, David, seriously, not a reason to turn it down."

"OK."

"No, I mean it."

"I know you do."

"Well—night, night. Sleep well."

"Night, night."

"I love you."

"Me too."

The spirit of her generosity stayed with him. She had become so confident as her work advanced, rising above, or sublimating the pain he had caused her, growing in dimensions that astounded David and filled him with pride. The Ph.D. course at NYU was rigorous, but she'd taken it in her stride, and still comfortably performed the tedious routines of a diplomat's wife. The degree would qualify her for curatorships almost anywhere.

WHEN HE CAME home to her after first meeting Francesca, returning to a February night in Ottawa, 20 below zero, his heart had been full of joy mixed with dread.

He saw Marilyn a long way off, in her winter coat and boots, and he melted with pity for her and with shame, but neither emotion conquered his private joy. His dominant thought was: Will she see it?

"Look at your tan, you lucky bum!" was the first thing Marilyn said, as she might have spoken to a friend back from holidays at boarding school. At thirty she would still look at home in the green gym tunic she wore as the head girl at Elmwood. The sort of school that might have expelled Francesca just for looking as she did.

Marilyn looked her prettiest, her sensible brown hair freshly washed, her blue eyes sparkling with the excitement of driving out to Uplands Airport on a cold night, her cheeks bright pink; but also so ordinary, so reassuring, so trusting. When they embraced, her scent enveloped him, its deep familiarity a reproach. Everything seemed a reproach; that she would let him kiss her, hold her hand, that she would go home and go to bed with him.

But every detail also said *difference*. She seemed huge beside his still vivid memory of Francesca. Her gloved hand in his felt large as they waited for his luggage. Her lipstick looked harsh in the unpitying neon. What a contrast in how many articles of clothing had to be put on and taken off to support life here in winter. Francesca wore a blouse and skirt, bikini underpants and sandals, nothing more, not even a bra. Marilyn would be wearing layers and layers in this weather. How white she and all the people looked at the airport.

"It's been freezing here, and the driveway's a mess. I couldn't get anyone to do it properly."

She eyed him with affectionate scrutiny. "You look different somehow."

"Different bad or different good?" Hiding in a weak joke.

She looked again. "Different—something. Cat that's swallowed the canary and trying not to show it."

"No canaries down there. Just parrots and things." And he gave her arm a Judas squeeze.

"No, it's the look you get when you've done something smart, and you know it. The essay you can't wait to show the teacher. Something like that?"

"I think our Cold Warrior friends have fouled up magnificently down there. If they'd let things take their course—"

"There's your bag."

Settling beside her in the five-year-old Volvo station wagon, he wondered, with a needle of fear, whether any of Francesca's Shocking might have lingered on his clothing. He had showered before leaving Guyana, but they had kissed a lot at the airport. On the plane he had scrubbed his face, even his ears and neck, with airline soap to remove any trace.

He also had the strongest urge to tell Marilyn. It would save all this deception.

Changing planes at New York he had passed a duty-free shop and thought of a present for Marilyn. The overly made-up salesgirl tapped her long red nails on the counter. The names and exotic perfume packages were a blur. Chanel Number 5. Very conventional, very expensive. It wasn't Christmas, and they were careful about money. Would such extravagance make her suspicious?

But what shocked him most was that the moment he was back in her presence, he wanted her, and in bed found himself, if anything, more avid. He wanted to prolong it, until she said sweetly, "I'm awfully sleepy, darling. Could we just do it and go to sleep?"

Everything made him aware of the difference; Marilyn's relative passivity and immobility. She was a bigger woman, her thighs were heavier, the sensations of being in her looser—she had had two children—the whole experience different. Whereas Francesca had curled her body to his, her pelvis articulate, Marilyn from habit simply let him do it. As though they had been to different schools of womanhood.

He wondered how much experience Francesca's active love-making implied. How many men had she been with? He knew that he was the only man who had made love to Marilyn, and there was a primitive reassurance in knowing that she was his alone.

When it was over and they had kissed good night like familiar lovers, he lay wondering whether he'd betrayed both women.

TEN

AALAND ISLANDS

ON THE CHART folded open on the cockpit seat, Francesca had highlighted the island with yellow marker. Decidedly unorthodox. Serious sailors would not approve. Past the hummocky island a few miles ahead, still small on the horizon, then leaving a long island to the right. The chart showed a cross for a church steeple as a navigation mark. Also highlighted in yellow. Then past a few tiny islets, nothing but rocks with a few bushes and grass, to the steep wooded island with a protected harbor—big yellow dot. That meant one more difficult test, anchoring safely, often the most difficult thing in a sailboat. Well, no way out of that. About three miles to the hummocky island, two to clear the church steeple island, one more for the islets. Two o'clock now. At least an hour's sailing. About three-thirty to be anchoring. That was good. Still plenty of daylight. The little anxieties about accomplishing it all began to mount, but they mingled with the tingling emotion that had been rising all day. "You see! You can do it!"

She felt competent, exhilarated. An hour to wait to be safe for the night, then plan the next stage. Some people were going to be very surprised.

"BUT YOU DON'T need the money," her brother had said when their father's estate was divided between them.

"Of course I need it."

"I mean, you'll just fritter it away."

"That's my business."

"You'd do much better to put it into some land here so's it'll be worth something when you're older and really need it."

"You mean put it into *your* land, Nigel."

They were standing on his farm in Barbados, looking at his fields of sugar cane and market vegetables.

"Well, there is a bit of land the fellow next to me might want to sell, over there, past the old sugar mill."

"To make your farm bigger."

"It would stay in the family, that way."

"Why don't you use your own share to buy it?"

"I am, some of it. But with yours I could buy more."

"It doesn't do me much good, growing sugar in Barbados when I live in Finland."

"You don't have to live there, freezing your bloody tail off. You could come back and have a decent life here. Settle down."

"You're getting to sound like Father." She also noticed how Ba'jan he sounded, how local. Her ear was keen for different accents, the formal correctness of Finns and Swedes speaking English. It revived her old fear of being trapped in this provincial world.

"The old man made good sense sometimes. It's because of him we've both got a few quid coming. And you're getting old enough to listen. You can't go running around the world like a kid forever."

It was annoying yet comforting to have him preach like this.

Listening, she thought of David, of the stupidity of her affair with Geoffrey.

"After all, you'll soon be forty."

She shrugged off the unpleasant memory. Now she would be forty, in two days, in Kaarina's house.

When David was ambassador in Helsinki, he had met Matti and Kaarina Koivisto at a literary evening for Finnish and Canadian writers. Later, when Marilyn was away, he had introduced Francesca. The Koivistos began treating them as a couple, cooperating in the subterfuges they had to employ, the discretion necessary in Helsinki's small foreign community. The old apartment near the university, where Matti taught English literature, was a place they could safely meet. The situation bred intimacy, their hosts becoming connivers in the affair. Few outsiders could be invited regularly, unless David wanted to be reckless. The isolation from other people heated up the atmosphere, while the Koivistos' tolerance legitimated Francesca and David.

On her visits to Helsinki, Francesca would go alone when David could not. It became almost a home to her, and she sometimes spent the night. Kaarina encouraged it, and the two women became very close. In her fifties, her blond hair silvering, Kaarina was still a Finnish beauty, with a taut and sensual face like the Aaltonen sculpture of the Karelian girl. Francesca was magnetically drawn to this handsome woman, older but still feminine and alluring in an austere way, with her firm chin and strong cheekbones, her breasts still shapely. She had a shrewd and affectionate way with Francesca, like an aunt who could talk bluntly but also seductively.

She was passing the hummocky island to her left, the wind freshening as she came out of its lee, making whitecaps, *Havsflickan* surging along, the speed alarming when the land was so close. Without the binoculars she could see the severe Lutheran church steeple on the low island coming up on the right.

ELEVEN

OTTAWA–TRINIDAD

DAVID IMMEDIATELY TURNED in his Guyana report to the Prime Minister's Office, pleased with its directness and irony, but heard nothing.

The reaction came from External. Ferguson, the assistant under secretary, called him in.

"I can see the game you're playing, Lyon."

"What game?"

"Toadying to the PMO. A little obvious, isn't it? Let me give you some sound advice. The worst crime in a foreign service officer—unless it's screwing some politician's wife—is to tailor your reporting to please the political bosses. If you want to suck up to politicians, go into politics. Just because we've got a prime minister with foolish ideas doesn't mean we have to corrupt this department to cater to his whims. Prime ministers come and go—even this one, thank God. We have to honor the traditions of this department for straight, unbiased analysis."

"That's what I thought I was doing," David said, flaring a little.

"You want to know what you have done? You have pulled the rug out from under our High Commissioner. Jim Evans is a good man ending a distinguished career. You've made him look like a fool. And that's just how Trudeau will treat him if he goes to Guyana —after this." He tapped David's report.

"If he goes?"

"*If* he goes. They cook up thirty ideas a day over there—get everyone scurrying around—and then forget twenty-five of them. But *if* he goes, how do you think he'll treat Evans? Those Jesuits in Montreal may have taught Trudeau how to ask clever questions, but they certainly didn't teach him any manners. He's the rudest, most arrogant bastard we've ever had in that job. Sweet as pie to the Russians or Castro but acts as though we're beneath his dignity. He'll treat poor old Evans with contempt because you've given him the ammunition. Well, we won't have him humiliated. We're going to recall him."

"Won't it humiliate Evans even more to be recalled just before the PM's visit?"

"Would you want to be in his position?"

David was worried—and furious.

"May I say something?"

"Yes."

"I think you're making an unwarranted conclusion because my analysis disagrees with department policy."

"I am reading the evidence, God dammit! You must be naïve not to realize there's a war going on between the PMO and External. We're fighting for our existence. If the PM and Ivan Head had their way, they'd get rid of us altogether. And work like this just helps convince them they're right."

"What if my reporting—as I believe—is the truth?"

"The truth?" Ferguson laughed. "Wait till you've had a few more postings abroad. You'll find that *truth* is policy carefully and deliberately arrived at. We don't send raw reporting like this to our own minister, let alone the PM. Do you know how many people have to sign off on something before it goes to the minister? Where have you been? Go back to your desk and think over what I'm saying. You're smart. You even write well. If you want to make your career in External, you make it our way. Is that clear?"

"Yes. It's very clear."

"I wonder what your father-in-law would make of this."

"I have a pretty good idea. He shares your opinion of the PM."

"Surprise. Surprise! Get along and let me figure out how to limit the damage."

Shaken and angry, David went back to his desk. Contempt for Trudeau among old External hands was widely rumored but seldom voiced as openly to a junior. Now they could hang him out to dry for a report the Prime Minister's Office might not even read. Trudeau was flirting with the European Community and absorbed in the constitutional struggle with Quebec. They might have forgotten the Guyana visit. The PMO might hang him out to dry as well.

"What's the matter?" Marilyn asked that evening.

He didn't want to discuss it with her.

"Oh, come on! Obviously you're stewing over something."

"I got a real raking over the coals from Ferguson for my report on Guyana. He thinks I was deliberately currying favor with the PMO with an analysis Trudeau would like."

"And were you?"

"No, of course not!" Her question cut him. He didn't want Marilyn to be right . . . but this was his career.

"I guess I was. I knew they hated Trudeau but not how vehemently. Ferguson said I've pulled the rug out from under old Evans, the high comm. They're going to recall him."

"Oh, David!" She was silent as the enormity of that sank in.

"I just loathe all that caution, all that protection of turf. No wonder the PM is sick of them."

"And how do you feel about *him* now?"

"Just the same. Trudeau has brought some life to this town. People hate new thinking, and that's what he's making them do. Think. Go back to zero. Ask basic questions. Why are we doing this? What is our foreign policy really for? That's why he's shaking things up."

"And when he's shaken them up, will it really all be better?"

Her questions annoyed him.

"Marilyn, it's a new generation. We have to think new thoughts."

"Well, you don't have to bark at me because you're upset."

"I'm not barking."

"All right. Obviously you're worried. Have some more coffee. Now, what can you do about it?"

"Nothing, I guess. Just wait it out."

She said, meditatively but affectionately, "Maybe you were a little cocksure when you came back from Guyana. You seemed awfully full of yourself."

Startled, David looked at her very carefully. He actually had a letter from Francesca in his pocket. His guilt had subsided once he was sure he had not given himself away, and as work and domestic routine consumed his energies. And as he found, unproudly, that he was good at dissembling.

He seemed driven to notice the little things that made the two women different. Marilyn pulling a slip over her head gave him a small negative feeling. Her upper arms and shoulders were fleshier than Francesca's and lightly freckled. David saw himself accumulating evidence, building a case. When he caught himself, he knew it wasn't fair. But the compulsion to compare did not weaken. Everything about Marilyn became not Francesca, another grain of sand tumbling from Marilyn's sphere in the hourglass to Francesca's.

David told himself repeatedly he would do nothing to hurt Marilyn. She was innocent; she must not be hurt. Given his imperative feelings for Francesca, it was not an argument he could pursue very logically. Something had to unfold to bring them together, without hurting his wife. Not the kind of analytical reasoning he was commended for at External Affairs.

He had written asking her for a photograph, pouring into the letter his joy at their days together and his agony at being separated. In writing he noticed a complete ease of expression, the same new ability to unburden his heart that he had felt in her presence. He noticed a certain grace and fluency; he liked his own letter. He gave his office address and was feverish for her reply. He looked every day, counted the days, imagined her writing tearfully the moment he'd left, going immediately to the post office.

Yet when her letter came, he saw that the delay had been hers. She had waited eight days to write, although her letter was as passionate as his.

He replied immediately then, waiting for her reply, studied her first letter as though it were a message to be decoded. Her bold handwriting, her flow of words, her extravagant punctuation, all were electric with her personality. It sounded just like Francesca talking—uninhibited, passionate, daring, funny, with an occasional simple phrase so intense in feeling as to make him swallow and breathe more rapidly. He had her second letter in his pocket now.

"Maybe you should talk to Daddy," Marilyn said. Odd, Francesca had said the same thing, sardonically, about politics in Guyana.

"No. It'd be just like talking to Ferguson."

"He might have some practical advice."

David knew Wallace Farquhar's opinion: "Trudeau's a popinjay. An intellectual poseur. A mind with no solid core. Everything's for effect. Look at the clothes the man wears! A middle-aged man trying to look like a Left Bank intellectual!"

"You're out of date, Daddy," Marilyn had said. "It's a hippie they're calling him."

"Highly appropriate!" Farquhar said.

"Is it inappropriate to observe," David had said drily, "that the Canadian people seem to love it?"

"The Canadian people!" Farquhar had snorted. "People like conjuring tricks—until they get weary of them."

Now gently, supportively, Marilyn murmured, "Well, perhaps you'll just have to trim your sails a little, till this blows over."

"Sound advice from the bureaucrat's daughter?"

"The bureaucrat's daughter who loves you."

A WEEK LATER, a call from Ivan Head, the man rapidly becoming his own Ottawa legend, some said cultivating the legend. It was common talk that he could call Henry Kissinger at will. Less charitable talk said he was trying to play Kissinger to Trudeau's Nixon.

"We thought your Guyana stuff was terrific. Right on the mark. Just what we wanted," he said.

David wondered who *we* was, whether the PM knew anything about it.

"I'm going to get External to spring you for the trip. We think it'd be useful to have someone along who knows the score. OK with you?"

"Sure," David said, swelling with joy at the chance of seeing Francesca. "When is it?"

"Not set yet. Probably late summer. I'll let you know. Got to go now."

Just as he'd hoped. Or almost. It wasn't an invitation to join the PMO, but it might be the prelude to one. On prime ministerial trips valuable relationships were formed. Who knew what this might lead to? A little thought nagged nonetheless. *Just what we wanted*, Head had said. Would going burn David's bridges at External? He couldn't worry about it. It was too exciting.

If his bosses at External knew of the call, there was no sign. Senior officials like Ferguson were immersed in another reorganization, coordinating with other government departments to produce "country plans" for each mission. Senior ambassadors overseas were complaining. The under secretary had to take the extraordinary step of cabling all missions, "We are not doing this . . . to be stylish or to imitate the Americans."

"How pathetic!" said Wallace Farquhar when he heard of it. "We're not imitating the Americans! Dear, dear!"

David thought Ottawa's bureaucratic squabbles very petty beside the momentous events in Washington, which he still followed avidly. He was fascinated by the torment of this great superpower, a gladiator thrashing helplessly in the coils of Vietnam, irritated (when it noticed) by Canada's nipping, clucking disapproval.

IN HER LETTERS Francesca grew more impatient, and David's agony mounted in the bursting of the Ottawa spring—ice breaking up, snow evaporating, a million Dutch tulips bejeweling the federal Driveways, trees exploding into leaf.

No word about Guyana. Trudeau seemed fixated on Quebec, calling the provincial premiers to Victoria to hammer out a new constitutional formula.

In July Marilyn took the girls to her parents' cottage at Mac-Gregor Lake, while Ottawa sweltered in leaden heat. Each day David arrived at the office with his shirt soaked with sweat.

Out of the blue President Nixon announced that he was unilaterally abandoning the postwar fix at Bretton Woods, pulling the U.S. off the gold standard, and slapping a 10 percent surcharge on imports. Taken off guard, Canadian officials raced back to crisis meetings in Ottawa. Ministers flew to Washington to protest about the damaging blow to America's closest friend and largest trading partner. The blustering treasury secretary, John Connally, talked to them from notes prepared for Japan—until the mistake was noticed.

Trudeau went on television to say he thought Americans didn't know or care much about Canada.

For the first time David thought Trudeau had struck the wrong note, sounding petulant and weak for the leader of a proud nation. For all the talk of a bold new foreign policy, all Canada could seem to do was react. Detractors noted with satisfaction that even Ivan Head's vaunted relationship with Kissinger had not spared—or even warned—Canada.

Then suddenly, at the end of August, the PMO called. The trip was on. Ecstatic, his energies revived in the rush to go, David phoned Francesca but was told—he guessed by her mother—that she was in Trinidad. He must have missed a letter. His hopes crashed. Then he learned that their commercial flight stopped in Port of Spain, and he had her phone number. Hope revived.

On the plane for the first time he saw Trudeau close up, the high cheekbones, the long teeth, the strangely tilted eyes that had mesmerized the country. He was a much smaller man than David had expected, almost dainty in his proportions.

Very junior in the delegation, David was introduced but not drawn into any prime ministerial conversation. He was dying to know whether Trudeau himself had read his report, but didn't ask.

There was an hour at Port of Spain. The prime minister's party was ushered into a private lounge. David rushed to a money exchange, got coins, found a phone—and was told Francesca was out. Agony. Just before boarding, he called again. Still out. He left a message—he was on his way to Guyana and would be back in two days. Miserable, he boarded the plane.

But at the BOAC hotel in Guyana there was a message.

"Call me immediately, do you hear."

Dressing for a reception, David called.

"Why didn't you tell me you were coming? It's stupid, your being there and my being here."

"I couldn't. I didn't know till the last minute."

"Can you stop in Trinidad on the way back?"

He took a deep breath. "I'll try."

"It's been seven months."

"I know. I'll do my best. Look, I've got to go."

"David?"

"Yes?"

"Mind you come!"

In the rush of official events, he had difficulty getting Ivan Head alone. Then for a moment they were walking together on a tour of the botanical gardens—where Francesca and David had spent magic hours.

"Do you see any problem if I stop off in Trinidad on the way back?"

"Not carnival time, is it?"

"No, an old friend."

"If you can square it with External, no problem. Just change your ticket."

No problem, but David knew he was taking enormous risks. Others in the entourage saw him leave the plane at Port of Spain and could mention it in Ottawa. At the airport he saw officers he knew at the Canadian High Commission in Trinidad. They were buzzing around the official party but might notice him leaving with Francesca. One of them might recognize him in town.

But the thrill of seeing her pushed his anxieties aside. Where guilt might have resided, he felt a kind of innocence. He underwent no moral debate. It seemed honorable to keep his promise to her to come back. It did not seem dishonorable to leave his wife and two children; they were at the lake, away from the late summer heat in Ottawa.

She persuaded David to stay at her uncle's house in the hills above Port of Spain, because her parents knew she was there and it would save him a hotel.

Her uncle was a bandy-legged little man obsessed with horses. In the three days David stayed, the uncle was ostentatiously discreet and nosy.

He managed never to be there when they came or went, but prowled his house late at night. He said he got up to eat ice cream. They suspected that he waited outside the doors of their adjoining rooms—listening.

They heard him once when they were in full embrace under the mosquito canopy in her bed. She said, "Ssh!" and they lay locked together, not daring to breathe, listening to the night dogs barking far off and Indian music from one of the Hindu houses down the road, until the tiny clink of a spoon against the ice cream dish betrayed him, and they heard him creaking away.

"Do you think he heard us before we heard him?" she whispered.

Then they made love more quietly, an ear on the door, half-imagining him there.

In the mornings her uncle and aunt remained out of sight, but possibly just within earshot. Each morning he left them ripe mangoes from the tree in his garden and Francesca prepared them in the sweet coolness of the tropical morning, the room open to the air on two sides, lush greenery visible in an unfocused blur behind her.

She cut the sides away from the large pit, leaving two saucer-shaped slices, then scored them through the fruit to the rind, making a checkerboard of small squares. Lifting one slice, she pushed the convex skin with her thumbs, and the scored surface exploded into a hemisphere of mango cubes.

In lingering bites, she nibbled them off, licking away the yellow fibers and the juice from her lips. She made eating the mangoes seem like a variation on themes they had enacted under the mosquito canopy on the bed. Under the perfume of the mangoes, David was aware of the smell of her sleepy body, with its trace of Shocking from the night before. As she ate the fruit, she consumed him with eyes so black that she remained invisible behind them, although he could see himself reflected.

So shy of her uncle in bed at night, Francesca was bold and teasing by day.

She wore a pleated cotton nightdress, leaving the top untied. As they ate the mangoes and drank their coffee, his eyes strayed naturally to her breasts visible through the opening.

"Uncle?" she called.

There was no answer.

In a louder, warning voice, "Uncle! I tell you what he's doing. He's trying to look at my breasts through my nightdress."

There was no sound in response, and David didn't know whether they were just there behind the open doorway, listening, or far off, minding their own business. Francesca didn't know either, but it was typical that she dared them to hear and, in daring them, dared him to be uncomfortable, as he was, but pretended otherwise to appear unshockable and amused.

She could find a way in the sweetest moments to pierce his delight with a little poisoned needle. Lying in his arms under the mosquito netting, their secret pavilion, surrounded by the thick tropical night, on the lovely, ebbing moments, their breaths still subsiding, she giggled and said, "You'd better come back and keep doing that to me or I'll find another man!"

David tried to rationalize that it was her insecurity, not his. Francesca's games were the price of attending her, of being enveloped in ineffable sweetness and mystery, feeling in her presence a higher energy of living, breathing purer oxygen, able to take on the world with confident amusement, as she did. The dissonant undercurrents only gave that rapture a spicier seasoning.

To escape the uncle's unnerving scrutiny, David rented a car for a day and they took the twisting road behind Port of Spain to the beach at Maracas Bay. That is where he first noticed that she could talk to anyone, instantly, as though born to their place and position in life, not just in the islands, but later in Europe, in the U.S.

In her brown bikini she strolled up and started talking to the women in bandanas who were grilling fish under the coconut palms. The hefty black women emphasized Francesca's slimness and golden color.

She kept glancing at him over her shoulder while laughing with them, like old friends. The Trinidadian accents were so broad, he couldn't follow. One of them slapped her thigh and wiped her eyes.

They carried their sandwiches down the beach closer to the turquoise water.

"Do you come here a lot?"

"Hardly ever. I never have a car here."

"You seem to know them so well."

"Those women?" She laughed. "Do you know what they were asking me?"

"What?"

"Are you going to marry him? Is he a good man? Is he a good lover?"

"What did you say?"

"To shut them up, I told them, 'He's got a big bamboo!' That's why they laughed. I said, 'You don't think a white man's got a big bamboo? Well, you're wrong!'"

The sandwiches were delicious, grilled fish on rough homemade bread sprinkled with a hot sauce. As they ate, several dogs appeared, creeping closer, sniffing extravagantly. They were thin and mangy, with sand in their fur, growling quietly, retracting black lips to show their teeth. David thought they darkened the mood of the day and tried to shoo them off. But Francesca said to the closest and ugliest, as though it were her own dog, "Come here! Sit down!" And it did. The others, uninvited, hung back. Francesca sat there, exquisite in her bikini, her knees drawn up, the dog patiently sitting at her feet, its head level with hers, while she smiled at it so affectionately, it must have been bewitched.

"Are you hungry?" She broke off part of her sandwich and the dog snaffled it in one gulp.

"That's it, then! Go!" A dismissive flick of her fingers, and it moved. In a second it was gone, and the others too.

She laughed and got up. "Those women. They probably train them to beg so they can sell more sandwiches!"

She ran into the sea, clean-limbed and free, exquisitely beautiful.

TWELVE

KAARINA'S ISLAND

IT WAS TIME to get ready. The church steeple was a mile astern, the little islets almost abeam, and Kaarina's island was rising ahead. The declining sun was already casting longer shadows, and the wind was freshening. Francesca put on her anorak and woolen cap.

She turned *Havsflickan* into the wind, the genoa luffing frantically until she subdued it by hauling in the roller furling-line. That quieted the ship and made her feel in control. She started the engine, letting it idle quietly, then went to the mast and uncleated the main halyard. The mainsail came down with a thump. She did a rough furl on the huge sail, which always seemed more voluminous down than up. With four canvas tiers it was lumpy but secure, and she could concentrate on navigation and anchoring.

She was half a mile from the nearest shore and the yacht was drifting comfortably, with the motor idling, so Francesca took a few moments to study the chart: around a point, along a rocky shore, then the cove would open up. There were big rocks on the left going in, but clear water if she kept to the middle. Five meters of water at the entrance, shoaling to two meters halfway in. Years before, Matti had sketched in for David the course line in pencil, 175 degrees, extending ashore to the house.

So, she should motor on her present course, 305 degrees, till the house lined up, then turn south and steer 175. There was a small anchor drawn in pencil where the cove began to narrow, opposite the bump in the shore on the right-hand side. The plan was clear: motor in slowly past that bump, turn in as small a circle as possible, come back to the center, and opposite the bump again drop the anchor.

She went back to the wheel, put the gear into forward, and advanced the throttle, bringing the boat back to her course of 305.

With the sun losing its warmth and the short day dying, the falling light created a forlorn feeling. She was impatient to be snug in her cabin with the heater on before the chill of the northern night descended.

She remembered she hadn't prepared the anchor, and while there was still room to drift, she locked the wheel and slowed the engine. On the foredeck, she found the lever that released the lock on the capstan gripping the chain, tried it, pulled through a few feet of chain to see that it ran freely, then fed it back down the hole and tightened the lock. Leaning through the pulpit, she slid back the stainless steel pin that held the anchor in place. So that was ready. Back in the cockpit, she resumed her course and speed.

Her training with Geoffrey had been very thorough. She had crewed for him for five months. Another whim. She was visiting Barbados . . . she couldn't model until she got her figure back after Samantha. Geoffrey's current girlfriend *cum* cook mate had just taken off on another boat.

He was a red-faced, stocky Englishman of fifty with a graying blond beard. He had chucked his staid career and left a wife in England; one of the charter fraternity who had run away from humdrum lives and put all they owned into their boats. Barbados was so small, you met everyone. She had dinner with him, went dancing to a steel band, then back for a nightcap on his large ketch . . . and to bed . . . half-drunk, not caring, experiencing a kind of pleasure in surrendering to his brute strength . . . then waking to the novel feeling of morning afloat on a well-appointed yacht. And later that same morning she had suddenly agreed to work with him.

Her brother, Nigel, was furious at her irresponsibility, but his wife, Delores, loved babies and offered to keep the children in Barbados while Francesca took off with Geoffrey. Now she could hardly believe she had done it, with no guilt, no remorse, feeling instead that she was paying someone back for something.

It was hard work, some of it very menial, learning to cook and perform basic seamanship. They sailed to Antigua, north to the Virgins and the Bahamas, south to the Grenadines, back up to St. Lucia, Martinique, Guadeloupe, Monserrat, St. Barts. At first she enjoyed the times when there were no charters to cook for or clean up from, when they were alone, and she really learned to sail as they moved the boat to a new location. But she quickly soured on Geoffrey, a loner, utterly selfish, even brutish, who wanted a woman only to fuck and cook for him.

In the spring she quit and returned to Paris with the children and work-hardened hands to pick up her modeling, resuming the strange routine with David, meeting when both could snatch a few hours or a night in the same city.

Later she and David had sailed in these islands alone for two weeks. Such a different man from Geoffrey but similar on boats— leaving nothing to chance.

The island was growing in size, and she could make out the sea, which seemed so friendly to the yacht, crashing angrily on the rocky shore. The fury of the waves made her steer very wide of the point. But once she was behind it, the wind dropped and the sea was reassuringly calmer. About five minutes later the little bay opened up suddenly on her left, and there, picturesque in its forest clearing, was Kaarina's house. Francesca slowed the engine and waited carefully until the house bore 175 degrees, then turned into the narrow cove, the wind and the sea growing quieter with each few yards she progressed.

The shore was already in deep shadow, so the little promontory halfway in couldn't be seen until she was almost there and the depth finder showed 2.8 meters of water. There was more room than it looked on the chart, so she swung the boat with no anxiety, then slowed to a crawl to line up again in the center. Oh, the damn dinghy! Again she had forgotten. She jumped back to the rail, gathered in the long painter, and hauled the dinghy up closer to the side of the yacht. That put *Havsflickan* past her anchor mark, so she had to make the circuit again.

This time as she approached the mark she switched into neutral and went up to the foredeck. The boat finally stopped moving against the trees on the shore. Francesca gave the anchor a shove, and it went down with a roar of chain. When she guessed enough had run out she locked the capstan, then raced back to put the gear lever in reverse. If you did it too timidly, the stern spun away to the right, so she shoved the throttle until the engine roared and the boat began to move quickly astern. In a moment, *Havsflickan* was brought up with a satisfying jerk. The anchor had bitten. She gave it one more surge of power hard astern to embed it firmly.

Pleased with herself, she went below, poured a glass of red wine, lit a cigarette, and came back on deck. She sipped the wine and smoked, sitting on the cabin top, smiling, looking possessively around the cove, with affection for her quiet anchorage.

Tomorrow she would take the dinghy ashore and follow the path up the meadow to the house. All she could see of it now in the shadows were the heavy shutters and the long ornate gable, its white paint standing out against the dark brown of the walls. She didn't want to go up there with darkness falling.

She was languorously tired. All her muscles had been stretched, her blood freshened by the heavily oxygenated air, and her face was tingling pleasantly from the wind, her palms burning from the work they had done. She wanted to eat and fall into a deep sleep, but just now it was blissful to sit on the boat she commanded, feel it swing daintily at anchor, in water that was calm except where a whisper of wind stole through the darkening woods to send ghostly ripples over the surface.

THIRTEEN

TRINIDAD–OTTAWA

ON DAVID'S LAST day in Trinidad, Francesca went to British West Indian Airways in Port of Spain.

"It's a way to get away, a job to get me out of Guyana."

David thought she could find something more fulfilling.

"I'm not trained for anything else."

He'd suggested she go to college in the States or Canada, a selfish motive operating beside the generous one.

"My father says girls don't need fancy educations, and he's already paying for my brother's agricultural course in the States. As soon as I start flying, I'll be going to New York all the time and it'll be much easier to meet you. If we have to depend on your coming all the way to Trinidad, we'll never see each other."

So she went to BWIA, delectable in a short pink skirt and white blouse, tanned legs, woven sandals, and sunglasses. He watched her cross the road, her head cocked in that defiant, disdainful way that

94

later made her so outstanding as a model. She could freeze out male curiosity even as she drew it, with a taunting, challenging look that said, *I dare you to make me an object of desire.*

He felt conspicuous, waiting in the street. There was a Bank of Nova Scotia next door and a Royal Bank of Canada farther down. He expected every white person passing to recognize him.

She got the job and came out excited but, typically, sardonic.

"Surprise, surprise! They said yes. They must be hard up!"

That night they went out dancing. She moved as though she were making the music, the reggae band playing to her lead.

David felt awkward, trying to dance as nonchalantly as she. She would say, "Just relax, don't try so hard." But it was impossible. He never felt the Zen of it, never came to the feeling that he knew well in skiing: the less attention, the smoother the turn. He couldn't let go enough or stop caring.

He worried that they might run into someone he knew. He also sensed competition. He assumed young men she knew would see her with some big guy who looked awkward. He projected his own feeling into their minds and into Francesca's.

When he apologized, she said, "Don't be stupid." The words sounded insulting, but she said them affectionately, like a caress. "It doesn't matter." But it mattered, because David was projecting another anxiety: that when he went, they would be dancing with Francesca. And, in the darkest corner of his anxiety, one of them might —to use her word—be poking her.

NOW AT FIFTY-TWO, feeling tired and heavy at 188 pounds, David thought of himself at thirty-two, a trim 155, and marveled at his insecurity. Yet it hadn't stopped him from taking more bold steps.

The telephone rang. Expecting Jean Luc, he heard Jenny.

"Hi, Daddy. It's Jenny. I hope it's not too late. I just got back from work. Whew! I'm out of breath from running upstairs!"

"It's OK. It isn't ten yet. How're you doing?"

The idiom he used with her. Both daughters were born in

Washington, but Jenny had really become American, living in San Francisco. So far, for cost reasons, they'd persuaded Peggy to stay at McGill.

"I'm fine. I just wanted to know how Granddaddy is. I didn't want to call Ottawa so late, and I have to go out in a minute."

"He's making a little progress. I talked to Mummy a while ago. He's saying a few more words but it's really tough."

"That's awful! I can't bear to think of it. Does he know? I mean, like, can he understand?"

"She thinks so, but she isn't sure. Sometimes people with this kind of stroke can get a lot better, and sometimes they don't. It just takes time." His daughter was three when he met Francesca, who was then younger than Jenny now. "Mummy said the Prime Minister's Office called. He wants to go out there and see Granddaddy."

"Wow, that's neat. Who is the prime minister, anyway?"

Canadian affairs were not her daily bread—unless she was saying that to tease him.

"Look, I'm sorry, Daddy. I've got to go. We're late for a thing. Bob says hi. Talk to you soon, OK? Would you tell Mom I called? Bye."

She hung up, but her personality lingered. She was determined to make a career as a writer, living with a man who wrote publicity for records, taking courses, attending creative-writing groups. She'd been published in small magazines. More than anyone in the family, Jenny had the single-mindedness of Wallace Farquhar, the old man now stricken in Ottawa.

Jenny simply cut through all the Canadian reserve and moved ahead. The family in Canada adored her.

A couple of minutes after ten. Five in the morning in Helsinki. A few hours until they would know anything more.

Who is the prime minister, anyway? His American daughter, who called Marilyn *Mom*, instead of the Canadian *Mum*. So did a lot of Canadians, who heard it all the time on the American television most of them preferred, part of the gradual erosion of Canadian distinctiveness. That process would probably accelerate now that Free Trade was a fact. The marriage Canada's wise virgins had so long feared, because it threatened too much intimacy, was now being consummated with a vengeance. It was far more likely that the offspring would be raised in the American religion of unbridled consumerism and individuality than the dying Canadian faith in self-restraint and collectivism.

David rarely indulged this private skepticism; professionally he was adept at countering such doubts. And there was no shortage of doubters. Even Gordon Ritchie, who had negotiated the Free Trade deal, now said he had very mixed feelings because the Americans were being so bloody-minded in resolving disputes.

Thinking about it clearly, putting ambition aside, did he have confidence that Mulroney was the man for this difficult hour? Not really. Then why even consider joining his government? For that matter, did he even want to move back to Ottawa?

He remembered how it felt returning that summer from Trinidad. Having grown up by the sea, David thought the inland city tasted stale and flat, like water left overnight in a glass. Despite its rivers, Ottawa in summer felt landlocked and stifling.

On his first night back Marilyn left the children with her parents at MacGregor Lake, and drove into the city to be alone with him.

Naked, without covers, they made love in the airless bedroom in Sandy Hill, their bellies sliding together in the heat. David's guilt again surfaced as renewed desire, wanting her more, again in the morning at the sight of her thighs in short shorts as she tidied the bedroom. As she bent over the bed to smooth the sheet, he slid his hand under the shorts, irritating her because she was impatient to get back to the lake, where guests were coming to lunch. He insisted, pushing her back onto the bed.

"What has come over you?" Half laughing, half annoyed. "Not now. It's too hot," Marilyn said, wiping her hair back from her perspiring forehead as she lay under him. "Besides, I've put the diaphragm away in my bag. It's already in the car."

"I could go and get it."

"No!" She rolled him off her. "Come on. We'll be late." She looked in the mirror, fluffing out her hair. "I shouldn't let you go to the Caribbean again. Something gets in your blood. You come back like an old goat. Come on. Use some of that energy to help me."

It left a little anger cooking in his mind and he drove too fast when they hit the unpaved road to the lake. He didn't want to be here, in this hot car, on this dusty road, with this woman.

"We've got to get air conditioning in the next car. It's crazy not to have it in this climate."

"It's never bothered you before. Isn't it even hotter in the Caribbean?"

"There's usually a cool breeze blowing."

"And we certainly can't afford a new car."

When he had driven a few minutes in silence her tone softened. "Never mind. It's cooler at the lake. You don't have to do anything except be polite at lunch. You can laze in the shade all afternoon." Life with her irascible father had made Marilyn, like her mother, a soother of ruffled male feelings.

"And Jenny's dying to see you," said Marilyn, following her own thoughts. "We're having a lovely time but we miss you."

Neither she nor External had remarked on the three extra days he'd taken in Trinidad.

When he didn't respond, she gave his thigh a comradely rub. "Don't be grumpy. Everyone has to come home and face his responsibilities sooner or later."

Her uncanny touch with sibylline remarks always left him uncertain of their innocence.

It would be a week or ten days till a letter from Francesca, perhaps months before any chance of seeing her. He could not live without her, and to say so was the honorable thing. Ask Marilyn for a divorce. Cruel and blunt, but honest.

Francesca thought not. She had said, "It's too soon. We don't know each other well enough."

"I know you're the person I want to spend my life with."

"Are you sure? Someone like me? You might regret it."

Or she could sound like his conscience. "But what about your little girls? What would happen to them?"

Francesca never seemed to argue just in her own interest. "What will happen to your career if you get divorced?"

His close friends at External would say that, but he answered, "It's not supposed to matter as much nowadays."

"How would I live in a place where there is snow half the year?"

"Not really half the year—and you lived in Switzerland."

"Be honest. How cold does it get in Ottawa?"

"Twenty below—sometimes."

"Twenty below freezing?"

"Twenty below zero."

"I couldn't stand it. I think we should spend more time together first. Even if you were not married, I wouldn't say yes right away. People should live together to find out if they are compatible."

"I couldn't do that."

She gave one of her deep chuckles. "What do you think this is?"

"This is different. I don't think of you as an affair."

"Your wife would. If it were me, I'd be furious. I'd kill you."

"We just have to find a way to spend more time together," he said.

"That's why I'm going to BWIA, remember? So I can fly to see you all the time. And if you can't come to New York or Miami to meet me, I'll transfer to an airline that flies to Ottawa. You watch out. I'll call you from the hotel and say, I'm here! Come and make love to me quickly before I fall for one of the handsome pilots."

Her customary little flick, unerringly striking his private fears. He'd seen the camaraderie in airline crews, checking into hotels, the pert stewardesses flirting with the men. All young, pretty, susceptible, away from home in strange cities—the male passenger's fantasy.

It worsened his mood at Sunday lunch to listen to Wallace Farquhar and his guest, Norman McDougall, both veterans of the Pearson years of the department, both retired. They were still chewing over *Foreign Policy for Canadians*, the statement of Trudeau's new policy priorities.

"Mike Pearson is fuming. He told me Trudeau didn't even have the courtesy to consult him . . . all the months they were drafting and redrafting that nonsense . . . never even rang him up."

"Intolerable."

"Damned insulting to the man who put Canadian foreign policy on the map."

"And gave Trudeau his start . . . brought him into government in the first place."

"But more than the bad manners is the sheer vacuousness of the policy. How do you labor for months and produce six pamphlets defining Canada's vital interests, and scarcely mention the United States?"

"And then whine on television that Americans don't care about us . . ."

"Well, Trudeau's had a thing about the U.S. all along—typical fuzzy leftist cant . . ."

The two older men, a little flushed from their gin and tonics, were enjoying themselves.

"And standing there in Moscow bleating about the overpowering presence of the United States and the danger to our national identity . . ."

"Come on, you two," Margaret said. "It's too hot. You'll give yourselves strokes. Let's see if the porch is any cooler."

LATER ON THE porch, even in the shade, it was intolerably close, with the feeling of thunder overdue, a white shimmering heat haze hanging over the lake, a cicada rasping in a nearby tree. The McDougalls had left from the dock, the whine of their outboard gradually receding, now replaced by another, around the point. The outboard and the cicadas blurred together in the thickened air. A scent of pine needles mingled with a soapy smell from the grove of

100

poplars by the water, even their restless leaves now limp and still. Wallace Farquhar was snoring in the hammock, just visible through windows across the corner of the living room. His wife was lying down in her bedroom with Peggy, the one-year-old. Jenny, nearly four, was on Marilyn's lap in a wicker armchair. Deep in a deckchair David was reading, observing them in small glances over his book.

Marilyn had changed to take Jenny swimming but was making her wait until an hour after eating. Every few minutes the leggy child squirmed around, making the wicker creak, to look at her mother. "Is it an hour now?"

"No. Quiet; you'll wake up Granddaddy," Marilyn whispered.

David looked at the two bodies in their one-piece bathing suits, the woman of thirty and the child of four. The idea of going up the path through the pine trees to the guest cabin, of Marilyn stripping off the blue bathing suit, came and went in his thoughts. He could look at her critically—and with desire. Her thighs bulged minutely below the elastic rim of the suit; her stomach swelled—slightly; her breasts were becoming pendulous—a trifle. The lean tanned legs of the child lay along her mother's thighs, whose flesh suggested a future doughiness. Beneath her upper arms, hugging Jenny's scrawny chest, was the hint of a lap of loose flesh. Her hair was nondescript brown, not chestnut, not auburn, not dark blond, nothing vivid. Her pubic hair—God, why did it matter?—was straggly, overgrown-looking, whereas Francesca's was a trim neat triangle.

Marilyn eyed him dreamily, holding the child possessively against her, despite the heat.

If her thighs were leaner, no bulge where the bathing suit ended, the skin browner, the tummy flatter . . . if she were not here . . . if he were not here . . .

He closed his eyes and lay back, letting the book fall against his chest, hearing the cicadas, the outboard motor growing fainter, the smell of pine needles and poplar leaves. Deliberately he summoned Francesca's image and held it in his mind, like a private screening, second by second commanding it to switch from bedroom to beach, from day to night, from one lovemaking scene to another, his memory a subtle controller. Francesca in her bikini getting back into the car at Maracas, no one else nearby, turning to him, his hand on her slim naked waist . . .

He felt soft lips on his and opened his eyes. Marilyn, intensely intimate in her bathing suit, was leaning down to kiss him. She whispered, "Jenny had to go tinkle."

She kissed him again. "I'm sorry about this morning."

Desire for her flooded through him. He reached to touch her, but Jenny was back. "It must be an hour now!" She was leaning on his deckchair arm and rocking it.

"Ssh, ssh. Not so loud. Come on. I'll take you now." Throwing David a little pout of regret, Marilyn led Jenny down the path to the dock. He watched her body, now erect, looking fit and trim for its proportions, altered by his desire.

It was unfair to judge Marilyn by her body. It was not what mattered about her or to her. People remembered her eyes, her calm voice, her humor, her infinite considerateness. She had many friends, the number constantly growing. For any kindness, she wrote careful notes so touching, so personally nourishing, that recipients kept them for inspiration.

She swam and skied well, skated, played respectable tennis, a good sport. But she wasn't glamorous and knew it. There were always girls in the group whose legs, whose bottoms, whose breasts you noticed whatever they wore, Elmwood tunics or heavy overcoats; the message got through. You did not notice, until you really got to know her, that Marilyn had all those attributes.

David had known her for several years before he noticed she was sexually attractive. That was when he saw her at sixteen in a strapless evening dress at a dance, was aware of her powdered but slightly freckled shoulders, and felt her naked back above the dress. When he came back with drinks to find her sitting with others on the floor, looked down into her dress and saw her breasts, she became a sexual object and he wanted it.

102

Jenny was swimming, her squeals and splashing magnified by the sound-reflecting lake.

That night the storm came and they made love in the little guest cabin, amid flashes of mock daylight and a downpour thunderous on the roof; the natural drama emphasizing how undramatic was their coupling—routine, familiar, domestic.

FOURTEEN

KAARINA'S ISLAND

FRANCESCA AWOKE WITH the feeling of a child on a treasure hunt. She could not suppress the pleasure of finding what she had come for, however dead the reason for its being there.

Sunlight beamed into the cabin through the square ports. She lay cosily in the bunk, listening to the small sounds of water against the hull, the sensations of being in bed afloat, the warmth of her feet inside the bedding, the shrill cry of a bird fishing, feeling pleasure in being alive and intensely hungry. For years she had eaten nothing for breakfast but fruit and black coffee, but the moment her eyes opened she noticed the loaf of bread and remembered the eggs in the ice chest. She had been too tired to cook the night before and had managed only a piece of cheese and another glass of wine before falling into the deepest sleep in years. She got up and looked out, noticing that *Havsflickan* had swung around with the tide. The bow was pointing towards the house, now inviting in full sunshine.

In the head she laughed at herself in the mirror, her hair tousled and spiky, her face sunburned. She had fallen asleep without even washing her face. Now she heated water in the kettle for coffee and used some to wash and comb her hair. Then she attacked the kind of breakfast that made her queasy to watch people eating in Scandinavian hotels: scrambled eggs, salami, cheese, bread, and coffee. She took a second cup on deck to find the day mild, with no wind. She sipped her coffee, smoked a cigarette, prolonging the pleasures of the morning, letting the suspense mount, even as she marshaled rationalizations against disappointment.

In case she had to break in, she took a large screwdriver and hammer from the boat's tool chest and put them into a canvas bag, with a flashlight and matches. She poured the rest of the coffee into a thermos and added cigarettes to the bag.

She found the oars for the dinghy and let down the stern ladder into water that was so clear she could see pebbles on the bottom. If it had been summer she would have dived in, but when she dipped her fingers over the side of the dinghy, they ached with the cold.

The sun was warm on her face as she rowed ashore, glancing over her shoulder, steering by the house. The sky was almost cloudless overhead, and the waves breaking at the mouth of the cove were gentle. She could smell the spruce trees and the nutty autumn odors of dead leaves and ferns before the dinghy grated on the sandy beach. She tied up to a tree root overhanging the little strand and climbed up to the path. The grass had not been cut for a long time. Between the beach and the house were several hundred yards of tall grass and dead wildflowers drenched with morning dew. Her shoes and jeans would be soaked. But she remembered boots with the foul weather gear and experienced an odd pleasure in forcing herself to row back and get them, just further postponing the discovery.

She found the yellow sea boots and decided, while she was about it, to pull on the trousers of the foul weather gear to keep her legs dry. Thus attired, she rowed back to the shore.

She was breathing heavily as she climbed the slope through the thick grass, and not only from the exertion. She knew she was excited and knew how absurd it was, but she didn't care.

The setting of the house was high and the climb long. From the sea it had looked small, like thousands of cottages and fishing camps owned by Swedes and Finns in these islands. But it got larger as she approached, growing from what appeared to be a small chalet to a substantial house.

From the unkempt garden, unraked leaves, the overgrown meadow it was clear no one had lived here this year and no caretaker had come by to tidy up. Despite a little sadness at the signs of neglect, she was unable to subdue a childish excitement.

The grass grew right up to the steps to the verandah running across the front, almost invisible from the water. The front door was around to the left on the side away from the sea.

Aware that she was again postponing the moment, Francesca put down her bag and caught her breath, gazing down the field to the cove, where *Havsflickan* sat as regally as a swan upon the glassy water. The elevation of the house gave it a spectacular view over the last islands of the archipelago and beyond to the open waters of the Gulf of Bothnia, to her left towards Sweden, Finland to the right. Yet it was hidden from all sides except the cove and sheltered by forest from the prevailing winds. An autumn fisherman in a motorboat speeding by might not notice the yacht anchored in the cove. Without it there to give her away, no one would know she was here.

She remembered precisely where the key was hidden but expected it not to be there. People changed hiding places. But the key was there, its brass green from corrosion. Holding the cold metal, she thought hers must be the first warm fingers to touch it in a long time.

Her heartbeat quickened as she opened the storm door. The key entered the lock stiffly, the tumblers resistant from disuse. But it turned, and she was standing in the gloom of the large open room, lit by splinters of sunlight cutting the darkness at different angles from chinks where the shutters fitted imperfectly. These mini beams created a pleasant twilight, making her flashlight unnecessary. For a house long empty, it smelled fresh, not musty, and there was little dust apparent on the floor or furniture. She looked carefully before advancing into the room, the interior of pale wood, walls and floor in blond birch finish, handwoven rugs on the floor, and fabrics of similar texture in curtains and covers for the chairs and sofa.

Francesca put her bag down. She crossed the living room and dining area and glanced into the kitchen, its appliances from another generation. It was a comfortable, well-appointed summer house, with no electricity. Throughout the downstairs living area were handsome oil lamps, and the dining room table was lit by a modern steel chandelier bearing a dozen half-burned candles. On either side of the large stone fireplace were shelves filled with Matti's books. It was just as she remembered.

The stairwell was enclosed with paneled wood. She glanced in each of the shuttered bedrooms, noting carved wooden headboards and colorful handwoven spreads. In the room above, under the eaves, she knew, was the loom on which all the fabrics in the house had been woven.

She left the main bedroom until last. It was large, commanding the two center windows on the sea. In the dim light she could see the massive four-poster bed.

Francesca opened one of the windows, released the bolts securing the shutters, and pushed them outwards. Sunlight flooded the room, dazzling her eyes, accustomed to the gloom. Emboldened, she undid the other shutter. The view down to the cove and out to sea was even grander from this room. *Havsflickan* had begun to swing again. The tide must be turning.

She turned back to the bed, which dominated the room. It was an eighteenth-century piece, built by a Swedish country cabinetmaker or perhaps a shipwright, almost like a miniature house, with its vertical beams and beveled paneling, a row of finely cut dentil molding along the top edge. The bed had a wooden canopy, divided into panels, with delicate floral carvings like those in the headboard. A subtle vine tendril with little blossoms crept down each face of the corner posts.

There were bed curtains of fine white linen, bordered with a handwoven ribbon, the same used to tie the curtains. It was the most beautiful bed she had ever seen. She pulled off the dust sheet, finding large pillows, their cases of the same handwoven linen as the bed curtains. On the bed was a thick eiderdown, also covered in white linen, embroidered in stitching to mirror the panels and flowers in the wooden canopy overhead.

Francesca stood back and looked. She had been dreaming of this bed. Besides the fine early workmanship and its probable value as an antique, it was a work of love. Two centuries ago, some craftsman had made it as the most important piece of furniture in a family, perhaps for a bride and then for her descendants. Many generations would have been conceived and born, and would have died in a bed like this. Young men and women, in the ecstasies of the bridal bed, would have climbed in here and closed the curtains on the world. In this bed the bride would have endured the horrors of unmedicated childbirth, her husband looking on helplessly. Perhaps she died in childbirth. If not, she had suckled her babies in this bed. As they grew, her children had snuggled in here with their parents. And the old or the sick had breathed their last, staring up at these carved flowers.

But for all the grimness it might have borne, this bed spoke to Francesca of love. Certainly Kaarina had thought of it that way. On her loom upstairs, she had woven these fabrics, and embroidered them by hand.

Francesca could wait no longer. She brought a chair close to the left-hand side of the headboard. She knew it was that corner. She stood on the chair, and her head came close to the ceiling. She reached over the ornate molding on the canopy to the depression inside and explored the dusty interior. Her fingertips felt paper, and she withdrew an envelope covered with dust. She took it to the open window and blew away the dust and cobwebs.

It was still sealed, and she felt a strange emotion now that she was actually holding it, a little chilly from the fresh morning air. She closed the window but left the shutters open and felt the sun warm through the glass. She knew just how she wanted to do it. She removed the rubber boots and the foul weather pants. In her stocking feet and jeans she climbed up onto the bed, leaned against the big pillows, and slipped her legs under the thick eiderdown. From there she could see out the window, down the meadow to the cove, and miles out to sea.

Then she opened the envelope and read David's handwriting:

OCTOBER 14, 1975

This will record a solemn pledge made on this day, in this old bed, with the ghosts of all its previous occupants as witnesses. We, the undersigned, Francesca D'Anielli and David Lyon, do hereby pledge to meet here sixteen years from this day, on October 14, 1991, no matter what difficulties, obstacles, or hindrances life may erect to prevent it. This we solemnly swear.

Signed: Francesca D'Anielli
David Lyon

"But why 1991?" David had asked as she dictated.

"Because it's my fortieth birthday, and in case I'm an old hag by then I want to make sure you're committed to turn up."

"You won't be an old hag but I'll be a balding old crock with a potbelly and flaccid withers."

"What are flaccid withers?" She laughed.

"You'll see in sixteen years."

Francesca put the letter down and settled back against the pillows.

They had come in the fall of 1975 when all the excitement from the signing of the Final Act of the Helsinki Accords had died down, Trudeau and the other heads of government had departed, and life at the Canadian Embassy had slipped back to normal routine. David took two weeks' leave.

When he told the Koivistos about the plan to charter a boat and cruise in the Aaland Islands, Matti and Kaarina insisted that they stop at their island and use this house. It would be a little chilly in October, they said, but very beautiful. Kaarina said quietly to Francesca, "When your time together is precious, don't spend it all on a boat. Use the boat to get there but go and stay in the old bed on the island."

Whether it was a slip or intentional, she didn't say, *Go and stay in the house* but in the old bed, as though it were the house.

"When you see it, you will know what I mean. It is the bed for people who are in love."

Normally the Koivistos took the large ferry to Mariehamn on the principal island, then their own motorboat to the cove. But for David, Matti marked the anchorage and drew in the bearing for a yacht entering the cove.

Matti, with his lined, bearded face and twinkling blue eyes, was the sort of professor Francesca imagined students adoring, gentle in his manner but passionate when he talked of books and music.

"No one will know where you are," he said. "There is no telephone. No electricity. If the weather is bad you can sit by the fire and read. A lot of my English books are there. You will be very cosy."

"So," Francesca said aloud to the empty room, "it is October thirteenth. Tomorrow is my fortieth birthday. I am here. But where are you?"

She knew where he was, and she knew he wasn't coming.

They had written the pledge sitting in this bed one night, with a bottle of aquavit and little glasses, giggling together like two children. She wondered whether he would even remember. Probably not. Their last break, in 1981, was final. After a lot of agony, no doubt, he had made peace with his wife, who must be a smart woman. David had her and his career and his children. Francesca knew that. She had known it in planning this whole escapade. And it had not deterred her. She had kept the pledge. She would spend the night to wake up on her birthday in the four-poster bed.

Downstairs she opened shutters to let in light. Nothing looked touched. Matti had not been there since Kaarina's death. The books were as she remembered, and the album of photographs on the table behind the sofa. But for Francesca the house was full of Kaarina's presence. A vase of dried summer flowers, the colors still vivid, seemed to breathe with Kaarina's pleasure in picking and arranging them. It must have been two summers ago. Shivering in the chilly room, Francesca took the photographs out into the sunlight on the verandah.

It was more an album of the house than of the family, recording summers there and visitors. Turning the pages, Francesca could guess the years from details of clothes and haircuts: Matti and Kaarina and their friends, Kaarina luminous as a younger woman, on a midsummer night, golden hair, healthy, smiling, athletic— fewer shots of her because she must have taken the pictures, Matti lean and muscular, without a beard, his hair still blond. They had aged imperceptibly. Just a few years ago she had seen Matti at sixty-five and Kaarina at fifty-seven flying across a frozen lake on their cross-country skis, leaving Francesca, only thirty-four, panting distantly behind them.

Then with a shock she found it. David had set the timer and propped his camera on the verandah railing where she now rested the album. Afterwards, they had sent the Koivistos a copy. She looked yearningly at it, registering indifferently the changes in her own hair and face but concentrating on David. That year his chestnut hair had just begun to recede in front. By now, he might be bald all the way back, but it wouldn't matter. The setting of his dark blue eyes, the firmness of his mouth, and the assured set of his head— assertive in humor and confidence—gave his face such strong defi- nition that it did not need hair.

For once she herself was not wearing the supercilious look she had learned to hate, after seeing it smirking out of so many fashion magazines. What had been a reflex and protection when she was young, later useful in discouraging lechers on planes, disgusted her in still photographs, frozen into a mask of arrogance.

David had once written to her: "You're like Circe . . . luring men to your island so that your look can turn them into swine." Rather than admit she did not know who Circe was, Francesca had looked her up in a library, then bought the Penguin edition of *The Odyssey*. She wrote to David:

To a woman, most men behave like swine if she lets
them. Like pigs. Whatever exciting things they do outside,
with her all they want to do is eat and sleep and poke.
That's all she sees of them, grunting and snorting and
wallowing in the dirt, so she has to wash their clothes and
pick up after them. That's most men. Very handy for a
girl to have a magic potion to turn them into pigs right
off and save her having to look after them while they turn
into pigs anyway.

So you think I'm like Circe? Well, be careful you
don't turn into a pig—you hear! Or I'll get my magic
potion out!

But in this picture the mask was off, perhaps because there had been no photographer present, only David and his camera. She'd even taken off her dark glasses, as he was always asking. And what stared at her now, in medium close-up, her face near his, was a vulnerable young woman who could not stop herself from behaving self-destructively. She gazed at her younger self as at the corpse of a murder victim, or the picture newspapers print after a young woman is murdered, and readers peer into her eyes to see the flaw that lured her killer.

FIFTEEN

NEW YORK

FATE CONSPIRED. WHEN the United Nations General Assembly con-
vened for its 1971 fall session, David was assigned to assist the
Canadian delegation in the deliberations on China's admission.
Francesca too was scheduled to fly to New York.

But then she telephoned; they had scheduled her first flight not
to New York but Miami.

"I'll be there."

"What?"

"I'll come down to see you."

"How can you do that?"

"What time does your flight get in?"

"Do you mean it?"

He'd been given an important position paper to write, which
had to be finished in two days, when the minister returned from a
cabinet meeting in Ottawa. Saying he needed privacy to finish it in

his hotel room, he took the documents to La Guardia and boarded an Eastern flight to Miami.

Fighting to subdue his excitement, he drove himself to concentrate, writing on the wobbly tray table, stopping occasionally to look out the plane window and feel a flutter of anticipation.

Her flight, making many island stops, was late. He waited for hours in the spartan Skyways Motel, cinder block walls sweating in the oily Florida night, chlorine from the too-turquoise pool mingling with the perfume of jet fuel from the airport close by. He waited, trying to continue his writing, but frequently wandering out to the lobby.

She looked older, more worldly in her pale blue airline uniform, striding confidently into the lobby with the air crew, some black, some white. His heart contracted with joy on seeing her.

The night was exhausting, overloaded. They tried to undo a month's separation, Francesca naturally exhilarated by the novelty of her first working flight, David trying to subdue his anxiety about the paper he had to finish. They were awed by each other's physical presence after weeks of touching only words on paper. In the coffee shop their eyes were hungrier than their stomachs, searching for confirmation.

In the tiny bedroom, the air conditioning roared, the mattress sagged, the foam rubber pillows were flat and smelly. They were too tense, too tired, too excited, but obliged to make love, terrified to waste their few hours together.

They disturbed each other by the unfamiliarity of sleeping together. His eyes in the morning felt dry in their sockets.

Still, naked in the dark, Francesca was his again, whispering endearments, murmuring, making one body with his, chuckling, gossiping about her crew partners. But in the morning, when she showered and put on the unfamiliar stockings and slip, the tailored uniform blouse, skirt, and jacket, each piece of clothing distanced her. When finally she peered into the bathroom mirror to apply mascara and lipstick, he felt alienated.

"Looking at you, I feel you've gone already."

"I have to do this. They gave us classes. It's part of the job."

"What is? To wear eye make-up?"

"To attract men, of course. What do you think?" And she chuckled wickedly.

Then, quite unself-consciously, in the motel lobby she introduced him individually to the pilots, flight engineer, and stewardesses, saying, "This is the man who came all the way from New York to see me." Declaring herself taken, off limits. David loved it.

"Ting's gettin' serious." A Trinidadian stewardess laughed.

"Ask him!" Francesca turned. "And you'd better say yes, you hear?"

"Well, soon you'll be flying to New York and he won't have to come here," the woman said.

"Perhaps I can be there on my birthday," Francesca said. "October fourteenth. You'd better write it down."

They took a taxi to the airport and he walked with her to BWIA, noticing how men and women looked at her, then at him, and back to her.

Her presence stayed with him all the hours back to New York, echoes of her perfume, her voice, her body against his. He felt her beside him, distracting as he sweated out more pages of his paper, thinking and writing almost automatically, while his emotions savored the few hours with her.

Again Francesca had given him the feeling of riding the wind, of mastering the elements, the petty fears and anxieties of life as diminished as the tiny towns and microscopic people on the American coastline miles below the aircraft.

There was a layer of uneasiness behind these thoughts: small voices saying, *We've being trying to reach you all day . . . They called a special meeting and couldn't find you . . . Your wife called . . . emergency with one of your children.* But the sense of special fate enveloped him so thickly that these voices were very faint.

Over the New Jersey coast the plane began its descent, the

cushioning air gently letting it down. David shared the sensations as though he were the aircraft descending, circumstances obliging him, air currents softly parting to let him return to earth.

There were no messages at the Beekman Towers, where the officials from Ottawa stayed. No one had been trying to reach him. He had got away with it.

He crashed into two final hours and finished the paper in time to take it to the office of the Canadian United Nations Mission to be typed. On the first re-read, he was pleased at the ease of the writing and the coherence of the argument. It was cogent and stylish, with traces of humor.

Two days later, several passages from his paper were delivered virtually unaltered in the minister's speech to the General Assembly. Particularly gratifying was the inclusion of several touches David liked, some lightly ironic words on the absurdity that a nation of a billion people, a fifth of the earth's population, should not belong in the United Nations while tiny Taiwan did. It fitted Pierre Trudeau's sense of the world—he had recognized communist China the year before—and it neatly counterpointed the rhetoric of the American delegate, George Bush, who was losing the battle to keep Taiwan a member.

However, Canada's lead was eclipsed by Nixon's dramatic opening to China. A lesson learned: when Canada acted, the importance was limited. If the U.S. made the same move, the earth trembled. Trudeau's initiative might have pushed Nixon slightly; it certainly irritated him. Each new Canadian government had to recalibrate its foreign policy gestures on a fine scale: political capital gained at home versus political capital lost in Washington.

WHEN THE ASSEMBLY sessions permitted, David took long walks to explore Manhattan. One day he found the jewelry center on Forty-seventh Street and had a long conversation with a Romanian couple in one of the booths.

They were concentration camp survivors and showed him the

117

numbers tattooed on their wrists. They had relatives in Toronto. David admired a small gold bracelet, and when he hesitated, they greatly reduced the price. He knew he could squeeze money out of his expense allowance; he had done it for the Miami air ticket. So he bought the bracelet for Francesca's birthday.

LIKE THE PAPER he wrote while flying to and from Miami, the more boldly David expressed himself, the more he was listened to in meetings. The feeling that he could dare more made his words flow colorfully, escaping from the dry, safe style of the foreign service bureaucrat, finding freedom in humor and metaphor. His superiors were wary; he'd be asked, "Are you quite sure of this?" But they liked the style, and his words found their way into more important speeches.

Francesca, he decided, made him feel his real self, the self he wanted to be—confident, daring, free of anxiety.

AS THE GENERAL Assembly session dragged on, she began flying to New York. Between visits, he missed her excruciatingly, cutting out of tedious diplomatic receptions, stretching out dinner in cheap restaurants, tiring himself with long night walks, making guilty duty calls to Marilyn, then lying frustrated on his hotel bed.

For all the anticipation, the joy of seeing Francesca was usually mixed. She was often late, frazzled from serving economy-class meals, soured on food herself, scornful of piggish passengers, wanting to get out of her uniform and the detested girdle they made her wear, have a bath, and sleep. Hard for David, full of pent-up desire, not to read indifference. If she had a day's layover, she would be amorous in the morning, but then he had to dash to his own hotel to shave and dress for work. If she had a second night, he chose a better restaurant and they relaxed with a bottle of wine, languorously anticipating the long night together.

On the first of those nights, he gave her the gold bracelet, and everything brittle about her melted into softness. She was obviously moved, turning her exquisite wrist to see the golden balls slide around.

"I couldn't wait for your birthday."

"No one has ever given me a piece of jewelry." Her personality receded into the shyest of her looks, chin down, face half turned, hair tumbling over one cheek.

"I'm surprised."

"Why are you surprised?" She raised her eyes.

"I would have thought you'd have inspired other men—"

"Don't be stupid." She said it softly but punishingly. "Do you want to spoil it?"

"Of course not."

"Then don't be stupid. You hear?" And she smiled her delicious smile, showing all her teeth. "Where did you get it?"

He told her about the shop owners and she listened intently.

"I'd like to meet them."

"I'll take you. They'd get a lot of pleasure, seeing their bracelet on such a beautiful woman."

She smiled. Harmony restored.

But in bed later, nestled together after making love, she asked, "Why were you surprised when I said no one had ever given me jewelry?"

The question felt surrounded by danger.

"Obviously you've known other men before me."

"I've told you. I have never felt this way about another man." And she pressed herself closer.

"Well, that goes for me. I have never felt this way."

"Not for your wife, when you were first married?"

"No."

"I'm glad. Not for her. Glad for me."

She was quiet for a few minutes. David could feel her breath warm on his neck.

Then she said, "You realize that I can't help seeing other men when I'm in Trinidad."

He felt it in the base of his penis, like the sensation of looking down from a great height.

"When you said you were surprised no one gave me jewelry . . ."

"Yes?"

"I thought you wondered whether there was another serious man in my life."

"I meant in the past."

"Well, it's true then too."

"And there isn't now?"

"Don't be stupid." She kicked him with her knee. "Would I be here in New York in bed with you if there were?"

"No."

Meaning . . . he hoped not.

"But, you understand, when I'm there in Trinidad I have to see people. I have to go out in the evenings. There's nothing else to do. I can't sit with my crazy uncle. And I have friends there, so I go out with them."

Images of young men Francesca's age in places they'd gone dancing were vivid in his thoughts.

"And you know, there are jump-ups and parties, and naturally I go to them."

"Sure."

He'd already assumed that. And found it quite reasonable. And hated it. And scorned himself for being so insecure. And admired her honesty. And wished he could put it all out of his mind. Which he decided to do.

Do you sleep with them? He did not ask, because she might respond, Do you sleep with her?

The next morning she was all business, rushing to shower and dress to meet the crew bus at seven A.M., the small room humid with soap and Shocking perfume. To go back to Trinidad, where others would smell it. To go back to the warm tropical nights with the laughing young men who danced as gracefully as she did. David felt excluded, a feeling he was coming to recognize when she dressed to fly away.

Do you sleep with them?

Do you sleep with her?

She had an odd way of putting on stockings. She wore them long after other women switched to pantyhose. She sat on the edge of the bed and turned the entire stocking inside out. Then, turning back a few inches, just enough to insert her toes, she would gradually work the reversed stocking over her foot and up her leg, smoothing it with her fingers flat. He had never seen a woman do it like that, practiced yet somehow unconfident. Of course, coming from the islands, she wore stockings less often than women here. It fascinated him to watch, but it made her more a stranger.

In the elevator, she showed him the bracelet on her wrist. "I can't wear it when I'm working. But I love it."

When they met the crew in the lobby, Francesca brandished the bracelet and said, "Ta-dah!"

The pretty black stewardess David remembered from Miami laughed. "Lookin' mighty serious, man!"

SIXTEEN

KAARINA'S ISLAND

KAARINA'S NIGHTGOWN LAY in the middle drawer of the chest in the bedroom. For a moment Francesca gazed at it, inhaling the herbal fragrance from the drawer. It was a warm Marimekko flannel in a sprigged design, for cold nights. It was carefully folded, as if about to be wrapped in tissue and boxed in a shop. It startled Francesca; the same inexpensive nightgown—or one just like it—had been there in 1975. She had worn it with David. It spoke of Kaarina's tidiness and modesty, but what pinched Francesca's heart was a sudden apprehension of continuity in these lives. One year after another, the same couple, coming to the same cottage, with the same possessions, from the same old apartment in Helsinki. The same people in the same place, knowing each other as they knew this old bed, as they knew where everything was in their lives. The old world, where people stayed in the places of their birth and died in the beds they were born in. People who knew who they were.

Not surprising that she had been so drawn to Kaarina's comforting contrast with her own vagabond existence. Typically, some of Francesca's clothes had been in a bag left with a friend here, another elsewhere, different cities, different countries; new articles bought because things she already owned weren't available. Clothes, books, records, small portable furnishings, candlesticks, place mats —casually bought, casually discarded. Bank accounts had been opened and closed, or left open with small forgotten residues of money, the statements not forwarded or lost. Telephone accounts opened, then closed months or weeks later. In moments of agitation she could forget her own phone number or street address for a taxi driver because it had changed too often and she couldn't bring the current one to mind. She'd had dozens of addresses since she left Guyana twenty years ago; no stability; sharing an apartment for a few months, moving in with a girlfriend or a man, moving out; hotels, studios, bed-sits, sublets, borrowed flats, shared digs; a room in a friend's place, sleeping on the sofa, avoiding a husband, dressing in the bathroom, no empty hangers in the closet. Even in the brief marriage to Federico they were always on the move.

Amazing that she never cared about it until the move to Helsinki. A need for stability had suddenly possessed her, and she had rented and carefully furnished an apartment.

Opening the drawer, enveloped in Kaarina's fragrance, she felt slightly dizzy. She picked up the nightdress and immediately sat down on the four-poster, feeling Kaarina's life in her hands and staring out Kaarina's window to the cove.

Every summer Kaarina had sat on this bed and looked at this view. When she got up in the mornings, if she came up here to rest in the afternoons, as she lay back on the pillowcases she had woven, made, and embroidered, she would see this view. And when she was not here she would see it in her mind.

Was it so many certainties that made Kaarina's spirit seem so free, so light? Francesca had always thought of freedom as moving, as never being tied to anything, people or possessions. But certainty of place and people permitted a different kind of freedom. Because of it Kaarina had always known who she was. Francesca, so sure of herself when she first met David, had been trying ever since to find out, borrowing this persona or that from day to day, depending on whom she was with or what book she was reading; assuming pieces of identity, like the vastly different styles of clothes she put on and took off when modeling.

The house was warmer and there was a pleasant smell of wood smoke filtering upstairs from the fire she had lighted in the living room fireplace. Dry wood cut years before crackled noisily and brightly. Living in Finland had taught her about fires, which she never knew about in the Caribbean. She felt a primitive, mystical attraction, imagining the life here in deep winter once dependent on wood fires. The clever Finns with their saunas created a hot womb protected from the fierce bite of winter, where they bathed, washed clothes, relaxed, made love, and where women gave birth while the wind snarled outside and the snow drifted up to the eaves. There was an old log sauna behind this house.

She lifted the nightdress to her nose, hypnotized by Kaarina's smell.

They had become much closer after David left Helsinki to go back to Ottawa. Sometimes Kaarina would be in bed when she visited and Francesca would lie beside her, talking more candidly than she ever had to a woman, feeling a delicious warmth and closeness, tempted often to remove her clothes and slip under the covers, sure she would be welcome to embrace her and lie together, secure in her warmth and friendship. There was something both sexual and maternal in how Kaarina touched her as they talked, holding her hand, letting her fingers fall on Francesca's leg. Francesca felt not just their spirits but their bodies drawing together, the barriers of feminine prudery dissolving, sliding inevitably towards some innocent but fulfilling surrender.

Then one night she was staying in the guest room and awoke to find Matti groping into her bed, putting his arms around her, his beard tickling her face, his mouth smelling of tobacco and drink. He was whispering, "I had to come, Francesca. It is too much. I had to come."

"No, Matti. Leave me alone."

"Please, Francesca, please. I am too hot." He tried to slide his fingers between her thighs. She rolled away but he pulled her back.

"Get out or I'll call Kaarina."

"No. No, little girl. Don't do that."

"I will." But she was still whispering too, afraid that Kaarina would hear.

"No, no," he crooned. "Make me happy. Please make me happy."

He forced himself on top of her, trying to push her legs apart.

Still she could not bring herself to call out in the small apartment. For a second she considered letting him, to have it over. Then, with an enormous effort, she pushed his chin up and squirmed out from under him and out of the bed.

"You must go back to your bed." She turned on the light.

He clambered across the bed after her, tried to rise, but his foot caught in the sheets and he fell heavily on the floor. In his twisted pyjamas and tousled hair, he looked comic and pathetic. With effort he got to his feet. Francesca opened the door and saw Kaarina, her hair down, frail in her nightgown, standing in the open doorway of their bedroom.

Matti slunk away to his study down the hall. Kaarina came swiftly into the room and closed the door.

Francesca sat on the rumpled bed, shaking, immediately assuming Kaarina would think she had lured Matti in. But the other woman sat beside her and stroked her hair like a child's.

"I'm sorry."

"I was asleep. I told him to leave. I had to push him off."

"Don't think too badly of Matti. He is worried about getting old."

"I think he was drunk," said Francesca.

"A little, yes, probably."

"I'll have to go."

"You can't go now. It's after two o'clock. It's the middle of the night." She made Francesca lie down and tucked her in.

Francesca had known, of course. She always knew, and she had seen Matti's interest from the first, although it was disguised by his scholarly diffidence. She had seen how his eyes twinkled below the bushy, sandy-gray eyebrows in her presence, how he fingered his beard in a certain way when he talked to her. And if she had noticed, so, obviously, had Kaarina. Perhaps neither of them was really surprised. But had she in some unconscious way enticed him?

In the morning Kaarina brought coffee and sat on the bed.

"You're very calm. Most wives would be furious to find their husband in another woman's room."

Kaarina smiled. "I don't mind if he slept with you. I love you. Of course I love him. It doesn't matter."

"He didn't sleep with me! I wouldn't let him."

"I'm just telling you, it doesn't matter."

"But nothing happened!"

"I believe you."

"Well, I can't keep coming here now."

"Yes, you can, if you want to."

"I think I feel guilty without anything to feel guilty about. That's a first!"

"I hope you will still be our friend."

"Do you want a friend who—you know?"

"Matti won't do it again."

"Is it the first time?"

"No."

Francesca looked at her and then at the snow falling past the long window deep-set in the old building. It made her think of Russian novels. A long moment passed.

"Why aren't you angry with him?"

"Dear Francesca, you are like a beautiful cat that everyone wants to stroke. If I were Matti I would want to make love to you, too."

A fearful deliciousness spread through Francesca. She turned and leaned against Kaarina. Their arms enclosed each other. Francesca felt their breasts touching, with a sensation both electrifying and soothing, an arousal deeper than she had ever felt, mingled with a sense of coming home, mingled with fear. The touch made Francesca feel she had taken a wrong road somewhere, that she was a different person from the mother of the small children with the nurse in Federico's apartment in Milan, different from the woman who had made these trips to be with David.

One slight move, she felt, might turn the embrace explicitly sexual. Did she crave that or dread it? Both. But she could not read whether Kaarina felt anything beyond sympathy. It was very ambiguous. She did not stir until Kaarina released her and kissed her cheek. But, yes, when she looked into the other's candid gray eyes, she could see the same ambiguity, and thought, with a thrill of certainty, that they would be impelled to resolve it.

With Kaarina's nightdress in her hands, the feelings of that snowy morning years before came back so completely that she could remember the sensations of the other woman's warm softness melting into her body, so different from the hard bodies of men. She had never wanted a man as she did Kaarina that morning. She tried to remember. It was years after Brussels, long over with David, after the abortion. She would have been twenty-nine and Kaarina in her early fifties—her body still beautiful—the body Francesca had later watched, day by day, melting away almost before her eyes.

It was not resolved quickly. The ambiguity grew because Kaarina began talking fondly about Matti, who had quietly left the apartment for the university. When she had dressed, Francesca found Kaarina in the dining room, precisely setting the plain teak table with mats she had woven, a slim vase holding a single yellow tulip, coffee cups and spoons as austerely plain as the other furnishings, lighting a large candle to dispel the winter gloom. The elegant simplicity, and Kaarina's unhurried pleasure in placing each article, gave the apartment a soothing serenity and harmony. Her deliberateness had the quality of making time slow down. The snow falling outside thickened the quietness within.

"On days like this when it snows and snows it makes me think of the war when I was very young—our Finnish war—before you were born, I think."

"I was born in 1941," Francesca said.

"So it was just before. We are a very little country. Stalin wanted to take us like Lithuania, Latvia, and Estonia. But Finland said no. It seemed ridiculous: tiny Finland, huge Soviet Union. So we fought. The Russian army sent many divisions and tanks into our forests. Their planes bombed Helsinki. We had a very small army but very clever. Our ski troops went out in the winter to fight in the deep snow of the forests. They circled the Russians and blew up their tanks, then vanished again on their skis into the dark woods. And they were so funny, our boys . . . so free in their spirits . . . as though it was a game. My brother was one of them. His name was Arno. And Matti. They were friends, students together, and they used to dare each other to do crazy things. And then joked about it afterwards. I still have the letters Arno wrote to us—before he was killed. They liked to sneak off by themselves in the woods to see how many Russians they could kill. Once Arno did not come back. Matti went to look for him. When he found him Arno was surrounded by bodies he had killed, about fifteen. He had surprised a lot of Russians and, instead of going for help, attacked them himself. He killed most of them but was shot many times. Matti found him almost dead. Then a lot more Russians came and Matti fought them alone, hoping Arno would stay alive. He held them off all one night, and when his company came to drive the Russians off, Matti was wounded too, but he had not left Arno. He was very heroic. But Arno died before they could bring him back."

128

Kaarina said all this, looking out the window at the snow, holding her cup near her lips but forgetting to drink from it.

"And you married him because of that?"

Kaarina smiled. "It was not so simple. I adored him like a little sister, but he had a girl. After the war, the Russians took all that land in Karelia, the part where we lived, the city of Viipuri, and we all had to move. Four hundred thousand had to move to other parts of Finland. We were city people. My father was officer in the army but he had been a teacher. My mother was a painter. They knew nothing of farms, but we made a farm on land taken from another farmer. It was very hard, those years. I married a young man from the other farm but we were not really alike. So—divorce. I came to Helsinki to go to the university and I met Matti again. His marriage was unhappy and I knew I had been in love with him all the time. He was very handsome—when his beard was all blond. The young women students fell in love with him."

"And he with them?"

"Sometimes." Kaarina smiled. "But not seriously. He likes women very much. Now it is hard for him—getting older."

It sounded as though she were both excusing Matti and making him more attractive. Francesca felt a little resentment that Kaarina was putting Matti between them.

She went back to Paris, as planned, the next day, to her modeling and traveling. Kaarina's words had an effect. The next time Francesca met Matti, she could see not only the bearded professor but the heroic student-soldier in the forests. She noticed not so much how old he was as how fit for his years, how clear his blue eyes, and how good his teeth when he laughed. She saw how rapidly he flew away from them when they took her cross-country skiing on Helsinki's frozen lakes. She liked him, but she yearned for Kaarina.

SHE PUT THE nightdress on the bed and got up to look in the cupboard. Several of Kaarina's dresses were there, an old-fashioned evening gown, slacks, a hand-knit cardigan for cold days, rough shoes for hard walking, and a delicate pair of high heels, incongruous as the evening dress in this rustic place. She touched the material of the evening gown and a painful longing possessed her. She felt herself wanting to put on Kaarina's life—to be Kaarina.

SEVENTEEN

NEW YORK—OTTAWA

NOVEMBER 1971 was cold in New York, and Francesca seemed to pull her own personality—like her thin raincoat—more tightly around her as they hurried through icy rain between museums, movies, bars, restaurants, her face often settling into marble, her golden complexion pallid in the gray light.

The Assembly session was over. Francesca had a week off from BWIA and moved into David's room in the Beekman Towers. They had planned it for weeks, he like a child waiting for a holiday, imagining the bliss of continuous days and nights together; no rushing off to another hotel to change; no hurried dressing and departures . . . lovemaking delivered of all anxieties. But life resisted the imagined script.

On the first night, a shyness replaced the automatic intimacy of her rushed overnights. Francesca retreated into the bathroom and emerged in a chaste nightgown, tied at the neck, her breasts widening the fine pleats. Her planning excited him, the element of ceremony she introduced, wrapping herself as though giving him a present. She was even wearing the gold bracelet.

They were rapturously alone, the rest of the world a distant hum of Manhattan traffic, the occasional whine of an elevator.

His desire for her was overwhelming in the dimmed light, the quiet room, the smell of her perfume . . . their coming together and kissing, but then knowing, before she touched him, that his penis was limp. He willed it to rise, kissing her, caressing her more urgently, but his body would not obey the fierce ardor of his thoughts. She murmured encouragement, but his body, his soul, felt as shriveled and diminished as his useless organ. Agony.

She retreated into herself. The beds were singles, too narrow to sleep in together. He had not asked for a room with a larger bed. The accountants at External would have seen the bill, assuming he had brought his wife down at government expense. As reckless as he had been, stopping in Trinidad, flying off secretly to Miami, underneath he had been more timid.

He lay miserably alone, wondering if Francesca was asleep, the weeks of anticipated joy evaporating, because his ridiculous sex, which leaped to attention at a flicker of interest from Marilyn, remained indifferent to this woman he wanted more than anything in the world.

Certainly he had taken risks. By now the Beekman Towers staff knew him as a resident, and he felt them watching. He had told himself he didn't care, as they came through the lobby, up in the elevator, Francesca, wearing her habitual sunglasses even in the diminished November light. She was so striking a woman that people in the streets, in restaurants, in the Museum of Modern Art, always turned for appraising looks. The hotel staff must have done the same.

How had he kept countenance with her, he wondered. Had they talked about it in the daytime? It must have been so painful that he had simply blotted it out, and now, twenty years later, couldn't separate one day from another. He couldn't remember what movies they saw, what restaurants they went to. As the days blurred together, so did the nights. Had they tried afresh each night? Had they by unspoken agreement let a night or two pass to reduce the tension? All he could remember was a knot of anxiety, of sexual agony that must have grown from day to day. How well he had repressed all this!

In the two months of the UN session he had telephoned Marilyn several times a week, talking to Jenny if she was still up, trying to sound sympathetic about leaf raking, installing storm windows, getting the Volvo serviced, the unreliable cleaning woman. But during the week with Francesca he had not called . . . yet was increasingly nervous about not doing so. Intending to, eyeing a pay telephone while waiting for Francesca, thinking, he'd do it tomorrow, he'd say he had to go to the office for some papers. Thinking, that would be deceiving Francesca and he couldn't lie to her, too. Thinking, Marilyn would be wondering. Thinking, if he left it too long she would phone and he would be forced to pretend, with Francesca in the room, listening.

She raised it. Typical of Francesca to say, frankly, "Won't your wife be wondering about this? If you have no work to do, won't she wonder why you're not going home?"

Clearly that was in the shadows of his mind. That and anxiety about work. He was stealing the department's time. He'd been meticulous about using their time and money. His expenses had always been conservative.

Yet he took Francesca to Forty-seventh Street to meet the Romanian jewelers, who told her extravagantly how lovely she was, how well the bracelet suited her. With a disarming directness—because it was obvious they were in love—the Romanians wished they could sell them a ring. Did they want to look at rings? Francesca did, and her interest must have given David a straw to clutch at, because he used it afterwards to construct a comforting rationalization: it was guilt that had rendered him dysfunctional.

They parted when he took her to the Lexington Avenue hotel the airline used to take a crew bus to Kennedy.

Back in Ottawa, sexual desire reawakened the moment he saw Marilyn, noticing—as he told himself—his stupid prick rising the moment she pressed against him in a warm hug, and an hour later in their bedroom fucking her—the verb he seldom spoke expressing his anger. All his chemical and nervous responders leaping efficiently into play at the sensual familiarity of her body; some moral censor relaxed. He lay angrily in the dark beside his pliant wife, amid the familiar shadows and smells of their bedroom, her soapy scent, their sheets, the texture of the blankets, the feel of his own pillow. Some Odysseus! Penelope unmanning him from afar, the mysterious threads she wove into his psyche, endlessly drawing him back after a failed fling with Circe.

As he walked to work the next morning, his desolation was heightened by a feeling familiar in the exhausted season between gaudy autumn and brilliant winter.

Emerging from Sandy Hill, he walked up the Rideau Canal embankment towards the impertinent Gothic profile of the Château Laurier and the Parliament Buildings, a fragile rampart at the margin of civilization, defining the world's coldest capital after Ulan Bator. Between gaps in the buildings, beyond the Gatineau Hills, the horizon was weighed down by pale green-gray clouds heavy with menace, where the spirit of the North assembled its implacable forces over two thousand miles of wilderness stretching to the Arctic. It was quiet today, with no wind, but a palpable presence, smelling of snow—and waiting.

No wonder there was in the Canadian soul a conflict between desires to endure and evade; to abide and to break out to all the sweet lures of the South. That is what David had done: break out. And now he was back, the first snow was imminent, and he did not want to be there.

On Parliament Hill, the ceremonial Mounties were already in

their buffalo coats. David entered the narrow Victorian corridors of the overheated East Block with foreboding.

TRUDEAU WENT TO Washington and secured from Nixon an assurance that the United States did not intend to gobble Canada up economically. The ecstatic prime minister called it "a fantastically new statement." His tone again made David wince. The incident was mocked by the press and detractors in External Affairs. So the U.S. recognized Canada as an independent nation? What a diplomatic victory!

LATE ON CHRISTMAS Eve, David helped Marilyn wrap small presents and fill stockings, but, as though two minds occupied one body, he was simultaneously trying to picture Francesca spending that evening. He was not sure where. She'd been vague.

"My parents want me to go to BG, but it's been such a relief escaping, I might go to my brother's in B'dos. I wish you could come. I want you to meet him and Delores. Or I might plead the work schedule and stay in T'dad with friends. I thought of staying over in New York, but not much point without you. I might fall in with the wrong kind of man!"

In a few lines she could toss him from heaven to hell.

Marilyn said, "I'm glad you didn't have to stay in New York for Christmas." As though she were sitting in David's brain, watching the same movie.

The filled stockings lay in the armchair by the fireplace, marked with tags, because this was the first Christmas Jenny could read her name. Marilyn put her arms around him, her face against his neck.

"It feels so sweet doing this, knowing how excited they'll be. I used to love my stocking better than anything."

David murmured. It made him sentimental too, close to tears, but he tried to hold the feeling back. He didn't want to like this so much, yet it was like a current pulling him. And he could feel her breasts pressing urgently, meaning that she wanted to make love. She was forward about it so seldom that it aroused him the moment he understood. He turned to kiss her and she responded hungrily.

"Let's go upstairs."

Marilyn whispered, "Let's stay here. It's so nice by the fire." She turned out the lamps and came back to him in the muted light from the flames and the bulbs on the Christmas tree.

"Do you mind?"

"No. No."

Her kiss had a new eagerness.

"Not worried about the girls?"

"They'll never wake up now."

"We've never done this before."

She laughed. "I think Christmas makes me feel sexy."

She never used that word about herself. He wondered how much she had drunk at the two parties earlier in the evening. But she wasn't drunk.

Deliberately, she undressed in the firelight, tossing her under-clothes lightly away, and drew him down with her onto the carpet. As he slid familiarly into her there came a thought he tried to put away. Wasn't this better than making love with Francesca, more natural, more satisfying, no inhibitions? He disliked the thought, but he also felt generous to Marilyn, wanting to please her; his desire, like hers, heightened by the powerful sentiment of Christmas, the children's stockings, the silly milk and cookies, the winking tree lights, the thickly falling snow outside, the sense of the whole city hushed by the snow and the mood of Christmas Eve.

Playfully, when they had finished, she rolled over on top of him, her hair, glinting in the firelight, falling around his face.

"I saw Mommy kissing Santa Claus," she sang under her breath and giggled. "Some kissing!"

She began thoughtfully planting kisses on different parts of David's face, saying between them, "Am I too heavy?"

"No."

"Comfy?"

"Uh-huh."

"Was that nice for you?"

"Sure."

"Sure? You're getting to sound awfully American."

"And you?"

"It was dreamy."

Dreamy! Like a girl at school.

"It's always dreamy when I think about it in advance and have hours to work up to it."

"And had you?"

"Yes. I've been thinking of it all evening."

"My goodness!"

"And what were you thinking about all evening?"

"I don't know. Christmas."

"I'll bet you weren't. I was watching you at both parties."

"So?"

"Whoever you were talking to, your eyes kept wandering off to devour any pretty woman in sight."

"Oh, come on!"

"No, it's true. I noticed it at the British party and checked at the MacDonalds'. It's as though you were looking for someone. Were you?"

"What?"

"Looking for someone?"

"No!"

But David knew it had become a little habit. At the round of diplomatic parties this year, if a woman seemed particularly striking or well dressed, he'd compare her with Francesca, a way of keeping her in his thoughts.

"I also thought you're a very attractive man and I should make darn sure some shiny little package from Uruguay doesn't try to tie a Christmas ribbon on your you-know-what!" She moved her hips suggestively.

"I've never met anyone from Uruguay."

"And don't you dare." She kissed him seriously. Among his confused emotions was a little new excitement aroused by Marilyn's aggressiveness. He felt desire returning, and so did she.

It was too easy, and it wasn't enough. David felt ashamed, as though he had taken advantage of someone defenseless. It was too easy. It didn't test him; it didn't stretch him as Francesca did, even when she teased him. He felt privately embarrassed that he had weakly fallen prey to the sentimentalism of Christmas, conniving in this contrived romantic scene, like a gooey Bing Crosby movie.

It was unfair to encourage Marilyn to feel romantic with him, but the physical intimacy reopened doors of spiritual closeness that he'd been closing to create distance—replying in grunts or monosyllables, withdrawing into politeness, not initiating the gestures that constantly nourish a feeling of shared experience.

Exhibiting a new ease at being nude in front of him, Marilyn picked up her clothes lazily, as though reliving the thrill with which she had removed them. She turned to him with a little smile of conquest that said all the clouds had been cleared away, intimacy rediscovered, their marriage restored. Her body had recaptured him. Like a young girl's, her attitude said, "Now we're best friends again, aren't we?"

David wanted to give her everything and give her nothing. It was worse than remorse over screwing a woman whom he didn't love when she abundantly loved him; worse than that. It was screwing a woman whom some perverse element in his soul was forcing him not to love. While another instinct was saying, Relax, stop straining. It's right here. Give in.

David would not give in. He stiffened when Marilyn curled up affectionately around him in bed and was soon contentedly asleep. He lay resentfully aware that, instead of advancing his affairs, he had retreated, remembering Wilde, *The coward does it with a kiss,/ The brave man with a sword.*

And if he slept with Marilyn, why shouldn't Francesca be sleeping with someone this Christmas Eve? Don't even imagine it! Well, why not? It's different; we're married. That's a cop-out, as the Americans said. Why? Is screwing a measure of loyalty, disloyalty? David had always thought so. Then enjoying Marilyn had made him disloyal to Francesca. But she was his wife.

Did you sleep with them?

Did you sleep with her?

Don't think about it.

ON CHRISTMAS MORNING, the little girls climbed onto their parents' bed to open their stockings, laughing and squealing over each little thing. When they had finished, Marilyn whispered to Jenny who ran out and came back with a bulging stocking—for David.

"There isn't one for you, Mummy."

"I didn't hang one up last night."

"Why didn't you, if Daddy did?"

Clever little girl, on the right track at four.

"I didn't feel like it. Did Santa Claus drink the milk and eat the cookies?"

"Only half the milk and only one cookie." She made Santa sound naughty. But she wouldn't be put off. "Well, didn't Santa Claus leave you anything, anyway?"

"Perhaps he thought Daddy deserved it more because he's had to be away from us for such a long time." Marilyn kissed him and patted his back. Her touch felt more informed, more authoritative. She looked her prettiest, fresh and healthy, her hair shining. Her look of trust and love was reflected in the faces of Jenny and Peggy, all caught in a moment of life-learning, a contented woman instructing two women-to-be, passing intuitive messages that would shape their sexuality and their womanhood. The idea touched him deeply.

With the stocking she had ensnared him again in her wifely toils, another sweet and affectionate gesture. He could do nothing but appear to enjoy it. He played out the charade for the children, rejoicing over a package of razor blades; casting Marilyn small glances of gratitude; and noticing beneath his resentment that he was also touched. It was the first time he'd been given a stocking since childhood. It awakened old feelings, as it also annoyed him to be made so vulnerable.

The idea came to him on Christmas afternoon, sipping port with Wallace Farquhar while Marilyn and her mother tidied up the kitchen. After listening to the Queen's message and eating the turkey, he was sleepily watching Jenny and Peggy play with their new toys. Outside, it was snowing heavily again, making the lights on the Christmas tree seem brighter.

His father-in-law had been complaining about the United Nations, when David suddenly saw the opening he needed. The committee he had worked on had adjourned in deadlock. Canada would come into the chairmanship when they resumed in January, well placed to offer an initiative to break the impasse. It was a role Canadians often played successfully, bridging east-west and north-south suspicions. And now he had *the* idea.

The rush of professional pleasure almost equaled David's excitement in knowing that it could get him back to New York—and Francesca.

The memorandum he wrote to the assistant under secretary the next morning was approved by the minister and cabinet within a week. He was instructed to go to New York, brief the UN ambassador, and guide the deputy who would chair the committee.

"Oh, what a shame!" Marilyn said. "Just when things are going so well."

"I know. It shouldn't be for long."

"It'll be weeks at least, won't it?"

"A few at most."

"Perhaps I could come down and spend a weekend with you. I haven't been to New York in ages."

"Well—maybe."

"I suppose it's better you going when we've got our marriage on an even keel again. It was listing pretty badly for a while, wasn't it?"

"Uh-huh." Anything he could say was a lie.

"Anyway, I'm deep in my French lessons." She kissed him. "I'm going to remember this Christmas Eve all the rest of my life."

EIGHTEEN

KAARINA'S ISLAND

FRANCESCA APPROACHED THE evening with a sense of ceremony. She examined the high tiled stove built into the kitchen wall, shared by the living and dining rooms. David had made it work to heat water and warm the house, but it looked too complicated. So she pumped water from the well and filled a large pot to heat on the cooking stove. When it was hot, she bathed and brushed her hair.

She took the old evening dress from the cupboard upstairs. It had puffed sleeves and a low neckline, so dated it must have been kept as fancy dress. Her figure and Kaarina's were almost identical. With the feeling of dressing for a fashion show, of putting on another personality, she got into the dress and the high heels, and swung the skirt in front of the mirror. Her face looked wan against the vivid color. Since she stopped modeling she had worn no make-up but felt the impulse now. In the bathroom cabinet she found an eyebrow pencil and a lipstick that looked years old. She outlined her eyes and darkened her brows and applied the unfashionable bright red to her lips, then put a dot on each cheekbone and rubbed it in, creating a faint blush. She shook out her hair and surveyed herself. A different woman greeted her. The haughty professional look was back, almost as outdated as the dress, and she laughed at it. "Stupid girl!"

She went downstairs with the feeling of making an entrance, then poured a small glass of aquavit. Outside there was a chilly night with bright stars. Below her in the little cove, *Havsflickan* was a faint smudge of white in the dark shadows.

She walked up and down the verandah as though on a ramp, turning professionally at each end, remembering the feel of doing it, imagining the upturned faces of fashion people and the usual voyeurs.

She had enjoyed it and felt contempt for it equally. True of so much in her life; true of men; true of her sense of her own beauty. True of the pleasure she derived from the contrast between the appearance—the glossy perfection of the fashion photograph, the glittery social life it could open—and the often grimy reality behind it.

There was Stan, the goaty photographer in New York, who insisted on being alone with a model and produced his best work only with a sexual current between them. If the girls refused, he told them to fuck off and not bother him. If they were ambitious, if they wanted stardom, covers, high fees, he'd deliver, but only if they played his way. And many played, some experienced girls tipping off the newcomers, some not, but making little jokes afterwards. Expecting it, but thinking it wouldn't happen to her, a girl sweated through the hour he took to set his lights and line up the shot, breaking to cool off and powder again during his endless tinkering, adjusting, the process moving him from hostile indifference to excitement. He would snap off a few rolls of film, muttering and complaining, then stop.

143

"I can't do it. It's lousy, it's boring. There's no life in your face. Your body looks like a fucking board."

"What do you want me to do?"

"I can make you look like a million bucks, but we got to get in the right mood. Understand?"

"No."

"Sure you do."

"I don't want to."

"OK, don't bother. Forget it. Don't waste my time."

"No. Be careful! You'll crease the dress."

"No, baby. Just take it easy. I like the dress. Just lift it up and slip off your little panties a minute."

"No, I won't!"

"No pussy, no pictures, baby."

He got his kicks in desecrating the perfect images he created for the public, for a few minutes destroying the cold serenity of their faces, the perfect drape of the clothes. When they succumbed, he pulled down his pants and pumped away furiously, pulled out, and said, "Now let's take some real pictures."

And he did. The results were brilliant. The anger or the erotic charge he provoked in the models blazed out of the magazines in smoldering eyes, pouting lips, haughty fury, and an energy in the limbs that in his models, for all the affected composure and indifference, reeked of implied sexual promise.

His was the best set of pictures Francesca ever had. They brought her new work in Europe and America. Her fees increased. Fashion houses asked for her and other photographers sought her out. But they couldn't produce the same hard edge, the sensual hostility that had become her trademark. The agency advised her to go back, but she rebelled.

"Everyone knows what he does. It's too degrading."

But the more she thought about it, the more it challenged her to put him down. She got the idea when Diana, a sweet model from

Texas, paranoid about safety in New York, confided that she always carried a little pistol.

Astonished, Francesca was shown a tiny pearl-handled automatic.

"Does it have bullets in it?"

"Sure."

Francesca laughed at this fragile blonde, whose face on magazine covers implied demure innocence, toting a lethal weapon with her make-up and cigarettes. In Guyana Francesca's father had kept his large service revolver and had shown her how to fire it "in case things ever get out of hand." Guns didn't frighten her.

"Will you lend it to me?"

"What for? You're not going to do anything crazy?"

"Just for a joke."

Francesca made a date for a session with Stan on a Saturday when other businesses in his loft building would be closed. He welcomed her knowingly.

"Hey, Francesca. I missed you, baby. You're the best-looking broad I worked with in years. Come on, let's get to work."

She let him go through his routine, but when he reached the ritual—"It's not working. We've got to get you loosened up"—she said, "Not this time."

"What do you mean, baby? You know the score."

"Just shoot the pictures."

"Come on, Francesca. I've been waiting for you. It got me hot just thinking you were coming."

"Take the pictures."

"So, you want to fight a little, first? OK. I like that too."

She slipped the automatic out of her bag and pointed it at him. "Take the pictures."

"Are you crazy? Stop the kidding around."

"I'm not kidding."

"Put the fucking toy gun away."

"It's not a toy."

"Sure, sure!"

Francesca pointed the gun at a huge enlargement of a model taped to the wall and fired. For a little gun it made a deafening explosion in the studio, and a small hole appeared in the model's bare shoulder.

"Jesus Christ! What are you doing?"

She smiled at him sweetly. "Now take the pictures."

He was sweating. "You think I can work with that fucking gun in your hand?"

"I could shoot your camera."

"God dammit, what's got into you?"

"Not you, Stan."

He looked at her for a moment, then laughed.

"OK. You got a deal. You are one crazy cunt but you've got a deal. No fooling around. I take pictures and you put the gun away."

He snapped away, constantly muttering, "That's great! That's fabulous! Jesus Christ. It's better than sex. Just like that but raise your chin. Too much. That's it. Just like that."

When she left he said, "OK, baby. You win. You take great pictures. Next time you come, no fooling around, OK? But leave the gun at home."

She told Diana she had fired one bullet for practice, nothing else. The agency and the magazines raved over the new photos, but she never went back. Whenever she saw one of those shots, she laughed.

"Fuck you, Stan," she said now into the cold night, and sipped her aquavit.

There were no conquests as pure as that and some she now regretted.

The atmosphere was exciting and sordid, the snapping, joking, highly strung girls, most of them very young, new to drinking and sex; dating older men who took them to expensive restaurants; occasionally one on drugs, hysterical that needle marks would show. The

146

frantic dressing rooms during a show, pulsing rock music from the stage, the odor of many perfumes and sweat; the tangle of thin bodies of all skin colors, constantly dressing, undressing; the dressers snatching off clothes, the scramble for shoes that fit; a furious couturier repeatedly slapping a girl who unexpectedly got her period and stained an original; the anger of the girls in one New York showroom having to put on clothes worn by a well-known model who brazenly refused to wear underpants; the girl from California who never had the proper liquid but spat into her contact lenses and put them into her rare turquoise eyes.

NINETEEN

NEW YORK

THE NEXT TIME in New York, it was the Hilton Hotel on Sixth Avenue, a queen-size bed, a view north towards Central Park.

David arrived wearing his rationalization like soul armor. Obviously guilt had wrecked the week in December and only honesty could purge it. Get divorced. Marry Francesca. They should be married. He would ask her. He would take her to the Romanians on Forty-seventh Street to look at a ring.

Francesca arrived exhausted, her normally close-fitting uniform hanging loose. She was too tired to eat. When they fell into the big bed, all his desire for her restored, she took him sleepily and gratefully into her as though bringing him home, and she was virtually asleep when her muscles gently extruded him.

He held her lissome body, so different from Marilyn's, awake in a room half illuminated by the glow of the city through the curtains, the muted roar of ceaseless traffic, smelling the Shocking, which already filled the space. His senses and mind hummed in resonance with the unsleeping, pulsating city and the slow-breathing woman, both electrifying to him. It was warm in the room, and they had thrown back the light blanket. In the dim light, he looked at her sculpted shoulder, falling to a perfect breast, the deeply indented waist above the hip, the lovely thigh, the tidy lawn of black curls, her hand laid in it like Manet's Olympia. She was perfection. Possessing her made him feel godlike, there on Olympus—on the forty-fourth floor.

With breakfast, the room service waiter brought a rose, and handed it to Francesca, who sat in a silk robe with one leg curled under her, her hair simply shaken out, her eyes, like Jenny's, as fresh from sleep as flowers newly opened.

David went to the bureau to find his pen, and saw among the scattered contents of her purse a letter addressed to a man on East Seventy-third Street. He felt a small panic, and knew everything—knew nothing. He looked up. She was smiling at the waiter, who had lifted the cover from the orange juice.

"Thank you, sir. Have a good day." The waiter left, and David joined her. Bright sunshine whitened the eastern faces of buildings outside.

She smiled at him and extended the rose to touch his lips. The letter was none of his business. She was posting it for a friend, but it looked like her handwriting.

"I don't remember falling alseep. You started to make love to me and then I don't remember. I'd better watch out. The next thing, I'll be so tired I won't remember who I've done it with, eh?" She was teasing, and he laughed.

"I wanted to ask you something last night but you fell asleep too quickly."

"You could have woken me up."

"I thought you looked too tired."

"It's no wonder. I was up half the night on Tuesday in Trinidad. One of the girls left to get married and they had a jump-up, and that led to another party . . . and so on . . . and so on." While talking, she got up to find her sunglasses and came back with them on. "It's too bright."

The glasses shut David out. "It's foolish, trying to carry on like this."

Behind the black stare of the glasses her face showed nothing, but she stopped putting a small corner of toast between her perfect lips. "You mean you don't want to go on seeing me?"

"No, no. I want to see you all the time. I want to end this crazy dodging in and out of hotels and get married. I want to go to the Romanians this morning and buy a ring."

Her smile below the sunglass mask was very faint.

"But you *are* married."

"I'm saying—I've thought about it endlessly—if you will marry me, I will divorce Marilyn—"

"And lose your job—throw away your career?"

"That doesn't happen these days."

"And your little girls?"

"They would get to know you—in time."

"Where do you mean we would live? In Ottawa? I've never even seen it."

"Until I get another overseas posting. That's bound to happen pretty soon."

"Where would it be?"

"I don't know—Africa, Asia."

"I couldn't keep flying from Trinidad to New York."

"I thought you already hated it."

"I hate the bloody passengers when I get tired. But it's my independence, you see?"

All negative. David was waiting for some sign that she liked the idea.

"How long does it take to get a divorce in Canada?"

"I'm not sure. A year, perhaps. I have to find out."

"Have you told your wife?"

150

"No."

"Did you fight with her over Christmas?"

"No."

"Can you afford to support her and the children—and us?"

He hadn't thought of that. He said, "But you haven't said whether you want to live with me or not."

"Don't be stupid! Of course I want to live with you." Said with an intimacy that took his breath.

"But?"

"I don't want to get married."

"Please take off those glasses. I can't see your expression."

"I don't want to."

He wondered whether she was crying. He had never seen her cry.

"Why?"

"I don't want to get married. How can I just tie myself to you, when I have lived nothing?"

"But you want to live with me?"

Francesca pushed the sunglasses up into her hair. Her mouth smiled at him, but her black eyes were impenetrable.

She was naked under the dark silk robe. One thigh was partly exposed, its golden smoothness awakening echoes in his fingertips. Physically he could touch her, but spirtually she had suddenly receded. Her flesh showed nothing of his imprint from the night before. Her face showed nothing. Love left no marks. They were sexual animals one moment, detached and indifferent the next. Circe's magic: changed into beasts, changed back.

He sat there, heartsick and miserable. "Well, I can't leave my wife and family—just to *live* with you."

"In sin?" Francesca laughed tauntingly.

"But you said you wanted to get a ring from your aunt in Georgetown."

"I didn't go there at Christmas."

"Is there some other reason?"

"What do you mean?"

He had to ask. "Like seeing another man."

"Don't be stupid!"

"There's a letter by your purse addressed to a man on Seventy-third Street."

"Well?"

"Who is he?"

"A man I met on a flight."

"And have you seen him?"

"I'm going to."

Again he felt that shriveling fear. "And do you want to see him again?"

"He talked to me about modeling. It isn't important."

"It's important to me."

"Well, do you expect me to spend all my time alone except when you come?" She paused. "How do I know that you wouldn't get tired of me as you are of your wife?"

"Because I have never felt about her as I do about you."

"You feel it, but perhaps you aren't sure. If you were sure, wouldn't you leave her and take your chances with me?"

"I'm sure enough to ask you to marry me."

She looked at him, her face exquisite without make-up but expressionless.

As though embracing, not repulsing him, she said, "I don't want to be tied down like my mother, you know? Trapped, bitter by the time I'm forty. I want to be free, to see you, to see other people. I have to be free."

"Do you love me?"

"Of course. But if I don't marry you, you'll stay with your wife."

He actually had not thought that—and was silent.

"Probably," she added.

David felt himself whirling away from her, a climber swept off the mountain by a gust of wind, an abyss beneath him.

"You see?" she said. "There's something wrong. If you'll only leave her to marry me, you're probably not sure you want to leave her."

They stared at each other, the gulf widening second by second.

"I have to go," she said at last, getting up.

"I thought you weren't to go back till tomorrow."

"No, the schedule changed. It's today."

For the first time, he didn't know whether she was telling the truth.

She went to the bathroom to shower, then dressed in front of him, as indifferently as if they had lived together for years. With each article of clothing she donned, he had the familiar ache of growing alienation. Finally he saw her pick up the letter and put it into her bag. Swept by anxiety and desire, he moved to embrace her, desperate to detain her. But she slid away to put on her uniform jacket. At the door, the familiar shy smile, a feather-light kiss on his cheek, and she was gone.

David looked forlornly about the thunderously empty room for evidence that she had even been there, the rumpled bedclothes, the nibbled toast. He picked up the rose she had held to his lips. It had no smell, but the smell of her perfume surrounded him. Her scent was stronger in the bathroom, with its used towels and a tissue blotted with lipstick. The mirror startled him. On it in lipstick she had written, *Give me some time. I need to think about it. Love, F.*

It took David hours to find the resolution to wipe off her words, then shave and dress. When finally he emerged from the Hilton into a bright, cold day, the snarling traffic on Sixth Avenue disconcerted him. He felt alien, purposeless. The committee was not meeting, and he'd made excuses at the UN office so that he would have the day free with her; now he had nowhere to go.

He walked through Central Park, then all the way down Madison Avenue, and back up Lexington, until in midafternoon, exhausted, he stopped at a cinema on Second Avenue. A James Bond double feature, *From Russia with Love,* was playing when he entered. Watching Sean Connery scything through villains and leggy women, David noticed his own good humor seeping back. The first film ended and the lights went on.

"It's ridiculous. Torturing myself with her. It's nonsense. Thrashing around like a fish on a line, played by her whims. I can be free of her. I can tell her. Enough's enough. That's it!"

The words were so loud in his head that he looked around the theater, wondering whether he had spoken them. The flush of angry pride melted into euphoria. She wanted to be free; well, so did he! And thinking it made it so. The realization coursed through him.

The lights went down and the title sequence for the next film began. David got up and walked out into the cheerful light, a prisoner released.

In the cleaned hotel room, all traces of Francesca had vanished. On the Hilton note paper, he wrote:

I cannot go on like this, twisted and jerked from mood to mood—alternately angry, perplexed, jealous, enervated, hurt, enraptured, furious, elated, depressed, cast up, cast down, sublime, abject; your lover, your prisoner, your companion, your fool. I must live my life too and I can't live it in such thrall to your whims. For sanity, I need to say goodbye. You need freedom, I need certainty.

The thrill of renunciation merged with the thrill of being in command of his life. He finished the note, addressed it to Trinidad, and immediately went downstairs, bought a stamp, and posted it.

He even felt purged of guilt, as though writing one letter had erased months of infidelity. With a clear conscience, he phoned Marilyn and felt a warming sympathy for her rising within him. For once he really listened to her domestic recital.

The next night Joseph Rogers, a member of the American UN delegation, with whom David had worked on the committee, invited him to join a small dinner party at La Grenouille. Rogers was a wealthy contributor appointed by Nixon, and he entertained gener-

154

ously. There were eight in the party, including a lean, tanned, carefully groomed woman named Raleigh, who sat on David's left and talked intensely in a Southern accent about horses and books.

"I love to read, especially in the winter up here. When I'm at home I ride. Those are my passions, reading and riding, ever since Sweet Briar—that's a college in Virginia—they have a huge indoor riding ring. I rode all the time. I took my own horse there."

"You must be very good."

"I used to compete a lot—now it's just for fun."

She looked like a thoroughbred herself, with her long neck and slim fingers.

"Do you like John Updike? I'm just reading his new book—*Rabbit Redux*—have you read it?"

"No, not yet."

"What I love is that everything is so real. I mean, I don't know the kind of people in the story—the man's a car salesman in Pennsylvania, for heaven's sake!—but Updike makes him absolutely believable. And he's so honest about things that other writers just, kind of, skate over."

"What sort of things?" David felt expected to ask.

"Like intimate things between a husband and wife. Well—sex, and money and all that. But he makes me feel I'm really learning something. I'll never meet those people—I really wouldn't care to—but feeling I know them, I've been inside every room of their home and inside their thoughts, I feel connected to them. It makes me feel more American because I know them. Do you know what I mean?"

"Well, I can feel that too with Updike, and I'm not American."

"Canadians are *almost* Americans."

"Perhaps. But we're constantly submerged in your feelings. If they read a lot, Canadians probably know more about what it feels like to be American than they do about being Canadian."

She registered that while studying him. "I have another passion besides good horses and good books, but it's harder to find."

"And that is?"

"Intelligent men!" She smiled deliciously, her upper teeth poised as though about to bite her lower lip.

He had turned to talk to people across the table, when he felt a touch and realized that Raleigh had calmly entwined her leg around his. She looked quite absorbed in talking to their host, but under the white tablecloth her leg slid knowingly against his and a tingling rose through his body. Across the table her husband was laughing with Mrs. Rogers, their voices lost in the excited hubbub of the restaurant.

Raleigh turned and from amused brown eyes gave him another smile of unmistakable intimacy as she withdrew her leg.

"You must be lonely, with your wife—where is she?"

"In Ottawa."

"Ottawa?"

"The Canadian capital."

"I thought Toronto was the capital of Canada."

"So does Toronto." He laughed.

"Are you by any chance free to have dinner with us tomorrow evening? Harold would love it"—she nodded at her husband—"not a party, just a casual little dinner at our apartment."

"Well, I am free tomorrow evening," he said.

As she shook hands when the party broke up, she gave him a card with an address on Park Avenue.

David went the next evening, wondering how he would behave with the husband in her seductive presence.

Raleigh greeted him, exclaiming, "Isn't it a shame? Harold had to go to Washington overnight on business, so it's just the two of us. I hope you don't mind. But we can have a real talk. I cooked supper myself. We go out so much, I can't tell you what a pleasure it is to stay in."

The apartment was like something David had seen only in movies; marble, gilt, and brocade, an ornate staircase ascending.

"None of this is ours. We're just renting it furnished while Harold's here for the UN. Come into the library, where it's cozier. I can't stand this Versailles look."

She led David into a room of polished red walls and dark bookshelves, with soft lamplight, a fire burning, and a table set for two.

"Who are the owners?"

"Some people with awful taste, judging by the books. I was having a bourbon, because it's such a cold winter night. Would you like that or something else?" She turned with the smile that had excited him in the restaurant.

"I'll join you."

She brought him the drink and clinked glasses.

"To our new friendship." She looked at him over the edge of her glass.

"David, I'll be honest with you. I hate beating about the bush. And I simply loathe coy women. I thought you were very attractive the moment I set eyes on you and I knew Harold was going to be away tonight. And here we are!"

"So I see."

"And now we can really get to know each other. Come and sit with me."

She was not beautiful like Francesca, but she exuded sexual energy in her toothy smile, her edgy gestures, the way she crossed her legs as she sat down.

"I'm going to ask you a very direct question." She turned to face him, raising one knee to touch his leg on the sofa.

"We can have drinks and dinner and talk and talk all night if you like, or—"

"Or?"

"Or you could make love to me first."

David laughed nervously.

"Honey, the last thing in the world I'd want would be to force you into anything—but I've been dying to do this ever since I saw you last night."

She leaned towards him, her lips apart, and they fell into an

157

embrace that quickly became fiercer until, in a fever, she began pulling clothes off. Her body was very thin, with almost no breasts, her ribs protruding, her hips' narrow, but there was no fragility in how she wrapped her legs around him and worked to the noisiest orgasm he had ever witnessed.

When she caught her breath, she said, "Now isn't that better than sitting here politely all the blessed night, pretending we're not thinking about what of course we're thinking about? Now we can relax."

"I've always thought of Raleigh as a place, not a woman," David said.

"Well, I don't guess you will anymore!"

But when she snatched up her clothes and retreated to the door, saying, "I'll just be a minute," a glimpse of her unpleasantly skinny thighs gave him a twinge of misgiving. When she asked him to stay the night, he excused himself and was glad of it the next day.

At the UN he ran into Joseph Rogers and thanked him for the dinner invitation. The older man pulled David aside to say, "I noticed Raleigh giving you the eye. If you'll pardon a word between friends, I'd be careful there. That filly's been over a lot of fences— and not very discreet about it."

David was actually relieved, when the committee adjourned, to be recalled to Ottawa.

TWENTY

KAARINA'S ISLAND

SHE SAT IN front of the fire, looking at her legs and feet in Kaarina's dress and shoes. On what occasions had the dead woman worn them? Francesca was sure she could imagine. Kaarina's life seemed so much easier to understand than her own; anyone's life than her own.

She poured more aquavit, not caring that she had no ice to chill it.

Should she have let Matti have his moment? Was it somehow disloyal to Kaarina to refuse him? Strange thoughts. She had done it more casually, for less reason, although, of the two, the one she felt drawn to physically was Kaarina.

The actual fucking was such a slight matter, more in the mind than in the act. She usually got less pleasure from it physically than from the sense of power in giving in because it meant so much to men. David. Barbados and New York nights with David. It didn't matter to her whether they actually did it. It mattered enormously to him. She felt diminished by that importance. He could have done that with anyone. So could she. What she could not have with anyone was the spiritual union she felt with David from the first moment, afterwards fleetingly, the feeling of two souls merging, not two bodies.

For him the souls didn't merge unless the bodies did. But if it wasn't important to her, why had she teased him about it, even when she knew the teasing lacerated him? What had she been trying to do? She had made it seem more important to her than it was.

With men the physical was essential, the lack prevented intimacy. She had believed it to be so essential, she had often initiated it, provoked it, with a little underfeeling of angry achievement, as though she were the man pushing the issue, instead of the woman pushing it away.

The upwelling of rich and comforting feelings in being close to Kaarina had gradually made her realize that physical love was not essential to deep empathy. It must have been out of habit with men that she had first reacted physically with Kaarina, automatically, her sexual antennae alert. But as time passed and Kaarina did not reciprocate in little touches of their bodies, did not by the slightest move seem to demand more, Francesca could relax her sexual early-warning system. It was both more tantalizing and less strained to know that you could do something but did not have to.

There was the moment at the graveyard.

On December afternoons the early darkness of the winter solstice descended on Helsinki, depressing to many but to Francesca making the city cozier. Shops and restaurants glowed more invitingly; reflected lights sparkled in the eyes of women beneath their seductive fur hats. The early darkness, the snow squeaking underfoot, gave her a sense of belonging she had felt in no other city. That, and the comfort she drew from the Koivistos, kept drawing her back on visits.

"Why don't you ever come in summer?" Kaarina had said. "It is so beautiful . . . light almost all the night long. You could come to the island with us."

"I will," Francesca said, but summer did not have the allure of deep winter in Helsinki, where she felt hidden, and liked the feeling.

On one of the dark afternoons, Kaarina took her to the graveyard for soldiers killed in the Winter War. It was Finland's National Day, and other families were there, also brushing snow from the grave markers. Like the others, Kaarina made a small circular wall of snow and placed a lighted candle in the center. She stood up with Francesca to watch the little flame burn serenely. Around them hundreds of other graves glowed with their snow lanterns. At one end stood the massive granite tomb of the wartime commander, Marshal Mannerheim, flanked by tall torches, their flames whipping and flickering in the wind. The wind blew a dusting of fresh snow over the stone at their feet. Kaarina knelt again, removed her glove, and with her bare hand smoothed the snow away from the letters,

ARNO KARKONEN
1921–1940

Impulsively, Francesca knelt beside Kaarina and put an arm around her. Kaarina turned, and in the candlelight her face framed by the gray fur of her hat was beautiful to Francesca. They rose and stood looking down.

"He was only nineteen?"

"He didn't seem so young then," Kaarina said. "I was so little, he felt very big to me. Only in the after years I realized he was just a boy. When I became old enough to be his mother—and did not have my own children."

They stood silently for a few moments, the light wind sighing in the fir trees enclosing the graveyard.

"I feel so much lonelier for them now—in winter."

Deeply moved, Francesca took Kaarina's hand and found it still without a glove. For a moment she thought of slipping it inside her coat to warm it on her breast, but instead put it against her cheek, although still feeling the intimacy of the imagined gesture.

When they turned to leave, Francesca asked, "Is your father buried here too?"

"No. He died long after the war . . ."

The thought sounded unfinished, but Kaarina said no more as they walked away to find a taxi.

In the apartment, when they had taken off their winter coats and hats, Kaarina made coffee and they sat as usual in the quiet dining room.

"There is something about my father I have never told to anyone." There was a haunted tone in Kaarina's voice that made Francesca shiver.

"In the war, he was the officer commanding a small post on the Soviet border, near Imatra. My mother and I went to live there with him. It was after Arno died. I was eleven. I had a friend named Britta. I don't remember how we heard of it, but we knew that our soldiers had captured some Russian soldiers and we were full of curiosity to see them. We crept through trees and deep snow to the top of a small hill. It was late afternoon, almost dark. We were hidden and we looked down. And we saw my father's soldiers shooting the Russians. They looked half frozen, not well fed, totally miserable. Our soldiers made them stand up in the snow and shot them and they fell down in the snow. We looked at each other, very frightened, and looked back. When they were finished, we crawled away and afterwards neither of us wanted to talk about it because we knew we were not supposed to know. It was like being in a dream.

"I knew our soldiers were good people, and the Russians were bad. I assumed my father knew about it—I assumed he gave the orders—but I never dared to ask him. Perhaps he was angry because of my brother's death. But my father was not a violent man. He was very thoughtful and gentle. Perhaps he had orders from his superiors. I couldn't forget it as I got older, and the more I remembered it, the more I was appalled. I know everyone does terrible things in war but this seemed to go against the image we cherish— brave little country, heroic against Soviet hordes. Those men were not communist monsters. They were just cold, frightened young men. I have never told any Finn, any other person."

"Even Matti?"

"Even Matti. I suppose I did not want to disgrace my father's memory, or Arno's . . . but I had to tell someone."

Kaarina got up and came back with a bottle of aquavit and poured two small glasses. There were tears in her eyes when she lifted her glass to Francesca's. "I am very glad you have let me tell it."

"There is something I have never told anyone about my father," Francesca said. "It's amazing, because I was almost the same age as you—ten—and I was also with a friend. Her name was Maria, she was from a Portuguese family in BG."

"What is BG?"

"Guyana. British Guiana it was then. Only Maria didn't see what I saw. And I have never told anyone."

"You don't have to tell me," Kaarina said, and put her hand on Francesca's.

"No, I want to. It was a very hot day. Maria and I dared each other to ride our horses out of Georgetown. We were not supposed to leave town. For somewhere to go we headed for the sugar estate my father owned, about two miles away. We knew it would be deserted on a Sunday. We rode through the narrow lanes. The sugar cane was tall enough to give an edge of shade from the hot sun. We came to the ramshackle jumble of buildings of the sugar refinery, storage sheds, and offices. It was very quiet when we got off our horses in the shade of a large banyan tree. To find some water for the horses—but I think it was as much for the thrill of exploring—I crept into the silent buildings. Maria was more timid and refused to come with me.

"It was cool in the dark sheds. They were piled with cane waiting to be crushed. There were ribbons of sunlight streaming through cracks in the walls. The air had the sour-sweet smell of spilled cane juice fermenting. Each building opened into another, and I wandered through them, a little nervous about snakes and rats, until I heard a noise and went towards it, thinking it might be a caretaker I could ask for water. The sound, like grunting, was louder through the open door of an office. I tiptoed to the door and saw my father, naked, lying on top of a young black woman. Instinctively, I drew back. I was astonished; my heart was beating fast. That both of them were naked and the woman was black meant more to me right away than what they were doing. I knew about that, of course, but I had never seen anyone doing it. I was very scared. I crept away back through the sheds and out into the hot sunlight. I didn't tell Maria. But the image I had seen, the black thighs wrapped around my father's hips, kept coming back back to me. I couldn't get it out of my mind.

"Of course, the meaning of it became clearer to me, and it gave me strange feelings to look at my father or my mother. When I began to attract boys, when she told me over and over what nice girls did not do, I thought, But Father does. And then I thought, If Father does it with one black girl, does he do it with others? If girls get pregnant from doing that, the black girls must get pregnant. So there must be children around who were my half brothers or sisters, half white, half black. My father called his workers 'black bastards,' and after that day I began to laugh to myself at the new meaning. And when he was exasperated by something and scolded me, I was tempted to throw back at him what I had seen. But I never dared. It was a weapon too dangerous to use.

"But the first time I let a boy go—you know—all the way, in the back of my mind there was a kind of wicked amusement at what my father would think if he knew, and if he found out, I could say, 'What about you—poking black girls on the estate?' "

Kaarina got up behind Francesca's chair and hugged her, leaning her face against her hair.

"That is such a sad thing for a little girl to see."

Francesca, with a rush of feelings suddenly released, turned to the other woman and embraced her, crushing her face against Kaarina's breasts, the intense longing to be closer to her overwhelming any restraint. The confusion of maternal and sexual feelings emanating from Kaarina made Francesca want to give her herself completely to this woman, whose presence gave her such delicious comfort; made her want to curl up in her embrace.

"I love you."

"I love you, my Francesca."

She raised her face to Kaarina, who knelt beside her, and they kissed. It was very strange to kiss a woman so. It was strange and achingly pleasant. But Kaarina stopped her.

Holding her shoulders, she looked gravely into Francesca's eyes: "We both know what might happen now. But we don't know what would happen afterwards."

Francesca was about to protest when they heard Matti's key in the lock and parted.

His face was bright from the cold and he said cheerfully, "What's the matter? You both look as though you have been weeping."

"We went to put a candle on Arno's grave," Kaarina said.

"Ah, yes." He noticed the bottle and brought another glass. "Well, let us have a drink to Arno. He was a brave fellow." There were tears in his eyes as he emptied his glass and wiped his beard.

"And so are you," Kaarina said, her kiss on his cheek so chaste to Francesca after the kiss she had just experienced.

WATCHING THE FLAMES curl around the birch logs, feeling a hot glow from the aquavit, Francesca raised her glass and said, "To Arno. To Kaarina. To Matti. To me."

TWENTY-ONE

OTTAWA—LUSAKA

LATE IN THE spring of 1972, there was a call from New York.

David was emptying his desk. He'd spent months wondering where he stood in the bureaucratic wars between the PMO and External. The so-called Third Option, Trudeau's opening to Europe to offset dependence on the United States, consumed the department, and he had felt left out. Of course, that initiative, like so many Trudeau ideas, ultimately fizzled for lack of follow-through.

Unexpectedly, David was named first secretary and acting high commissioner to Lusaka. A very small mission, but important. Next door in Rhodesia, Ian Smith's white settler rebellion was fracturing the British Commonwealth. Trudeau was pushing Britain to accept the inevitability of black majority rule or risk destroying the multiracial association.

At thirty-three, David had his first senior posting—a plum. He must clearly be in the slipstream, as they said in the department.

He was exhilarated to be flying out the next day. Marilyn would follow later, after renting their house and coping with the hundred details of transferring small children to a strange and exotic new home. Foreign service wives, unpaid and largely unthanked, carried as heavy a burden as their husbands. Younger women were complaining that the rigors of managing households and children on increasingly tight allowances, often in housing well below the Canadian standard, was not worth the small glamour of calling themselves diplomatic wives. Some were flatly refusing to go. But Marilyn's upbringing had conditioned her. Indeed, when the department held training sessions on the duties and social graces required, she'd known more than the instructors. And, unlike her parents, she was determined to take her children everywhere.

David's desk was cleared, his colleagues were about to take him to a farewell lunch at the Château, when he was told there was a call from New York. Full of knowing apprehension, he answered.

"I told you I needed some time to think?" Francesca's accent hit him as though a waft of her perfume had come through the phone.

"Yes?"

"Well, I was stupid that day in New York. I should have said yes."

His heart made a small leap, but he suppressed it and said carefully, "I see."

"You haven't changed your mind?"

"No, I haven't."

"Too bad." Francesca was silent for a moment. "I wish you'd given me more time."

"I'm sorry. I'm leaving tomorrow for Zambia."

"For a long time?"

"Probably about three years. I'm going to be acting head of mission."

"What does that mean?"

"Like acting ambassador."

"Congratulations. Are the family all going with you?"

"Yes."

"Well, good luck. I wish I hadn't been so stupid."

"Are you still flying?"

"Yes, but I'm sick of it. I'm going to do some modeling. A man introduced me to an agency."

David remembered the letter in the New York Hilton.

"Well, good luck in that."

"Goodbye, David."

"Goodbye."

He put the phone down and went to lunch, where he drank some wine in celebration, proud of his self-control. He needed to apply himself fully to justify the new level of responsibility. There were men in the department who would be watching carefully. A promising career left no room for reckless behavior, like his with Francesca. He was lucky to have escaped unscathed, no one the wiser. He had really put her behind him, a conviction made the more poignant because, under the crust of his determination, for a tiny second with her on the phone, he had felt regret, a whisper of temptation.

Marilyn and David went to a farewell dinner, and he spent the last night content with her and with himself.

"I feel in a way that you've come back to me again, just as you're going away," she said as they settled for sleep. "I suppose it's because I'm going with you this time."

"I'll do everything I can to make it fun for you there," he said— and meant it.

Later it became obvious, for all his resolve, that he'd been hasty in rejecting Francesca. She'd asked for time; then a few months later she wanted to say yes. But it was she who had walked out on him. He had urged her to marry him and she had walked out— although she'd left the message on the mirror, asking for time. Perhaps he'd been unconsciously relieved to escape from her spell, to go home to Marilyn.

168

DAVID LOOKED AT his watch. Two hours since he had spoken to Jenny. Just after midnight—seven in Helsinki. They'd be starting the day. No point in calling again, two hours after he had spoked to Jenny. If Jean Luc knew anything, he'd call.

He was aware of being hungry and tired, but his anxiety was greater. He wandered into the living room. Tomorrow it would be filled with businessmen all convinced Ottawa was doing too little to help them crack American markets. They tended to think that External Affairs was still an effete culture irrelevant to the tough and real world they inhabited. Impossible to convince them that trade was now God.

How could he get through tomorrow's schedule with all this uncertainty—and that image in his mind . . . Francesca's body floating in gray waters?

Without thinking, David opened a silver box and removed the package of DuMaurier cigarettes kept for rare guests who still smoked. He lit his first cigarette in years.

On the table were framed photographs, dominated by the autographed portrait of the Queen. Near it was a picture of David with Kenneth Kaunda, the president of Zambia, in colorful African dress. Below, Kaunda had written, *To David Lyon, a true friend of Zambia and the African people.* Somewhere in his boxes in storage were extravagant Zambian newspaper accounts of the incident behind the photograph—another of the times he had started smoking again.

A blazing hot day, the air conditioners in the high commission in Lusaka feeble against the equatorial sun, but noisy enough to mask the first commotion outside David's office. Then shouts, several gunshots; and the office door was kicked open. Three Africans in camouflage uniforms and berets, two with machine guns, one a pistol, burst in.

"You are the prisoner of the Zimbabwe National Liberation Front," the man with the pistol shouted, nervous, sweating, highly charged.

David stood up, taller than the Africans, more surprised than frightened.

"You are on the territory of the Government of Canada," he said. "This is a diplomatic mission. I must ask you to leave immediately."

The leader pointed his pistol, his arm straight, at David's chest. "We are leaving—with you. Come!"

The two with machine guns gripped his arms and frog-marched him out of the office. There were more men in uniform, their guns holding the few members of the high commission staff, with frightened faces, against the walls.

Shoved out the front door, David called over his shoulder, "I don't know what's happening. You'd better tell Ottawa and the Zambian Government."

Three dusty Land Rovers waited outside, a small crowd of civilians watching, no sign of Zambian police. In a second they had propelled him into the covered back of one vehicle and were driving off. It had all happened in less than a minute.

"I demand to know what you're doing," David said to the leader. "I am a Canadian diplomat. What you're doing is against international law."

The young man ignored David, watching nervously for pursuers through the open back of the truck. There were no pursuers. Raiding parties from the guerrillas fighting Rhodesia's white government used neighboring Zambia as a base. But they had never kidnapped a diplomat. The Africans eyed him coldly. Their forces had killed many whites in Rhodesia—raiding and murdering on lonely farms— and these eyes showed complete indifference to one more white life.

They were quickly outside the small city, then left the highway, jolting over a dirt road through bush country with sparse trees, reddish earth, and ant hills taller than a man. After sweating for half an hour in clouds of dust, David could see thicker forest ahead, lusher vegetation. They passed men with a mounted machine gun guarding

170

the road. The Land Rovers jerked to a stop in a village of mud huts thatched with leaves, shaded by a heavy canopy of trees. He saw more men in camouflage uniforms, women in bright kente cloth dresses, small children. He didn't know whether he was still in Zambia or had crossed the border into Rhodesia.

Incongruously, on the hard-packed earth among the huts was a folding metal table and two chairs, one occupied by another soldier, older, bearded, obviously a commander. David was led to the table and made to sit facing him. At least it was cooler than in the stifling Land Rover.

"If you are the leader of these men, please order them to release me at once. They have obviously made a mistake. I am the Canadian high commissioner."

"They have not made a mistake. They were ordered to arrest you, Mr. Lyon. You are the prisoner of the Zimbabwe National Liberation Front." He sounded British-educated, with little local accent.

"This is absurd. I have nothing to do with the Rhodesian Government. I repeat, I am a Canadian diplomat, and what you have done violates all the norms of international behavior and diplomatic immunity." It sounded puny, but it was comforting to have something conventional to say.

"Are you thirsty, Mr. Lyon? You've had a very hot ride. Bring some water! Would you like a cigarette?" From his uniform pocket he took a flat tin of fifty Rhodesian cigarettes and held it out, politely. "You are going to be here for some time. I invite you to relax and make yourself comfortable."

A woman brought a small gourd of water.

"It is perfectly clean. There is a spring in the village."

His mouth full of red dust from the journey, David took a sip. The water was cold and delicious.

The cigarettes were offered again. This time he took one and the officer lit it graciously with his own match.

David's heart had slowed its furious beating. It seemed he was not in any immediate physical danger.

"There were shots when your men broke into my office. If you have shot anyone, my government will hold you responsible."

The officer said to his inferior with the pistol still guarding David, "You shoot anyone?"

"No, sir! We just fired in the air—to make them afraid."

"So, no one was shot and you have not been harmed, Mr. Lyon. Please relax. We have to do business." He waved the inferior away.

"The Zambian authorities have been alerted. Their forces will be out hunting for you."

The officer laughed. "Zambian forces are not a problem to us."

Unfortunately, David knew that was true. Kaunda deplored the violence of the Rhodesian nationalists but sympathized with their goals. David's staff knew that. They would have no power to free him. And Marilyn would know by now . . .

"Then what is the purpose of all this?" David said impatiently.

"The purpose is to hold you as a hostage. To make the British Government revise its policy and withdraw its support from Ian Smith's illegal seizure of power."

"Canada has nothing to do with the British Government."

"Oh, we think differently. When you write a letter, we will take it to Lusaka, to Salisbury, to the newspapers, the BBC, saying that Mr. Edward Heath's goverment must change its policy or a Canadian official will die . . ."

The man had stopped smiling, and, for the first time, David felt real fear.

"I think it will have a tremendous effect."

"My government has made its position extremely clear. Repeatedly. We are against the Rhodesia's unilateral declaration of independence. We are in favor of majority rule, achieved through free elections. My prime minister, Pierre Trudeau, has said so."

Thank God, David thought, it was true.

"But he has not said it very loudly. When he knows that a Canadian diplomat's life is in danger, he will call on London more forcefully. He will call on the whole Commonwealth. He will go to the United Nations . . ."

David tried to imagine such an ultimatum reaching Ottawa . . . the reaction of Trudeau's government, weakened by the recent election, the New Democrats holding the balance of power . . . how tiny and faraway this incident would look.

"And"—the officer added his trump card—"the Commonwealth Conference opens tomorrow in Ottawa. Prime Minister Heath will be there. Even the Queen will be there!"

He was right. For soldiers camped in a primitive village in the African bush, these guerrillas were astonishingly well informed and, David realized looking about, well organized and well equipped. Probably Soviet or Czech weapons. It was not an entirely stupid plan.

"I cannot write such a letter," he said. "I am not in a position to tell my government what to do. You may send any message you like. It is not my function."

"It is your function to advise your government."

"Not to advise it to submit to threats."

It scared David a little to say this, but he felt no immediate risk.

"This is not an empty threat, Mr. Lyon," the leader said with emphasis.

"You would bring no honor on your cause to . . . to put my life at risk. In the end you would be condemned. You would gain no sympathy in world opinion."

"In a war, sympathy is useless. What we want is action."

The argument continued as the light faded. Nearby, women pounded grain in a hollowed tree trunk, using a heavy carved log as a pestle. The smoke from small fires was pleasant. David smoked more of the officer's cigarettes and drank more cold water.

"We need the letter tonight, Mr. Lyon. No later."

"I will write that I am being held by you and that I have told you my government's position. That is all I can write."

The officer rose and disappeared into the shadows. Perhaps he made contact with someone by radio, because when he returned, he said, "You write what you said. We will supply the rest."

He produced paper and a pen and David wrote:

I was kidnapped at noon today by armed men saying they were from the Zimbabwe National Liberation Front. I am being held in a village about 30 minutes' drive from Lusaka. I have stated to them the position of the Canadian Government on Rhodesia.

The officer, shining a flashlight over David's shoulder, objected.

"No. You cannot say thirty minutes from Lusaka. Write it again and take that out."

Not surprised that he'd been caught, David rewrote the note and signed it.

"We will attach this to our own communiqué. If London does not condemn Ian Smith and withdraw support, you will be killed."

Repeated now in the heavy darkness, the threat was extremely unnerving to David. Otherwise, there was nothing unpleasant in his treatment. By a fire, with flattened logs as seats, they gave him a gourd of a hot mash made from the grain. It lacked salt but tasted like Red River cereal he'd eaten as a child.

They cleared one of the huts and a woman laid fresh-cut leaves on the sleeping platform. Soon after dark, with no artificial lighting, the village retired. An armed man was posted outside the hut.

David lay in the close darkness of the hut, smelling the smoke from the dying fires, listening to the sounds of the bush coming alive in the night, trying to be calm.

He thought of Marilyn scared out of her wits. He tried to imagine such a message reaching Ottawa and the Commonwealth heads

174

of government. How far, David wondered, had Trudeau actually pushed the British . . .

And then, incongruously, he had a memory of Pierre Trudeau sliding down a bannister at the Commonwealth Conference at Lancaster House in London.

The image annoyed David, and the more it played in his mind, the more his irritation grew. What pathetic need in a grown man to show off like a child! Like his pirouette behind the Queen at Buckingham Palace. Exuberance, joie de vivre, fine. Photographers ate it up, and some Canadians loved the jaunty impertinence . . . for a while. Perhaps it gave expression to a pent-up Canadian desire to say, We are not stodgy and dull . . . we too can be frisky, avant-garde, and sexy. We are not conformists . . . we dress unconventionally. We are not Cold War Manicheans like the Americans . . . we skin-dive with Castro and make deals with Moscow. We are not the prisoners of the American economy . . . we can develop our trade with Europe. We are not in thrall to the Queen . . . we do pirouettes behind her back. We do not take ourselves too seriously . . . we slide down bannisters for the world press.

Trudeau's antics, his glamorous dates, had dominated the popular press coverage of that conference at the expense of the real issues. The political instincts David admired always seemed to be at war with Trudeau's need to mock, to show off, and thus to trivialize whatever serious intentions he had. If a Canadian diplomat like David doubted his own prime minister's seriousness, why should other nations take him seriously? Why should the Zimbabwe National Liberation Front?

And then he found himself wondering what Francesca would think if she heard he had been killed here. Until this moment, he had really put her out of his thoughts, firmly closing that door. But now in the darkness of this thatched hut in Africa, the door of memory opened and she was vividly with him. She would be splendid in a situation like this, he was sure; disdainful; not frightened. She had made him feel life so much more more acutely, more on the edge of living, he who had always lived well back from the edge. And thinking of her actually made David less anxious, as though, from halfway around the world, he had again borrowed some of her existential bravado.

He fell asleep, wakened when his hips protested at the hard sleeping surface, slept again . . . wakened . . . slept.

A long time later, it seemed, there were shots: abrupt staccato concussions—mechanical burps of sound—tearing the night apart. Then shouts. Then firing from heavier automatic weapons . . . from a distance. No . . . close at hand, too. Gunfire flashes lit up the doorway of the hut. Alarmed, David got off the platform and rolled underneath as close to the mud wall as he could squeeze. More heavy firing, hoarse shouting, engines starting, revving loudly, driving away . . . then quiet. David didn't know whether to move. Then he heard more engines, different voices shouting . . . in English.

"Search the huts! Be careful. How many'd we kill?"

He recognized the flat accent. They must be Rhodesian soldiers. He crawled from his hiding place to see a flashlight blinding him.

"He's here," a voice shouted. "He looks all right! Are you the Canadian?"

"Yes, I am. Who are you?"

"Rhodesian Defense Force. He's here, sir! Looks all right. Not hurt, are you?"

"No, I'm fine."

An officer came up. "David Lyon?"

"Yes, thank you."

"No danger. They've all cleared off. We spotted this camp days ago. We were listening to their wireless. Just getting into position to move in when word came you'd been kidnapped."

"Are we in Rhodesia?"

"Well, let's just say very close. Technically we're not supposed to be over the border. So we're not. Right? Like a smoke? Afraid we'll have to take you back with us. We can't very well drive into Lusaka in a parade."

"Do you think you could get word to my wife . . . and the Canadian Government?"

"No problem. I'll send a message from the half-track. Must have been quite an ordeal. I'm glad we were able to get you out of it."

"So am I. Extremely grateful."

"They don't usually stand for a fight. Usually cut and run if we turn up with any kind of force."

"Were any of them killed?"

"Two we've found. Maybe others, but we'd need daylight to be sure, and we have to pull out. There's one."

He shone his flashlight on a twisted form, a large wound in the black face. David shuddered and felt sick. It could have been his body lying there, with ants already moving in the congealed blood.

"OH, SWEETHEART, THANK God you weren't hurt," Marilyn said, when he telephoned. "It must have been terrifying."

"Sure. But I sort of liked the guerrilla leader. There were fellows like him at LSE."

"Maybe he was there. Daddy always said it was a hotbed of leftists."

"Like Trudeau?" David laughed.

The irony of being rescued by the forces his own government condemned was a point he underscored in his report to Ottawa.

The Rhodesians kept quiet about their troops' presence in Zambia. David's note and the guerrillas' ultimatum never got to Ottawa, so never became an issue at the Commonwealth Conference. It was years before Ian Smith gave up the battle for white supremacy and Zimbabwe became an African-ruled nation.

David's superiors took his kidnapping very calmly, commending his devotion to duty, as though this happened to Canadian diplomats every day. He even had a fight with the accountants at External over the cost of repairing two doors smashed in by the guerrillas. As he learned the craft, David was learning the pettiness of running a minor mission, endless little battles with Ottawa over furniture and allowances.

Only Zambia's leader, Kenneth Kaunda, and his controlled press made a fuss. The prime minister paid a personal visit of apology to the high commission, deploring the outrageous infringement of his country's sovereignty by the guerrillas (though pointedly not by the Rhodesian army). He invited Marilyn and David to a dinner in their honor, and later sent the inscribed photograph. For a few weeks, two Zambian policeman languidly guarded the high commission.

David's thoughts during the hours in that hut lingered in his mind. On the practical level, how effective was Canada's new independent foreign policy if those most affected didn't know? Thereafter, he made sure it was known within his orbit in Central Africa.

Otherwise his years in Lusaka were quiet, and he felt far from big events—the Vietnam War climax, the oil crisis after the Arab-Israeli war, the Watergate scandal and Nixon's resignation.

On the personal level, probably fed by his own fear that night, his admiration for Pierre Trudeau had suffered serious damage, although he remained fascinating, puzzling, worthy of study. Canadians liked to think of themselves as a modest people, ill made for strutting in the world. Perhaps Trudeau personified the arrogance hidden in that modesty.

There must have been some envy in his ambivalent feelings. Trudeau had escaped the entrapments of family until his fifties, David's age now. With family money, Trudeau had been free to prolong his education, to explore and fulfill himself—as David had not.

And Trudeau had panache. Yes, to people brought up like David and Wallace Farquhar, Trudeau's dress looked outrageous, outré, absurd—therefore undignified. It was one of the interesting changes in Canada since Trudeau that how you dressed mattered less and less.

But if Trudeau's clothing was a challenge to his own generation, it was a clever gesture of solidarity with the young. Like Francesca's dressing, a kind of taunt. The Caribbean warmth reinforced it, seeming to say, Your northern climate makes you uptight, constricted, overdressed, overly formal. If you could relax as we do, wear less, take life less punitively, you would be happier. Come, I'll teach you. Take it easy. All that . . . and more.

He had been intoxicated by Francesca's apparent freedom. There he was, fettered in every way, circumscribed by habit, upbringing, cultural conditioning, professional environment—and she had seemed unfettered.

She made him wonder whether, given other choices, he might have been more creative, might have become a writer, not a drone in the dusty hive of External. His professional circumspection, the constraints of marriage and fatherhood, might well have slurred the free flow of talent within him. Perhaps that was why, when he began taking such risks with Francesca, his work reflected more daring, more panache.

Perhaps that was why he couldn't resist her when she came back.

TWENTY-TWO

KAARINA'S ISLAND

SHE PUT TWO more logs on the fire. Its warmth and the aquavit had suppressed any desire to eat. She lay back on the sofa in a comfortable haze, staring with unfocused eyes at the bright flames, the room illuminated by their dancing light, echoing to the crackling of the dry wood.

If she died like this, how long would it be until anyone found her? She might stay here all winter . . . the ice princess frozen in an ancient evening dress. Someone with imagination might suppose she had been here since the dress was in style in the 1960s, thirty years ago, when she was ten or so, too young to wear it . . . just the age when she found her father with the black woman.

Lying like this, her mind foggy, slipping from one thought to another, she could hold her entire life in her mind at once, one scene nudging another, people sliding by . . . voices advancing and receding as in a play on the radio . . .

180

"You're getting drunk," she said, and heard her voice naked and alone in the empty room. "And what of it? It's your birthday!"

She refilled her glass. What would Colin and Samantha think if they heard she had died? Rid of an embarrassment? Or sad that their father had taken them away when her life was such a mess ten years ago? To have a better life. Federico and his family had just taken control. She couldn't argue; indeed, at first felt guiltily relieved. But what better life? They wrote infrequently, dutifully, grudging with words and sentiments, about their bourgeois life in Milan. Federico had remarried well, some family connection, and they lived in one of those dark, high-ceiled, heavily ornamented apartments well-to-do Italians found comfortable. They kept up their English but were more at ease in Italian. *"Caro mama . . ."* How odd Colin would seem now in B'dos with his glossy black hair and long eyelashes.

Sleepily she saw that the aquavit bottle was almost empty. Tomorrow she would set off to complete the plan . . . all carefully worked out . . . the course plotted . . . must remember to remove the marked charts . . . add to the mystery . . . sail clear of the Aalands, make for the Swedish coast . . . the tiny summer resort she had picked for its easy harbor . . . come in at night, get up the rubber dinghy she had brought . . . inflate it with the foot pump . . . work the yacht in close to the the beach in the darkness, lower the inflatable alongside . . . set a course out to sea . . . lock the wheel . . . set the throttle to slow ahead . . . tricky to get down into the dinghy with the boat moving . . . cast off and watch the yacht head out to sea . . . to run until the fuel gave out . . . row ashore . . . pull the dinghy up the strand to the deserted cottages she had checked . . . one with space underneath, where she could hide it behind some latticework . . . walk up the road to the American-style motel where she had rented a room, flying over three days ago from Helsinki, leaving a bag with city clothes . . . change and leave quickly . . . bus to Malmö and ferry to Denmark . . . lie low and see when they found *Havsflickan* with the clothes

181

and the envelope . . . pretend to be missing just long enough to scare him.

She loved the plan . . . it was brilliant, and handling the boat had been easier than she'd feared. She would say to him, "We had a date on Kaarina's island and you didn't come!" Well, she thought, I showed up! She thought of raising her glass in a toast and saying, You see? I showed up! She thought of it several times . . . You see? . . . I showed up! . . . When she thought of it again . . . she thought she had already done it . . . but couldn't be sure . . . too sleepy . . . and she had a confused feeling that now she did not feel *in* her plan, but someone outside, watching herself go through with it.

She watched the flames purring and curling around the logs, making her almost too hot, lying in Kaarina's dress, on Kaarina's couch, in Kaarina's cottage . . . on a lonely dark island . . . miles from anywhere . . . the chill of the Scandinavian autumn settling outside.

SHE AWOKE A few hours later. The fire had burned down to a white ash. The room was dark and very cold. When she climbed the stairs, the bedroom was even colder. She looked out, but the sky was murky, with no stars. Shivering violently, her head aching from the drink, she slipped out of the evening gown, rapidly pulled on Kaarina's flannel nightdress, and got into the ancient bed. She pulled her knees up, wrapping her icy feet in the skirt, then lay curled up and trembling, her hands pressed between her thighs, trying to make her body create a cocoon of warmth under the thick eiderdown. If it was after midnight, this was her fortieth birthday. It was the day she would sail to Sweden.

Oddly, remembering her plan now did not bring the earlier tingle of excitement . . . it came to her in negative colors . . . but she could concentrate on nothing but the desire to be warm— and to sleep.

TWENTY-THREE

HELSINKI

AFTER LUSAKA, DAVID thought the cross-posting to Helsinki a poor career move, not the leap a high flyer might have expected.

In 1974, Helsinki seemed a backwater, an outpost in Cold War tedium, once a useful listening post, now a sideshow, definitely off the fast career track, out of the slipstream. David felt some resentment.

It was uncanny; either the coincidence of Francesca's timing, or her ability to divine his mood. Although she had been silent for two and a half years, the sound of her voice instantly reawakened everything.

"I ran into a Canadian who told me you're now ambassador to Finland."

"Where are you calling from?"

"Quite close. I'm in Stockholm. You know I'm a model now. Very glamorous!" she said, self-mocking.

"Uh-huh."

"I'd love to see you. I could come over to Helsinki. It's not far."

For a second David stalled. "I thought you hated the cold."

"I've changed. Do you want me to come?"

Without hesitation or thought. "Yes, I do."

"What hotel should I go to? I've never been there."

Again David found the answer as though he'd prepared it in advance.

"The Torni. T-O-R-N-I. It's a little more private than some others."

"Do you think we'll *need* to be private?" The familiar teasing in her voice was exciting.

"Well, we'll see, won't we?"

"I'll call you when I'm there."

It was simple. Marilyn had taken the girls back to Ottawa to see her parents and ease the transition from Lusaka.

The next afternoon, in a small dark hotel room, Francesca and David looked at each other shyly for a moment and shook hands. Then she kissed him lightly on the cheek, a replica of her farewell in New York, but a kiss of coming back, closing an emotional bracket.

She was glamorous indeed at twenty-four, noticeably more sophisticated in her hair and make-up, the sharp edge of her lipstick, her controlled way of sitting down, elegant knees together, one fashionable shoe slightly advanced on the other. What had not changed was her way of glancing intimately at him, hair falling over one cheek, then looking back with new intensity.

Eyeing each other curiously, with shy hunger, they answered simple questions.

"You have a wedding ring."

"I'm married. His name is Federico D'Anielli. And I have a son!"

"Congratulations."

"Does that amaze you?"

"Tell me about your husband."

184

She made a face. "He's handsome and he's very boring."

"The name sounds Italian."

"He's Italian and he sells cars. He knows a lot about cars. I made a stupid mistake—not for the first time."

David felt a different kind of desire for her; not the lyrical spell of their first encounters but an uncontrollable craving for her company and for sex with her. All hesitations of the past had vanished during their years apart. She had come back.

They became lovers again that afternoon. To be discreet they had dinner in her hotel room and David spent part of the night with her.

And so began a pattern that lasted for seven years. She was frequently in northern Europe and could come to Helsinki or Stockholm, and David began to travel more.

As it happened, the posting to Finland gave him fascinating work. He was drawn in to assist in the negotiations for the Helsinki Accords, which hastened the decay of the Soviet system. The moral force of civilized nations demanding minimal performance on human rights encouraged those, like Sakharov, who were fighting from within. It was an achievement David felt proud to share, diplomacy perfectly suited to Canada's taste for multilateral, nonmilitary solutions.

As negotiations intensified, he had to travel often to Geneva, with connecting stops on the way. In between, he and Francesca wrote letters. Too disorganized, too impatient, she sometimes telephoned. But they always knew approximately where the other would be, and how, sporadically, they could meet.

The relationship never recaptured the freshness he had felt with her in the islands, but it was more knowing, both carnally and intellectually. With her, David could discuss anything, a license he enjoyed with no one else. He wrote long unguarded letters, often funny and indiscreet, about colleagues and issues.

Because he never lived with her, Francesca never became a habit; he knew her only with the sexual excitement a stranger provokes. He never felt habit obliterating feeling. Domestication dampened desire because it removed risk, fear, guilt—all abundant with Francesca—and this referred back to Marilyn as the risk of discovery, and perhaps beyond Marilyn to his boyhood. As though sex and desire had to be surreptitious to be exciting. The habit he needed for security was the habit that killed desire.

In those years, it was he who avoided commitment, as Francesca had in the past. And looking back now, he found it impossible to know how seriously she had wanted a commitment from him. But if she had, how gravely had he disappointed her, had he let her down? At the core of David's private history was one conviction: he had loved her, would have abandoned everything for her, but she refused, then reconsidered, then drove him away with more and more bizarre behavior. She had driven him away.

She and her husband moved briefly to Brussels and she became pregnant with her second child, Samantha. David had to brief a NATO committee on the progress of the Helsinki talks. On a cold rainy afternoon, she came to his room in the old Métropole Hotel. Her belly was large and she looked uncharacteristically sad and defeated. She could stay only two hours, and lay with her feet up on his bed, in a drifting, melancholy conversation, most of her sentences beginning, "I wish . . ."

"I wish we could make love . . . I wish it was your baby, not his. Sometimes I imagine it is yours."

"Are you sure it isn't?"

"Yes. I wanted it to be but it didn't happen in Helsinki." She smiled at him wistfully, a small echo of the shy smile that he always felt in his stomach.

"I want it to be over. I can't do any work like this, so I have to stay at home, and if I'm not working, he expects me to be the dutiful housewife. Imagine! I'm learning to cook. I'm quite good, but I won't cook anything Italian. Only French." She smiled mischievously. "I should invite you to dinner, say you're an old friend who just turned up." It was the only time she brightened that afternoon.

"But you sleep with him?" Her condition made David feel tender with her yet bolder.

She flared up with something of her usual quickness to challenge. "Well, you sleep with Marilyn!"

"Yes."

"Stupid for the two of us to be sleeping with them when we'd rather be sleeping with each other."

Their eyes met and the sexual current was intense in the silence, the traffic noises in the rain outside muted by the heavy drapes.

She said softly, "If we did it gently, it wouldn't hurt the baby."

"Do you want to?"

"Yes."

David moved to the bed and kissed her, but after a little she stopped him.

"No. I don't want you to see me naked like this."

"You're beautiful like this."

"I'm ugly as hell. My hair is all limp. My back aches and I've got to go and cook dinner. I haven't even done the shopping. And it rains all the bloody time. No wonder the Belgians are so gray and boring. I hope it's a girl this time. I want to bring her up and tell her the truth about things."

"About Belgium?"

"It's all right for you to laugh. You don't live here."

"What are you going to do with Federico if you're so unhappy?"

"I'm going to make enough money so that I can be independent and get away from him."

"Does he know that?"

"Well, if he doesn't, he's a bloody fool. And when I'm slim again and have my freedom, I'm going to pursue you, do you hear? I'm going to come and make you make love to me until you're blue in the face."

David laughed. "Why blue in the face?"

"I don't know. My mother used to say that."

"How are they, your parents?"

"They're moving to Barbados. My father's fed up with Guyana. The government makes it impossible for him to run the estate. He can't stand kowtowing to them. He's going to sell out. I've got to go. I left my car on a meter."

At the door, she kissed him and said shyly, "Are you poking other women?"

"No."

David had been tempted. At a party in Helsinki he had lit a cigarette for an attractive young woman.

She said, "You blew out the match!"

"Yes?"

"In Finland that means you want to go to bed with me." Prudently, he had not pursued it, but the incident stayed alive in his imagination.

Francesca said, "Well, you'd better not be when I find you again, do you hear?"

He watched from the window as she walked heavily across the square and unlocked a small car. She sat in the driver's seat and slowly pulled her legs in. Then she shot off, making the car seem angry. He'd felt both the usual ache for her and relief that she was not his responsibility.

At the time, he'd been intrigued to feel such physical desire for her when she was so huge with Federico's child. If she hadn't demurred . . . but how grotesque it would sound to anyone else. He'd actually been a little shocked that she had even considered it . . . shocked yet eager for her, as long as the moral responsibility was hers. Before she rejected him in New York, he had assumed the moral responsibility. After their reunion in Helsinki, he had unconsciously transferred it to her.

TWENTY-FOUR

KAARINA'S ISLAND

FRANCESCA AWOKE, SNUG in the old bed but feeling on her face that the room was freezing. Sensing that the day outside was gray and unfriendly, she lay for a moment, looking at the panels of flowers carved in the wooden canopy. How many people over the centuries had awakened to their birthdays in this bed, full of fresh hope or old despair?

For months, the idea of becoming forty had seemed a momentous divide, the crest of a hill from which she would be able to see forwards and back to both ends of her life. Now, on the day, she felt both anticlimax and impatience.

Her parched mouth and growling stomach drove her out of the warm bed. She dressed hastily and breakfasted on the salami and cheese she had intended for the previous evening. She couldn't be bothered to light a fire. She would make coffee on the boat.

Quickly she tidied up, carefully folding the nightgown and re-

189

placing it in the scented drawer, which she closed with a feeling that she was interring Kaarina with a new permanence. She hung the evening dress in the cupboard.

She had gone downstairs, and was ready to leave, when an impulse sent her back up to the bedroom. Again she pulled a chair to the head of the bed and reached for the envelope on top. She would take the paper they had both signed, proof that she had kept the promise.

With the strange feeling of closing a grave, she shut the door of the house and locked it, returning the key to its hiding place.

A chilly wind followed her down the field and ruffled the waters of the cove. *Havsflickan* swung in a different direction on the gray water. In her plans she had imagined another day of bright sunshine, but the sky was all scudding clouds. The anticipation of harder, colder sailing ahead made her steel her courage against a feeling of apprehension, but rowing quickly to the boat made her warm and more cheerful.

She lit the stove, noticing she had forgotten to turn off the gas supply from the cylinder in the cockpit, and heard David, years ago, saying, "You have to be deliberate at sea. One small carelessness can mean disaster. Everything careful and deliberate." Geoffrey had been more casual, because he did it for a living, but in the Caribbean everything was easier, and you could navigate almost by the color of the water. David had learned to sail in Nova Scotia, where the sea had many moods. "Everything careful and deliberate," he would say and it reflected the personality he struggled against, surprising her with his willingness to take the risks he did with her. But that was the essence of sailing: you had to take risks and you had to be careful, a constant little war between prudence and daring.

Even that memory could not subdue the impatience she felt to try herself against the day and the sea, to force her plan to work. She started the engine and, while it was ticking over, freed the sheets of the genoa from the self-tailing winches. She made a cup of instant coffee and, to soothe her nervousness, lit a cigarette while studying the chart.

Out of the cove, make a wide left turn to clear the rocks that extend well out under water, then steer between two low islands. That would clear the Aalands into the Gulf of Bothnia. Slightly left again, course 265 degrees for Sweden. The wind was over her shoulder as she faced the stern, looking out of the cove, then again at the chart. If it held outside, that would mean a broad reach all the way. Perfect; perhaps no course or sail adjustments all day.

Taking a few minutes more to calculate, she went below, where the vibration of the diesel made small plates and glasses tinkle in their lockers. She unrolled a chart and stretched the dividers on the scale of nautical miles, as Geoffrey had shown her when plotting a longer passage. Six knots a good average for his boat, but that was much larger. Say five knots for *Havsflickan* and easier to count, anyway. She squeezed the dividers to span five nautical miles, found the pencil mark outside the last island where her course to the Swedish coast began, and walked the dividers along the line, eleven times, fifty-five nautical miles . . . eleven hours if the wind held.

It was now eight A.M., say one hour to clear the islands, plus eight hours in the open sea. With luck, she'd be off the harbor at midevening.

On deck, the feel of the freshening wind gave her another frisson of anxiety, but she subdued it by walking forward and testing the anchor line. The wind in the cove was still light enough to let her pull it up easily. She fitted the handle to the anchor capstan and cranked back and forth. The chain clanked up a foot at a time and flopped down the pipe to the locker. The action warmed her more.

The boat was turning its head towards the nearest shore. She'd have to be quick not to let the wind carry her too close when the anchor came off the bottom. She thought methodically: bring the anchor up, run back to go into reverse to come back to the middle of the cove, into neutral while she goes up again to secure the anchor, then back to the wheel to head out to sea.

The step-by-step planning calmed her. She resumed cranking until the anchor shackle bumped the roller on the pulpit. Dashing back, she threw the gear into reverse and revved the engine. *Havsflickan* resisted, then began moving astern, the engine roaring, and then, suddenly, with a loud clunk, it stopped. She shifted to neutral and pressed the starter button. The engine turned over but would not fire. The yacht was still moving rapidly astern and the wind was pushing the bow around. She tried the starter again, but this time there was no movement. She looked astern. The shoreline was growing closer. And suddenly she realized she couldn't see the dinghy. She looked over the stern rail. The little boat was half under water. Its painter had been been dragged down, obviously wound around the propeller shaft, jamming the engine.

Stupid! Stupid! Stupid! The one thing she was always forgetting. The engine was useless. The boat was drifting quickly now with the wind. She was frightened. What could she do? Put down the anchor! There wasn't time to fiddle with it. The rocks were getting too close. She looked at the wind on the water. She had to sail! As the boat swung, the wind came over the port quarter, quite fresh now. Quickly she freed the furling line and hauled on the starboard genoa sheet. The huge sail crept out a few feet, then suddenly ballooned out, and *Havsflickan* took off. Panting, she swung the wheel and steered for the cove mouth.

Thank God the wind was out of the cove! She would never have tacked out. But the genoa was out of control, billowing out in front of the bow. She grabbed the end of the sheet and got a turn on the winch. Steering with her left hand and hauling in the sheet with the right, she got the sail trimmed, the boat speed increasing with each metallic whirr of the winch gears. Breathless, she jammed the line in the self-tailing gear. At least she had saved the ship.

She let out a long breath, listening to the loud hissing sounds, as the boat sliced through the water. But what could she to with the dinghy, dragging half under water? Glancing astern, she found her answer. Already small in the distance inside the cove the dinghy floated upright again. The force of the propeller must have severed the line. Well, no going back.

The only thing she could do about the line wrapped around the propellor shaft was dive under the boat with a swimming mask to cut it off. She'd seen it done, but in the clear green water of the Caribbean, as warm as your skin, not this paralyzingly cold, iron-gray water, frightening just to look at.

She had told herself to be careful and deliberate. She had thought of everything, but kept making this stupid mistake. Now she'd have to come into harbor without the engine. "Remember," Geoffrey said, "every big boat is just like sailing a little boat, only heavier and less nimble." But she had never sailed little boats. She had learned on his huge ketch, then on a boat the size of *Havsflickan* sailing here with David.

Count your blessings, she told herself; you're safe so far and you have time to think. You wanted a thrilling fortieth birthday—and you got it.

"Stupid girl!" she shouted, her voice puny in the great wide air, snatched away by the cold wind under the racing clouds, white on top with dark gray undersides, the bow of the yacht now rising and settling with a loud swish, making the spray fly after each wave.

She was well clear of the cove. Time to make the left turn to the correct course. She hadn't set the mainsail. Now she had to do it without the engine to steady the boat.

You have to bring her into the wind, go up by the mast, use the winch handle, and crank up the main halyard. But the huge genoa would go crazy while she was doing that. Just keep thinking. Perhaps you were supposed to furl the genoa to calm the boat, hoist the mainsail, then release the genoa. It would be much better in a calm place, the shelter of an island, where the waves were smaller and the wind subdued. The nearest island on her course was three miles away. She had time to think. But she had to turn to avoid the rocky island ahead.

The boat could sail quite well on the genoa, but it wouldn't be balanced for the long run to Sweden. One thing at a time. She turned the wheel to the left on a reach and checked the course. The genoa luffed and she trimmed it, inserting the winch handle and cranking. It was hard work but by going backwards on the low gear she could slowly bring it in, the thick braided line creaking with the strain.

Francesca's fear subsided. The great thing about sailing was that the task at hand focused your mind. No time to regret anything. You had to push on, do what was needed, do the regretting later. Not unlike her own life. Only with a boat, you had to know where you were going. And that was the trouble with her life. She had never really known where she was going.

The wind was colder out here. She left the wheel for a moment to duck below to pull on her anorak and woolen cap. She lit a cigarette and came back to notice that the well-behaved boat had gently come into the wind and was curtseying gracefully to the waves, while the genoa thrashed noisily but harmlessly. So, with the genoa down, in sheltered water, the boat would calm down. She would have time to set the mainsail but also finish securing the anchor. She'd forgotten it but heard it now, dangling, banging against the bow. Couldn't leave it that way. When the sea got rougher outside, it could do real damage.

Then she thought, if she could bring the boat to a calm enough place, with enough room, she could drop the anchor and give herself time to think about the propellor. The man at the boat yard had said there was a wet suit on board for emergencies. If she put it on, let down the swim ladder, and tied herself to a line for safety, she could at least have a look. She was a very strong swimmer. And the wet suit would be cold only for a moment. That was the idea. The water came in and your body warmed up a thin layer and insulated you from the sea temperature. If there was a wet suit and mask, she could try it. Better than trying to land on the Swedish coast in the dark without an engine. A little apprehensive, but the delicious feeling that came with conquering fear was making her warm. She threw her cigarette to leeward and saw it snatched astern by the speed of the surging boat.

Glancing occasionally at her course, she studied the chart. There was one island with a curving shoreline making a broad bay to seaward. If the wind held, it should be calm there in the lee of the island. She'd have to change her planned course to pass between two different islands, but the passage looked clear, with deep water.

She laughed to herself at the contrast between this and mincing about in high heels on a fashion runway, wearing extreme make-up, showing off slinky clothes to bored professionals. All the chaotic wrestling in and out of gowns, the moaning when they couldn't find shoes, the hissing and shushing of the invariably tough women who ran shows behind the scenes, the preening, mirror-hungry girls, each a lonely island of vanity, each alone in her ambition to shine, even as they were jammed as close physically as they could be. An arm reaching into a sleeve hitting an elbow raised to fasten a hook, a hand stretching across the mirror to grab a powder puff blocking the view and jarring a hand poised with a lipstick. Tears, giggles, sneezes, laughter, and curses worthy of stevedores in many languages. She had acquired a vocabulary of obscene language from the glossy lips that smiled demurely from *Vogue* and *Harpar's Bazaar*. Diana, the Texas blonde who had lent her the pistol, used to drawl, wide-eyed, "You kiss your mama with lips that talk dirty like that?"

To turn quickly she should jibe, but it made her nervous to let the wind pass astern, so she did it the long way, coming about, loosening the starboard genoa sheet, then hauling in the port side, changing over the winch handle to crank in the last few turns. Didn't want to have to do that too often. Each time left her breathless, with her heart pounding. But with each successful maneuver her confidence, shaken by the dinghy accident, surged back. Now the boat was running before the fresh breeze, the genoa bellied out to starboard.

She remembered David quoting Shakespeare—comparing a sail

to a pregnant woman, "full bellied with the wanton wind." He'd always made her yearn to be better read, to know such things herself. The low rocky islands were rushing by on either side—lonely, deserted houses, their windows boarded up for winter, rickety wooden docks empty of their summer boats.

The island she had chosen was opening to her left, a long arm stretching ahead. She'd have to round that in another tack, reach to the middle of the bay, then sail close-hauled up into the middle. With joy, she could see across the low shrubs that the water inside was flat and still. A few more minutes on this leg, then the turn. Damn, she was hungry again—ravenous. She ducked below and grabbed a box of crisp bread and came back to the wheel, steering with one hand, crunching the hard biscuity stuff between her teeth. Now, time to turn.

Leaving enough room beyond the point, she turned, trimmed the genoa on the new tack, and cranked the sail in hard to sail close to the wind. The boat was still moving fast, but immediately she could feel the smoother water. The anchor was ready to go. All she had to do was choose her spot, come up into the wind, let the boat stall, then release the lock on the capstan. She'd forgotten to switch on the instruments, but the chart showed plenty of water almost to the beach. Time to turn again. A quick head to the wind, huge flapping of the genoa crossing the bow, sheet in other side. Thank God for self-tailing winches. Winch handle over, crank in. Sailing softly now, no up-and-down motion, the small trees on shore getting closer, the wind dropping in their lee. Once more: come about, the genoa now lazily shifting sides, sheeting in much easier. A few more yards. This was it.

She released the genoa sheet, headed into the light wind, and hauled on the furling line. The genoa wound up neatly around the forestay, and the boat gently glided on. She could see individual small stones on the beach as she hurried forward and unscrewed the capstan lock. The boat slowed, creeping on. When it was barely moving, she lifted her shoe, and the anchor obediently fell, the

196

chain rattling through the gear with a loud roar. She let it go by in a blur until she saw the shackle where the nylon line began, and quickly tightened the lock. With no engine, she couldn't go astern to set the anchor but had to let *Havsflickan* drift back on the light breeze.

Finally the nylon line sprang up taut and dripping, and the boat was anchored. She released an enormous sigh of relief.

Before she did anything else, she must eat. It was only just after ten, but she felt she had been sailing for a whole day. She lit the stove and heated a package of dried soup. There wasn't much food left. She'd also better prepare something for the long trip. She hard-boiled the remaining four eggs, sliced the rest of the salami and cheese, and made enough coffee to fill the thermos.

After eating, she searched the lockers in the forward cabin and found the wet suit, which covered everything except the face, hands, and feet. The shoes and gloves were a little large, but they'd have to do. She stripped down to the ski underwear, shivering at the imagined first shock of the water, squeezed herself into the suit, and zipped up the front. The head fitted her snugly. She tried on the face mask and tightened the straps for her head. Finally, she pulled on the shoes and gloves and couldn't resist waddling into the head to look at herself in the mirror. Nothing of her showed but her mouth and chin, and she made a grimace at her reflection.

She took off the mask and gloves to look for a sharp knife but could find only a kitchen knife with a serrated edge. Well, that would have to do.

Pulling a long spare line from the cockpit locker, she put on the safety harness over the wet suit and tied the line to the ring in front of her chest. A bowline, they always said, but she couldn't remember how to tie it. So she tied the one knot she knew, a round turn and two half hitches, added a few extra hitches to be sure. With the same knot she tied the end of her safety line to one of the stanchions. Then she let down the swimming ladder.

So—all was ready. The sea looked frightening and uniniviting.

The day was too cloudy to let her see the bottom. For courage, she went below, trailing her safety line, uncorked the bottle of red wine, and took two swigs, then climbed back into the cockpit. Carefully she coiled her safety line so that it could run free. When she pulled the mask over the head of the wet suit, the glass immediately steamed up. Oh, yes, you had to spit in it, then rinse it out in salt water. Her spit looked a little pink from the wine. She went down the ladder to rinse the mask, and the water on her bare hands was perishingly cold. But that was what the suit was supposed to protect her from. Standing on the ladder, leaning against the stern, she donned the mask and gloves, took a deep breath and climbed down one rung, then another. The water immediately flooded the shoes, stingingly cold. She couldn't do it! No, she had to! She descended to the last step. The water came up to her thighs, making her wince, but it did quickly feel warmer. Dreading the final immersion, she stepped off the ladder and plunged.

Freezing water filled the suit with a quick shock that brought her gasping to the surface to grab the ladder. She held on until she felt the water around her arms and chest lose its shocking coldness, took a deep breath, and dived under.

The underside of the boat looked strange and hostile, spotted with barnacles. There was the big rudder, and ahead of it, the propellor. She rose, out of breath, steadied herself against the side of the boat, but now, quite warm and confident, dived again under the large curve of the hull and came to the propellor. There in a huge tight coil, one frayed end floating loose, was the dinghy painter. But as she tried to reach it she kept rising against the hull, her buoyancy lifting her. Her lungs were burning. She had to come up for air. She went down a third time, steadying herself by holding the coil around the propellor shaft, and tried to unwind the loose end. One turn came off and another, and she had to go up to breathe.

On the fourth dive she unwound two more turns and was thinking this was going to be easy, but the next turn was jammed in tight as steel wire. She couldn't unwind it. It would have to be cut. She came to the surface and clung to the ladder to catch her breath, then climbed up. It was difficult to pull the waterlogged suit up the rungs and she had to rest at the top of the ladder. She noticed that the wind was cold on her face and the tops of the fir trees ashore were tossing. Obviously the breeze was strengthening. She needed to get this done and get on her way.

She picked up the knife and climbed down, not frightened now by the dark water, excited by her progress and determined to finish. It was harder swimming and staying in position with the knife in one hand. She sawed away at the coiled line and could see no impression. She came up for a breath and went down again. This time the hard sawing began fraying the rope, releasing tiny strands. Another breath and down again. By the fifth and sixth dives, she could see only minute progress and had to pause to rest. It was really tiring. She went at it again, angry at the puny effect she was having, cursing that she didn't have a really sharp sailor's knife. She kept sawing away, coming up for air, diving again, until she had to take another rest.

When she went under the next time, it was strangely dark below. The sandy bottom had disappeared. Then she saw a large rock pass by. Panicked she thrashed to the surface. Incredibly, the boat was sailing! The genoa was billowing out to the side, its sheet caught by the self-tailing ear on the winch. But it was anchored! She swam a few strokes to the side and saw the anchor line looping out over the bow, with more fresh new rope pouring out. Oh, God! She had forgotten to cleat it down. The capstan stopped the chain but not the smooth nylon line. The yacht was turning to head out to sea! As rapidly as she could, in the stiff suit, she raced back towards the stern ladder but missed it.

The boat was sailing past her! She could see her safety line uncoiling off the side. The boat was gathering speed. She tried to swim faster. Only a few feet to the last rung of the ladder, now lifting with the movement of the boat. She was terribly frightened—

but thought, The anchor line is tied at the end. The boat will stop. The bow will jerk to it and come up. Any second now. She had no idea how long the nylon line was. She tried her fastest crawl, but the boat was getting farther away.

Then, with a jolt of absolute fear, she saw the curled end of the anchor line, brightly new, as if fresh from the shop, fall lazily off the bow and into the water. The yacht was sailing away from her, the sail full and pulling hard. She felt a jerk through her body. Her safety line pulled taut and was dragging her through the water. She had to keep her mouth closed against the water surging around her face. Its pressure on the mask was hurting her.

Frantically she grabbed the stiff line in front of her chest and tried to pull it in. She felt exhausted. She got a hard grip, pulled herself up, got a new grip, but the boat was still about ten yards away, the ladder splashing behind.

I'm going to drown, she thought. This is the end of everything. I'm going to drown. I can't stand this surging through the water. I'll have to open my mouth to breathe. I have to.

She tried to turn her face like a swimmer to gulp down air but her mouth filled with icy salt water. In real desperation, she reached forward again and suddenly felt it easier to work her way up. Through the water-splashed mask she saw the genoa luff, collapse slightly, and hang loosely. The gust of wind must have passed. Rapidly she reached and pulled again and again. She was two yards from the ladder, but the sail filled once more and the yacht surged forward. Water was again rushing past her face. They were out of the bay. The waves were bigger, slapping into her mask, each blow of the water hurting her face.

I can't do it . . . my hands are burning . . . I can't hold on . . . I can't hold on . . . I'll have to let go . . . I'll have to let go. No! One more minute . . . I can't hold it . . . I can't . . . I must let go . . . I'm going to drown . . . how long will it take to drown if I let go. I must reach once more . . . one more reach . . . one more reach.

With her arms and hands aching unbearably, she stretched forward and grabbed. She gained one foot! Her mouth was full of water as she gasped for air. Coughing, spluttering, she tried again. The ladder was there, skipping over the waves. Almost within reach.

You can do one more . . . I can't . . . My arms and hands hurt too much . . . I'm choking . . . another mouthful . . . so salty . . . I have to swallow it . . .

Her open mouth taking in more water, her body surging forward.

You must try once more . . . before you give up . . . hold on for a second . . . rest . . . one last try.

She reached and made a few inches. The ladder was two feet away. If only the wind would drop again. She had no more strength. She clung there, coughing, but noticed the waves were calmer in the wake of the boat. It gave her hope. This was the chance. She had to do it. One more reach. A few inches. One more. A few inches! The ladder was a foot away. One more. One more. One more. She touched the ladder but couldn't grasp it and almost lost her grip on the lifeline. She dragged her hand forward and her gloved fingers closed around the stainless steel rung. Oh, God! Oh, God! She had caught the boat! She forced her other leaden arm forward, and it too closed on the ladder. She clung, her fingers numb in the hard gloves, trailing there, feeling the stern above her now rising and falling with bigger waves. They were really out to sea. Ahead was nothing but miles of vast empty sea. And how could she reach the next rung?

She tried leveraging herself forward on the almost horizontal ladder. Another second of terror because her weight pushed it down and she felt herself falling. But there was another rung in front of her face. She grabbed it with one hand, then the other. She had gained one rung. It gave her courage to try again, pushing herself forward, pushing the ladder down and grabbing the next rung. Two rungs! Now if she could bring her feet forward. But the boat's speed made that very hard. Each time she tried to raise her knees, the rush of water pushed them back. She must get up one more rung. Her hands could barely hold on now, so numbed and aching were her fingers, but she levered forward, the ladder went down, she curled her body up, and felt the lower rungs hit her legs. As though lifting a hundred-pound weight, she placed a foot on the bottom rung, then the other, then slipped and found herself sitting with her legs through the rungs, safe, staring at the large painted letters, *Havsflickan,* on the stern.

She sat there several minutes, coughing out seawater, trying to get clean gulps of air, waiting for the strength to move.

She couldn't give up now. Carefully, she brought one foot back, fumbled for the rung, missed, and then found it. Heaving herself up, she stood on the bottom rung, the ladder now flat against the stern, and grasped the backstay at the top. She waited again for strength, then climbed one rung, waited again, and raised herself another. Now the top of her body was lying through the gate in the lifelines along the flat deck of the stern. One more rung, and she slithered into the cockpit, banging her head on the wheel, her face mask hitting the edge of the seat, her lifeline snagged on something, dragging her safety harness up.

She was unable to move, lying in a heap, coughing and vomiting seawater, but knowing she had survived.

She was headed out to sea. The wheel was jerking back and forth, the boat rising and crashing on the waves. For the moment she couldn't care. She had nearly drowned. She had never been so close to death. She vomited again and saw red wine and morsels of salami by her face on the cockpit grating.

TWENTY-FIVE

LONDON—PARIS—GENEVA

USUALLY DAVID COULD keep his thoughts and feelings compartmen-
talized, but tonight, when he tried to force himself to think through
the prime minister's offer, his mind snapped back to Francesca.

He couldn't go to work for Mulroney and expect a clean policy
slate. There was too much history; if he bought Mulroney, so to
speak, he necessarily bought Mulroney's baggage—his economic
record, tax increases, personal unpopularity, the sleazy reputation,
all the scandals and resignations . . . and there in his mind's eye
was Francesca, driving the red Jag in London.

Mulroney's baggage included the Free Trade Agreement—no
way out of that. David had pushed his personal doubts aside to
defend it; now he had to be sure of his own position. He'd never
bought the scare-mongering of the nationalists who said Free Trade
would destroy Canada. Maude Barlow said Canadians were "sleep-
walking to extinction." Good phrase. In Canada today the naysayers

203

had all the good phrases. But what if she was right? Or Mel Hurtig? A few days ago he'd been skimming Hurtig's anti-Mulroney diatribe, *The Betrayal of Canada*, automatically rejecting the bombast and overstatement. But what if Hurtig's judgment was sound, that delivering the nation to the raw market forces *would* erase much that gave Canadian society its distinctive flavor? In effect the FTA could annul all the socially progressive legislation that had shaped Canada since World War II.

In its first effects, Free Trade seemed to be screwing Canada: closing factories, raising unemployment, and aggravating the recession. Government took in less tax revenue and had to borrow more to support the social services. Financing that borrowing meant higher interest rates, which further stifled economic recovery. But the only serious way to cut government spending was to slash the social services that Canadians were so proud of.

The warm side of his mind was remembering what happened in the Jaguar.

If Francesca always seemed to have another man in the shadows, David was usually too occupied to care. Only when they actually met did his jealousy flare up, and then it seemed just to intensify desire.

That time in London, they had a few hours together but nowhere to be alone except the red Jaguar she had borrowed.

"Do you remember the man I wrote to in New York? The letter that upset you so much? This is his car. His name is Anthony. He got me into modeling."

"And?"

"And nothing,"

"You must be good friends if he lends you his flashy car."

"Just business."

"Really?"

"If you met him, you'd see it's just business. He's a shady character, a smart little Cockney who always seems to have lots of money and I don't know where it comes from."

David didn't quite believe her.

They drove through Kensington, Francesca aggressively shifting gears and zooming through impossible gaps in traffic. All signs of the last pregnancy had vanished from her slim, vital figure, her skin tanned from a long stay in Barbados, her beautiful legs tantalizing him as she moved them to work the pedals.

She parked by the Serpentine bridge in Hyde Park and they got out to walk. Under the trees by the Long Water they embraced, a strange sight, he supposed, he in a blue pinstripe suit and she in a red miniskirt. They were pressed tightly together, both aroused.

"This is terrible."

"I should have got a hotel room, even for a few hours."

"We could go to Anthony's, but his wife may be there. She's a model. You'd like her. Very slinky."

"You're the model I like."

"Well, you had your chance."

"And you had yours."

"I haven't given up trying. I'm going to divorce Federico."

"In your last letter you said he wouldn't hear of it."

"He doesn't have a choice. I've left. I'm moving to Paris. Will you come and see me there?"

"Yes."

"You promise? I'll get a flat. Then we can really be alone. And you can poke me all day long."

"I want to now."

"So do I."

"There's nowhere but the car."

"Wait!" she said. "We could put the car in his garage! Come, let's go!"

Francesca drove rapidly out of the park to Gloucester Road, then turned into a mews.

"That's Anthony's garage. The house is two streets away."

David got out to open the doors and, when she had driven the car in, closed and latched them from the inside.

"What if he comes for the car?"

"He won't. He's out of town today."

She smiled at him and slipped out of her skirt. His heart beating rapidly, David removed his clothes and they screwed in the back seat of Anthony's Jaguar. Not lovemaking: rapid, brute copulation, he plunging, Francesca whimpering, both still panting loudly when they had finished.

After they dressed, she saw a patch of moisture on the black leather and wiped it with a tissue.

"Don't want him guessing what we've been doing."

Half an hour later, his quiet tie neatly knotted against his crisp white collar, David was on time for his meeting at Canada House.

SORDID, YET TO David now it had a residue of excitement, some erotic heat rising from the memory. How sexually ravenous he had been in those years. All that part of him had gone in the bitterness, then reconcilation, with Marilyn. Often now he didn't feel like it. Hard to imagine that would have happened with Francesca, but at what intolerable cost to his peace of mind. Perhaps instinctively, he had protected his middle age. Still, he couldn't help wondering . . . Now and then he'd glimpse a young woman, like the one who lost her shoe at the UN reception, and feel a quick stab of desire. But it never had the urgency of the past, and a placid home was a great consolation at fifty-two, in a profession in which he was almost never not working.

WHEN HE GOT to Paris months later, on an overnight stop between Geneva and Helsinki, he sensed another presence. Twice in the night the phone rang beside her bed and in rapid French she was obviously putting off a man who had expected to see her. She didn't explain and David didn't ask, suppressing a small sense of grievance. He had no exclusive right to her company. They had made no commitments. Yet in their letters and together they pretended that no one else existed for either of them.

An uneasy feeling was forming itself. Obviously a little grievance must have lingered from each episode and accumulated until it finally boiled over. But was it fair to her to hold these grievances?

His last sight of her on that visit was from a taxi window as he left her small flat. She had mounted her motor scooter and caught up with the taxi in the traffic, whizzing alongside, her model's bag slung over one shoulder, the wind blowing her skirt provocatively. She blew him a kiss and roared ahead, nipping through a traffic light that halted the taxi.

"*Quelle fillette!*" the driver said.

"*Vous l'avez dites,*" David said, immediately thinking his French sounded formal and stiff. Francesca would have known an earthy bit of Parisian argot.

He really wasn't comfortable with the idea of handling the rough and tumble of Parliament in French as well as English. Under Mulroney the House of Commons had become a raucous, locker-room brawl, losing dignity and respect.

And yet, David had to admit, there was also a lot to like about Mulroney. At first he'd seemed refreshingly pragmatic and easy to be with, compared with the condescending Trudeau. And Mulroney had guts. He was one of those Irish fighters who wouldn't stop, lolling and bloodied, taking more punches, whereas Trudeau wanted quick victories, a paralyzing kick to the groin, or he got bored.

David heard Francesca say, *I think's Trudeau's sexy, not like a politician.* He was trying to concentrate . . . like the early morning in Geneva with her in her nightgown.

Knowing that David would be there, she had surprised him when he entered his room in the Hôtel de la Paix.

"I said I was your wife and they gave me a key."

He had a moment of alarm. The hotel dining room and corridors were full of officials he knew. He had papers to study, a report to write for Ottawa, and an early conference the next morning, but he put them aside. They ate dinner in the room overlooking Lac Leman and slept together until he awoke anxiously before dawn and resumed his work under the small desk lamp. At one point he looked up to see her sitting, hugging the blankets to her chin, her hair gorgeously disheveled, looking at him intently.

"I had to finish some work."

"I love being with you." She got out of bed in her nightgown—a vision from a fashion magazine—and padded across to kneel on the floor and put her head in his lap.

"This is the first moment of peace I've felt in months."

He kissed her bare neck and shoulders, torn between desire to go back to bed and the absolute need to finish his preparation.

"Go back to sleep for a while and we'll have breakfast when I'm finished."

"I can't sleep, knowing you're here. We always have such a short time. What would it be like if we were together all the time?"

"I think about that."

"And what do you think?"

"I can't think now. If I don't finish and get this off to Ottawa and approved by the time the committee meets, we'll lose the initiative we've begun."

"What's it about?"

"Getting the Soviets not to be so brutal to their own people."

"Are they any worse than the Americans, the way they treat their black people?"

"Much worse in many ways."

He noticed that he was irritated by her political innocence, and by the maturity that separated him from it.

"I tell you what; after the conference I'll skip the official dinner. We can drive around the lake and have dinner on the French side. If you're interested, I'll tell you about it."

"I'm very interested."

She rose and kissed him. But a few minutes later from the bed she added, "But I'm more interested in talking about what we're going to do from now on. Do you hear?"

All day that sentence haunted him. He tried to push it away,

208

forcing himself to listen to tedious speeches rehearsing well-worn positions, waiting until his delegation had an opening. If they managed it deftly, they might show a way out of the impasse that was satisfactory to the West yet saved enough face for the East Bloc delegates to accept. The timing and nuance were crucial. David had to listen carefully.

She had dressed elegantly for dinner, and when the official car deposited them at the small restaurant, the eyes of other diners, male and female, kept straying to her. She knew it, but for once gave David all her attention, eating little and not finishing a glass of wine. In the soft candlelight, she had never looked more beautiful to him. Her presence destroyed his interest in food.

"Being realistic," she said, "you're so busy, and so am I. We're both traveling all the time. Even if we were married, we wouldn't see each other very much. So we can't really know how it would be together."

Almost independently of his will David felt challenged to be daring.

"We could try some time together. I have leave accumulating. These negotiations have prevented my taking any time off. In the summer, Marilyn and the kids will probably go back to Ottawa. We could find somewhere alone. Finland is very beautiful in the summer."

"Would you do that?"

"Yes, I would."

The negotiations stretched on. They kept making and breaking plans because of her travels or his. It wasn't until after the final round and the signing in Helsinki that David became free.

Trudeau himself came for the ceremony, was gracious with David and Marilyn, and, as always, graceful with the other heads of state. His magnetic news aura gave the Canadian presence extra sparkle, but in his media wake he left some disgruntled diplomats. As resident ambassador, David gave a dinner and it quickly turned into a major grousing session. Ambassadors who for years had painfully defended Trudeau's reduced NATO commitments grumbled that now he had just as casually reversed the policy, making their arguments look foolish.

One colleague said, "All these lurches in basic policies don't breed confidence in our steadiness. It makes Canada look skittish and unreliable. Half the time I think all he wants is to grab a headline. He gets it and then moves on to something else."

Later, back in Ottawa, David was asked by the Policy Planning Group for a confidential evaluation of Trudeau's foreign policy. It was a painful exercise.

He concluded that the thousands of hours of research at External Affairs, the drafting and redrafting of position papers, fierce cabinet battles, announcements, appointments, reorganizations, conferences—supposedly to forge a brand-new foreign policy—had achieved little. When you blew away all the political smoke, what was left, beyond recognizing China?

Trudeau had reduced the commitment to NATO, only to increase it a few years later. Flirted with Moscow, then made up with Washington. Wooed the Third World, but not so that it hurt financially. Lurched towards Europe to reduce U.S. economic domination—then forgot it. Embraced economic nationalism—then abandoned it. Repeatedly marched the nation up the public relations hill, and marched it down again.

His peace initiative in the winter of 1983–1984 was the last straw, an odyssey of vanity. Like many of his colleagues, David was embarrassed by the spectacle of the prime minister dashing from one capital to another with a plan to save the world, being treated with polite indifference or ridicule.

It was true that domestically Trudeau had made Canadians feel good about themselves. He had brought a sense of wider possibilities—Canada as an adventure, a touch of the poetic, the romantic. His elfin ways, his flirtatiousness, his boyish charm, had all worked the country's stodgy glands like a surge of hormones, making people giddily fond of their country, until Trudeaumania evaporated into a kind of postcoital tristesse.

No one had mentioned David's Trudeau paper until Mulroney two nights before. So it must have been brought out for a purpose. Obviously that was why he wanted David in government. It was all so transparent, so opportunistic, so improvisational.

FINALLY THAT OCTOBER their personal timing had coincided. Marilyn took her delayed trip to Canada. Francesca canceled a job, and David chartered a boat to sail in the Aaland Islands.

The two weeks were idyllic and serene. Even her teasing, taunting reflexes were subdued in a cosy tranquillity. They had sparkling skies and tangy air, anchoring in secluded coves, cooking dinner, watching the cold stars on deck. On a deserted island farm they found some late apples. Back on the boat she baked an apple tart with a little cognac for extra flavoring.

The island . . . but now he remembered—*the island*. Matti and Kaarina had insisted that they stop on their island and use the house. By their fire David had read to her from Matti's library of English books. On chilly nights they had slept in the ancient bed.

Christ! They had sat giggling like two kids, sipping aquavit on her birthday. And now he remembered it all . . . the heady night they'd agreed to come back for her fortieth birthday. He'd wiped it out of his mind. They had actually signed an agreement. It was hard to believe he had been so childish. Astonishing that he'd locked that door in his mind so firmly. Her birthday was October 14. That was Monday—three days ago.

That was what this was all about. She had emerged from ten years of silence to go there. She could be there now, waiting in the house. Or she had tried to go there and had had an accident, falling off the boat.

He could call Beaubien and suggest the authorities go to that island. She'd behaved very strangely when he'd last seen her; she might have suffered a real breakdown. She might have been in an institution or on drugs. For a wild second David imagined himself going to the island, walking up to the house to find out for himself.

Well . . . his fatigued mind was slipping into fantasy. And it wouldn't explain the envelope with his name on it. He could imagine the words in her flamboyant handwriting:

David Lyon, Canadian Embassy, Helsinki

Perhaps it was an envelope she had addressed to him years ago and never sent. Not a direct message to him now but a sentimental relic of the past. But why would she still be carrying it with her?

They would have searched her apartment. They'd be back to the embassy asking logical questions: Who is David Lyon?

David lit another cigarette and paced between the living room and the study.

They'd say, We have checked our files. David Lyon was your ambassador from 1974 to 1977. Where can we reach him now?

And Marilyn, asleep in Ottawa, knew nothing. Marilyn, whose worth it had taken him so long to understand.

Almost one o'clock. He had to try to sleep so that he'd be alert in the morning.

But in bed in the dark he thought, If Francesca was alive, what would it be like to see her again? No, impossible! Yes, impossible, but . . . and behind his anxiety David began to feel a different emotion. To see her at forty. Would she arouse the feelings that had overwhelmed him years ago? And how would he look to her, the middle-aged man—rather overweight?

Absurd how even stale, outdated desire tricked the mind, like tobacco addiction, dormant but never dead.

David rolled over to change his thoughts. Don't be ridiculous. They're sure she's dead.

He saw Francesca as she was during the two weeks' sailing. But the peaceful, unthreatening atmosphere hadn't revived his desire to make it permanent. They had turned a corner after New York. Something had been disconnected the day she left the Hilton Hotel.

212

He could not remember analyzing it so coldly, but he must have decided—after the reunion in Helsinki—that he couldn't tie his life to someone so rash and uncertain. He could have her when it was possible and have her in his imagination when it was not, without abandoning the safety of his other life.

She must have been on her best behavior during those two weeks precisely to overcome that reluctance in him. She must have expected him to raise it, as he had so often in the past. They had taken this time because she had pressed for a commitment in Geneva. But they never discussed it openly.

The two weeks he remembered as idyllic could have been far from idyllic to her—if she was looking for the commitment that he failed to give. Why else sign the agreement to come back in sixteen years? It implied sixteen years apart. It would explain her deep anger.

That night, his getting half drunk on aquavit and signing that paper had amounted to dismissing her as a permanent mate. She must have known that right away.

TWENTY-SIX

AT SEA

SHE WAS SHIVERING in the cockpit, still coughing and retching, but she had to get up, get warm, take control of things. Painfully she removed the gloves and, with water-puckered fingers, untied the line that had saved her life.

In the cabin, she peeled off the wet suit and the sodden underwear. She wrapped herself in a blanket and poured coffee from the thermos. Through the companionway she could see the wheel jerking back and forth, the stern rising and falling to the waves. And she saw what had caused all her terror: the twist in the genoa sheet that had snagged in the self-tailing winch was still holding. The sail was luffing and filling as the boat bent to the wind and out to sea. Well, there was nothing ahead to bump into.

Her body was still shuddering from the fear that had convinced her she was doomed as the boat dragged her through the water. But also creeping through her, like the new warmth in her body, was a nervous elation. She had come close to death and survived. Her own carelessness had nearly killed her—but her own strength and determination had saved her life. It was a feeling she had never experienced. She dressed again warmly, putting on dry ski underwear, warm socks, jeans, sweater, and her anorak. As a final gesture, she went into the small head, bracing herself against the movement of the boat, and took out her comb. She looked at her bedraggled hair and combed it out. Then she smiled at herself in the mirror and said, "Return from the dead. Ta-dah!"

But as she looked at her laughing face, a different thought quenched the elation. She saw it fade with her smile. The plan was stupid. To sail all the way to Sweden and cast a boat adrift—to show David what? That she was insane? In an instant the idea that had occupied her gleefully for weeks, each little detail added with rising excitement, was stripped of any glamour.

The boat was rolling and pitching violently, the motion making her head ache. She needed to hold on with both hands to stand up.

It was clear. She had to turn back. She had to bring the boat safely back to the boat yard. Go back to her calm apartment and forget this nonsense!

Forcing her way into the main cabin, balancing against the galley counter, she shakily poured another cup of hot coffee, lit a cigarette, and looked at the chart. To turn back with no engine she'd have to tack against the wind through the maze of islands. Even in daylight it would be tricky. Long before she could retrace her voyage from the marina, it would be dark, with few lighted buoys. There was nowhere to stop. The channels between many islands were too narrow to tack in. Even in full sunlight, sailing with the wind, she'd had to watch constantly for the hundreds of rocky skerries scattered among the islands.

She climbed into the cockpit and looked around at the restless gray sea. Astern, the low islands were already a misty smudge on the horizon, visible only when the boat crested on a wave. There was nothing to do but keep going. The only open water free of islands was her course to the Swedish coast, with the favorable wind. The only practical course, the only safe thing to do. Use the daylight and the wind to get there as quickly as possible, anchor safely, then call for help to bring the boat back to Finland.

The supercilious Swede who had checked out the boat said there was a spare anchor. Slipping past the jerking wheel, she opened the lazarette locker. Yes, there was a gray folding anchor and a large coil of line. If she could lift them and carry them to the bow, she could anchor.

So that was it. No real choice if she was to be safe. She had to go to Sweden to the harbor she had chosen. A lot of boring explanations afterwards, but better than losing the boat altogether. The decision made her calmer.

Now, quickly, she had to get the boat under control and on course. She looked back again and guessed she had come two miles, perhaps three. She went down to the chart table and split the difference. With the wild plunging motions of the boat, the parallel rulers skittered on the chart when she tried to draw the course again. It took four tries, leaving a mess of wrong lines. With no time to erase, she scribbled them out and found the new course from the guessed position, 260 degrees, making a long narrow angle with the original course line.

To make the passage quickly she must hoist the mainsail, too. She dreaded that, but it was nothing to be feared compared with what she had gone through. Grabbing a winch handle, she went out to undo the mainsail ties and free the main sheet. With *Havsflickan*'s head into the wind, the genoa would flap all over her, so she decided to furl it and turn into the wind. In her rush to look after the anchor, she'd also forgotten to cleat down the furling line. That was why the big sail could roll out when a puff of wind caught the corner. A third mistake. Now it rolled up easily, and she made the line fast.

Forcing herself to be prudent, she put the wet webbing of the safety harness over her bulky anorak and clipped its snap to a ring on the mast. With the boat now wallowing crazily, she had trouble holding on, swaying several feet from side to side, while she loosened the halyard and began hauling down. She got the mainsail halfway up, wrapped the halyard on the winch, inserted the handle, cranked it up the rest of the way, and cleated it. It looked fine. Back in the cockpit, she unfurled the genoa and winched in the sheet. Now she could swing the boat around to 260 degrees and sheet in the main.

Happily balanced on a beam reach, *Havsflickan* sang along. With one hand on the wheel, Francesca sat down and considered. It was almost one P.M. She had wasted hours in all that panic. But she had come through. If she had survived that, she would manage— then remembered with another little stab of fear that the engine was still useless. Well, she would manage. She just had to think it through carefully—and make no mistakes. Plan it and go over it, again and again.

She remembered Geoffrey putting an anchor over the stern to hold his boat steady against the current for the night in the Grenadines. If she could lift the spare anchor a few feet to the stern, she could tie one end to the big cleat and push it off. If necessary, she could use it to stop the boat as she went in close to shore.

Then she'd have to drag up the heavy bag with the inflatable dinghy. There was plenty of time to worry about that. When it grew dark she would switch on the navigation lights so that some ship would not run her down in the night. She looked around the horizon. Nothing in sight but cold gray waves. And it would get colder. She would have to put on the foul weather gear over her anorak. But for now she was warm and secure. The boat was sailing swiftly, faster than the five knots she had guessed. Stupid, there was a speed indicator! She climbed below and flipped the instrument switches. When she re-emerged, all the LCD displays on the cabin bulkhead had come alive with figures. Steadying the wheel, she saw almost seven knots. The wind was holding around eighteen knots.

She imagined someone asking, "How did you spend your fortieth birthday?"

"I nearly drowned," she would say, "and I sailed across the Gulf
of Bothnia to Sweden—alone—all night."

A wild thought came. She could buy her own boat, get to know
it well, and sail anywhere she liked. Many women had sailed single-
handed across the Atlantic—and farther. Geoffrey had talked about
the easy route from Europe, down the coast of Spain to the Azores
or farther south to the Canary Islands, then west on the trade winds.
How delicious it would be to do this in warm weather and sunshine.

In Barbados she would anchor off the yacht club, row the dinghy ashore, and take a taxi to Nigel and Delores's.

What a suprise! You came all the way across the Atlantic by
yourself? How did you get the boat?

I sold the shop. I got bored and I wanted to see the world!

She could take Colin and Samantha, teach them to sail and how
to be brave. Imagine Federico's mother having hysterics when she
said she was taking them off to sail the oceans!

"I'm getting lightheaded," she said, noticing herself laughing.
Her hands were cold. She ducked below and got her gloves. With
warm hands on the wheel, she felt another notch of rising confidence.

She could not abandon so beautiful a boat; now she felt real
affection for *Sea Girl*. Touching the ladder, finally climbing it, flopping into the cockpit, had given Francesca a sense of home
and safety. Although she knew enough Swedish to translate it,
Havsflickan still felt foreign. It had no connotations. *Sea Girl*
sounded better. The familiar words were comforting, even exciting.
Francesca and *Sea Girl*. Girl of the Sea.

Even now she could feel the terrifying sensation of icy salt water
forced down her throat, through her nose. The back of her nose still
burned from it. She shivered and had to remind herself: But you
made it! You got out! The sea was her friend, and she felt love for

the beautiful boat, heeling comfortably, gracefully lifting and dropping, cutting easily and prettily through the waves.

On one of the days before she died, heavily medicated, drifting
into consciousness and slipping away again, Kaarina had said, "Oh,
dear Francesca, don't torture yourself. If you cannot live without
him, do something to tell him and make him believe it. But only if
you are absolutely sure. He has a wife and children. Don't do it
unless you are sure. Be sure you won't capture him and then spoil
it again . . ." She faded into sleep without completing her thought.

Spoil it again. She had spoiled it many times, like the weekend
he had come to see her in Barbados . . . some mission about Canadian interests in the British Caribbean. She was thrilled, tidying
the small house she had rented on the beach. She met him at the
airport and put him on the motor scooter behind her, loving the feel
of his hands holding on to her waist.

"You keep your hands there or I'll go off the road!" she had
teased, full of joy that he had come to see her. And then she ruined
it. They were going out to dinner, but first she said she had to go
and see the skipper of a boat who could take them for a sail around
the island.

"Couldn't you phone?"

"It's better to talk to him in person."

"Then I'll come with you."

"It's better if I see him alone."

She kept David waiting in the house for nearly two hours while
she found Geoffrey, who had been drinking and did not want to get
his big ketch under way to take some boyfriend of hers for a day sail.

But David was hers—not for a few strained hours in a gloomy
European hotel room, but for a long weekend in the tropics. Nigel
and Delores both liked him. They spent a day at Nigel's farm. She
remembered David and her brother in shorts, squatting beside
something that had just been planted, drinks in their hands, talking
earnestly. They had got on immediately, which was strange, because

Nigel disliked everyone else she went out with. It had pleased her to see David so accepted.

"That's a good chap you've found; I'd latch on to him," Nigel said.

"He's married and he's got two children in Canada."

"I know; he told me."

"I'm suprised he told you."

"Didn't seem ashamed of it. He's got a damn interesting job. Diplomat. Traveling all over. International conferences. Meeting all the bigwigs."

"That's how I get to see him."

"Any chance he'd chuck the wife in Canada and marry you?"

"He asked me years ago."

"And you said no?"

"Stupid, wasn't I?"

"Compared to what you did marry, the Eye-tie with the greasy hair. Fredericko, what's 'is name?"

"Federico. You never met him."

"Because you were too embarrased to bring him back. His picture was enough. Bloody gigolo he looked. And what's he done for you?"

"Them." She had pointed to her small children, Colin and Samantha, playing with Nigel's.

"They need a father," Nigel said. "Colin's old enough to wonder. You watch the odd look in his eye when there are men around."

She had noticed it. She had awakened early that morning, listening to the sound of the surf on the beach outside the window of the rented house. David was sleeping, facing her. She felt something and turned, startled, to see Colin standing by the bed, staring at them through the mosquito canopy. He said nothing, but his eyes took in the man in her bed.

"Go back to bed," she whispered. "It's too early."

"No," said Colin, stolidly. He was a sturdy little fellow, brown from the sun, looking suddenly very manly, planted firmly on his legs, his black eyes more expressive than words. She slipped out under the netting, further embarrassed because she was naked. She snatched up a robe and led Colin out of the bedroom, his eyes looking back to David's form in the bed.

That day he was surly in David's presence, then forgot and became seductive, showing a toy, leaning against a knee, clearly looking for masculine attention. But if Francesca was attentive to David, the little boy sulked again. She remembered watching, with a flutter of tenderness in her stomach, as David lifted Samantha—still a baby —onto his shoulders to carry her into the sea . . . Why had she spoiled it by going to Geoffrey?

The morose Englishman was still angry at her leaving his boat— and his bed. They argued a long time. He wanted to make love to her, grabbed her wrist, and pulled her down to sit on his knees. He was overpoweringly strong. She tried to break away, but then, to avoid a long fight, gave in. They copulated quickly as always on his tousled bed. She promised to see him again and he grudgingly agreed to take his boat out.

Then she drove the scooter back to her house. David was sitting there, solemn, obviously not believing that her errand was innocent. Colin and Samantha were standing by the door to the sitting room, eyeing him suspiciously, while the Ba'jan woman who looked after them sang to herself in the kitchen.

Going sailing wasn't vital. She could have anticipated what would happen. Now she had to spend the evening and the night with David. And he knew. He knew something, and their conversation that night was full of silences. When they went to bed in her room, the breeze through the window louvers stirring the mosquito canopy, both were tense and wary. She tried to satisfy him, feeling ashamed and inhibited. The next morning she again found Colin staring through the canopy at David.

The day sail was agony. She tried to be gay with David, but Geoffrey's proprietary interest was obvious. David was tensely polite, talking boats; the Englishman was gruff and condescending. To get away from Geoffrey she took David to the foredeck, where they lay in the sun. She had on a new bikini she had bought to please him. David's eyes devoured her. She saw him eyeing her waist, her thighs, her breasts, while from the cockpit Geoffrey kept shouting orders as though she were still his mate, treating David like a tourist.

She took David dancing that night, and he looked awkward, trying to keep up with the reggae band, while she let her mind drift away with the odd syncopations and the relaxed, rum-drinking crowd.

Why? She could have made it really nice for him. She could have left Geoffrey out, as she thought she wanted to do. Whatever he actually knew or guessed, David left for Ottawa plainly unhappy. It was amazing that he didn't end it then.

The afternoon was fading and with it her courage to face the vast loneliness of the darkening sea.

She had to force herself to be brave. There was still hot coffee in the thermos. Leaving the wheel for a moment to pour a mug, she remembered the cassettes she had brought. She pushed the Beethoven back into the player, but the sonata was too melancholy for her flagging spirits. The boat was beginning to move awkwardly, without a hand on the helm. Instead, she inserted a cassette of steel band music from Trinidad and it cheered her instantly. Over her anorak and jeans, she donned the lined foul weather pants and jacket, with warm socks and her woolen hat. Then she regained the wheel, stilling the luffing sails by finding her course.

The wind was dropping a little—thirteen to sixteen knots on the digital display. That was good. No danger of having to reef.

The romping music was loud in the cockpit, filling the darkening air around her, partly drowning the sound of the waves and the hiss of the sea at the bow, making a bubble of optimism, as the boat ploughed on into the gathering night.

The music brought back the image of David trying to dance to this rhythm—so tall and stiff, so Canadian, she used to think—awkwardly trying to match the fluid movements of the West Indians. She sang with the rollicking calypso. Calypso was the siren who had entranced Odysseus before he was ensnared by Circe. The Greek story put all blame for men's weakness onto the alluring women, who held them in their magic power, lured them off the straight course of their lives—as she had with David, then, having lured him, did her best to chase him away.

The incident after the *défilé* in Brussels, turning David away by faking the attraction for the young black Frenchman. Henri his name was, very good-looking. She had her arm around him, snuggled up. Obviously gay. She heard a few years ago that he had died of AIDS.

Months later—when she told Kaarina about it—it sounded crazy. She had wanted to annoy David. When she saw him looking, she pulled the black man's arm around her and his hand around her breast. She turned her face into his neck and kissed him. It was obvious that he wasn't interested.

She was so self-destructive. She wanted to be loving to David, but she had known the moment she saw his face that he had made a decision: he was not going to leave Marilyn. Even if he didn't know it himself, Francesca knew it. She had lost him—and she had lost her children.

She could see David through her lashes and knew that the sight of her avid necking was shooting through him. She could feel the pain it was causing him. She wanted him to feel it. He tried to glance away nonchalantly, sipping his drink, the cool diplomat, surveying the crowded smoky party, looking back at them, then turning to slip into the crowd.

She must have had a lot to drink and no food. And pills. Sipping from the bottle of cognac in his room. Her mind was swimming but perversely fixated on getting the Frenchman really interested. He was talking to the model on the other side. She began kissing him, determined to arouse him, and when she opened her eyes, David was again standing there.

"We'd better go, Francesca."

"I don't want to go now."

"Then I'll see you later."

"Perhaps not! I might go somewhere else tonight."

"Suit yourself!"

He was furious, but he controlled it very well. She loved him for the way he handled it, flicking the words at her and leaving. She had provoked the anger she wanted him to show, but it left her feeling forlorn and empty. She wanted to get up, stop him, run to get her coat and go with him, but felt paralyzed. The black man saw a friend and slipped away. Someone gave her another drink. The party dwindled. She lay back on the sofa, and when she awoke, it was morning. Someone had put a blanket over her, and madame's maid was offering her a cup of café au lait. She was still in the evening dress she had borrowed from the collection.

She ran into the bathroom to drag on jeans and a sweater. No time to remove the heavy make-up she still wore from the show. Tossing the evening dress over the shower rail, she ran out to find a taxi. She had to see him, to apologize, to make it up—again.

But when she got to the hotel, David was out. She looked around the room, festooned with stockings and blouses she had flung about in a fit while dressing the night before, seeing the mess through his eyes.

"Stupid!" she said aloud. She saw the cognac bottle on the dresser and carried it into the bathroom to find her Valium. She looked at herself in the mirror and saw, vividly made-up, the disdainful look of a model on the ramp.

"Stupid girl!" she said to the mirror.

No wonder Federico had taken the children.

She put two Valium capsules on her tongue and washed them down with a swig of cognac.

"You like a stupid girl, you!" she said in her island accent, then, feeling ill, went into the bedroom and collapsed on the mussed side of the bed where David had slept, pulling the covers over her clothed body.

The calypso cassette had ended, and she didn't put on another. Time had passed unnoticed. The distance traveled slowly mounted on the log—33.3 miles. It was comforting to see the pink glow from the compass, the white masthead light rocking in the blackness overhead, the green reflection from the starboard riding light in the waves approaching and passing under the ship.

Sea Girl ploughed on.

There would be lights on the Swedish coast. There were lighthouses and buoys to watch for, and the lights of other ships. With a flashlight, she looked at the chart, and counted the five-mile segments on her course line. If her starting point was right, about twenty-two miles to go. There was a lighthouse on a point. She should begin seeing its flashes. If the night were clear. But the sky above her was black murk. No comforting stars. So the light might not show this far.

She started in panic. Right ahead was a towering buoy! Bright green against the waves. She was going to smash into it! Terrified, she swung the wheel hard to the left. The sails flapped violently. But she saw nothing. There was nothing. She looked hard, disbelieving her eyes, but there was nothing. Then she saw the green riding light illuminating the next wave. She turned back to her course to steady the sails. She was shaking with fear. She must have been asleep with her eyes open, hallucinating on the reflection of the riding light. There it was again—exactly like a huge green buoy about to crash into the boat.

She must stay awake. She had to be alert. Her heart still beating violently from the fright, she reached for her cigarettes and stooped in the companionway to light one. She had to stay awake; 38.9 miles. Nothing visible ahead. Even in the glove her hand was cold on the wheel. She changed her seat and steered with the other hand. It was harder to see the compass on this side, so she changed back. She was terribly sleepy. She needed something to keep her alert. More music. Casual now about leaving the wheel, she went below and put on the Beethoven. What had sounded gloomy and unnerving before now gave her a feeling of grandeur . . . of being in command. She was going to be all right.

She'd come a long way from that scene with David ten years earlier. Her periods had been so mixed up by the way she was living that it wasn't until she was three months gone that she knew she was pregnant. For a day or so she had a fantasy of having the child, of using it to lure David back. But she wasn't sure he would believe it was his. And she was in no condition to mother a baby. Everything was a disaster. The children were with Federico's mother. She should have left them with Delores and Nigel in B'dos. She wasn't in fit shape for anything. She simply couldn't have another child and work—and she had to work.

Someone had told her about the clinic in Stockholm. She saw a woman doctor, young enough to make Francesca feel awful that her life was so messed up. In a nice way, but firmly, the doctor gave her a hard time. She wouldn't perform the abortion until she had done a full examination and taken a medical history. She did the abortion, but then lectured her seriously. "You are in quite depleted condition for a young woman. You need to eat better, get more rest, get some outdoor exercise. From what you tell me, you smoke, you drink, you take many pills. You should look after yourself better."

When she left the room, Francesca felt washed out and depressed, very low, a bag of bones no man would ever want, and sick of men anyway. Sick of women, for that matter—or women in the modeling game.

She was very low about David. She had pushed him to the edge, and he had jumped. He wasn't coming back, and she had to get used to it.

She thought of Kaarina and Matti. She had a feeling that Kaarina would be a comforting person to be with. She couldn't go back to work right away; she looked too ghastly. She called from the hospital.

When Kaarina saw her in Helsinki the next day, she wouldn't let her stay in a hotel. So she moved into the little guest goom in the old apartment. It was lovely and soothing, particularly in the long afternoons, when Kaarina and she could talk, sometimes in her room, or over coffee, and she told her all the messes she had got herself into.

She wanted to be more like Kaarina. There was a mysterious serenity in her that Francesca envied, besides the sensuousness that made her want to touch her.

She went back to Paris, to work, much healthier and with warm feelings about Kaarina and Matti. She began thinking about another trip as soon as she could spare the time.

And she began to clean up her act. She drank less, just wine or Evian, started walking more and eating sensibly, and even, quite suddenly, gave up smoking. Her figure came back, her periods were normal, she looked a lot healthier, even her hair felt thicker and shinier—

Was that a light? No. Must have imagined it.

When she went back to Helsinki a few months later, it was winter. She had always dreaded the cold, but suddenly took to it as though she had been born there. She loved going out with them on the flat frozen lakes, skiing hard until she was gulping down the icy air, every part of her glowing and hot except her face, then coming back into the warmth and hot drinks, a sauna or bath, feeling luxuriously tired, but every cell in her body vibrant. As she got better at the balance on skis she could take those long gliding strides as well as Kaarina. Now and then, David would come into her thoughts, and in her mind she'd say, You see? I can do this too. And she would have a moment of imagining suddenly running into him somewhere where she was working and starting all over. But the only contact she had was seeing his picture in diplomatic groups once in *Paris*

Match and once in the *Herald Tribune*. Each time it gave her an ache of regret. And no one replaced him. There were men—modeling made them impossible to avoid—and she went out with them, but they had begun to seem unnecessary.

Matti and Kaarina made her realize what pleasure it was to stay at home quietly and read. She began reading. She found she could make time because it was so absorbing. Even on the road, it was more fun not always to go out with the others on parties, but to eat something in her room and read for hours.

She went to concerts with the the Koivistos and listened to their recordings. She became as passionate about Sibelius as if she were Finnish herself. She was learning their culture as she never had her own, although Matti's professional interest in English literature steered her to Dickens and Thackeray and others she had not read before. It was funny that it took a bearded Finnish professor, talking on those dark nights, with the snow deep outside, with his nice singsongy accent, to really wake her up to the treasure of English writers.

Her visits to Helsinki became delicious holidays away from the silly life she led. She wrote to Kaarina, or phoned her from here and there, and in her voice could feel the warmth and calmness of their lives enveloping her. Yet part of Kaarina remained beyond her. As much as she made Francesca feel drawn to her, she also seemed to be, gently, pushing her away . . . although once or twice later she relaxed her strong sense of privacy . . .

There it was! A faint flash, low down near the water. Very faint. A long way off. It must be a lighthouse. Or a flashing buoy. But surely she wasn't close enough for a buoy.

There it was, quite clear as she rose on a bigger wave. The Beethoven had stopped. She shone the flashlight at the cabin clock. Nearly ten P.M. Distance 45.6 miles. Speed 4.2 knots, slower now. Count the groups of five miles to be sure. About nine miles off. But which lighthouse? She had to count. There! No, she'd missed it.

Wait for the next. Where in hell was it? Ah, there, a bit to the left. She must be off course. Difficult, because the bow kept swinging back and forth, causing the compass to swing. Now 260 degrees more or less. Farther to her right the light showed, just past the starboard stays. Wait for the next flash. There! Count one—and two —and three—and four—and five—and six—and seven—and eight —and nine and—there, it flashed. Nine or ten seconds? Better do it several times to be sure. She waited. There. Counted again: eleven seconds. In her anxiety to be right, she was counting too fast. Nine seconds. Well, ten. She shone the light on the chart. And there it was, exactly the light she had been aiming for! Joy possessed her. Incredibly, whatever the tides or winds, she had hit it. Well, no. If it was on the right, she was sailing past it, too far south. The light was only a mile from from the large bay, then a little sticking-out bit, then the harbor. Steer more to the right. Not directly for the light but a little to the left. There was a buoy marking the bay. She looked again at the chart. A red flashing light. Steer just to the left of the lighthouse and look for the red flash. She turned the boat's head closer to the light. Never mind the compass now. Keep the white flashes between the starboard stays and the forestay, just under the genoa. She had to bend down to see. If only it were a clearer night, she would be able to see lights on the shore. But how many lights would be on this late in October, with the cottages and hotels deserted?

She sailed on, more nervous now, feeling the land so close. What if she missed the red flashes? The white flash was a brighter glare each time it swept by. She could see it reflected on the waves and through the sails. When it flashed, the genoa grew luminous for a second, then dark gray again. If only there were another person to help. There were too many things to think of. The illuminated log showed 46.9 miles. She had come another mile. The buoy must be less than three miles away. Keep sailing. Keep looking. Keep the lighthouse sweeping the sail just there.

Now, calm down, she said sternly. Everything is right so far. Don't panic. You've come this far. You can make it. Be calm and keep looking.

The land stuck out beyond the big bay and the harbor. That should break the wind and the sea, making it calmer. Then she could think about leaving the wheel to get the anchor out on the transom. Put the coil of rope beside it and tie the end to the big cleat. Geoffrey had taken two turns around a winch to be able to crank it in to be sure it had bitten in the bottom. She could do that. The port winch was free. But she might have to use it to tack into the little harbor. Never mind. She'd tie it to the cleat and worry later about putting a loop on a winch.

Still no red buoy. Look at the chart again. A long line of rock came out from the point to the left of the big bay. That's what the buoy was there for. Stupid. She was looking too much ahead. It would be more to the left. She saw nothing. Keep steady; 48.4 miles, still sailing at four knots, but the waves seemed bigger, choppier close to the coast, and their angle was different. They kept pushing the bow to the right, and she had to make it swing back. God, she was cold. Inside all the clothing she was shivering from cold or fear.

There was the red light! Still farther to the left than she been looking. Now head for that.

The wind was now close on the port bow. She had to haul in. Stiff from sitting still so long, she fitted a winch handle and cranked the genoa in tight, then the mainsail. Now the bow crashed into the waves it met on a sharper angle, slowing her speed to 3.7 knots. To see the light, she had to keep it just to the left of the forestay. The bright sweep of the lighthouse now came aft of the genoa, illuminating the whole cockpit for a second. The red flashes appeared and disappeared as the waves tossed the bow up and down. Hard to keep it in sight long enough.

Still no lights on the shore. Just the white sweep of the lighthouse and the winking red buoy ahead. It was growing clearer, easier to keep in position, even through the spray that shot up from the bow, made red by the port riding light. The waves were more vicious. Somewhere to her right they would be crashing on the rocks. The idea made her shudder. Keep going. Won't be long now. It was colder heading more directly into the wind. She was freezing.

The flashing red light grew closer. It was far enough out from the rocky point that she could pass it close on the left. Now it was continuously in view. Now it looked almost taller than the boat, red flashes turning the sails pink for an instant. Ease off a bit to the right. Don't get too close. Hitting it could sink the boat. Now she could see as it flashed that the huge buoy was rolling lazily with the waves. And it was ringing. She could hear the dismal clank of its bell over the wind and the crash of the bow. *Clang-clang*. Mournful and awful, but comforting.

At 49.9 miles on the log it swept by, clanging and flashing. There was a huge white number. Just to be sure, she shone the flashlight on the chart. Right. She was past the point. Wait a few minutes to be well clear, then in. She was hungry for the calmer water and softer winds inside. The lighthouse flashes were now dead astern, still washing the cockpit with moments of daylight. The land was a dark shadow on her right. A cliff a little higher than her sail. Now it should be safe to turn in. But there should be some light on the shore, a streetlight, or the motel just up the hill from the beach. Nothing but blackness ahead. Well, she had to turn. She edged the wheel to the right and eased the sheets. Already quieter, the boat moved on at three knots. Soon she'd have to slow down.

Unable to see the shore, she'd have to judge by the depth. The gauge showed twenty-two meters. She shone her light on the chart. There was a ten-meter line farther in, then a five-meter dotted line, then all the tiny dots for the beach. Go as close in as possible. Anchor on the five-meter line. Now nineteen meters. Getting shallower, the waves much smaller, and the wind was dying. She had to have the anchor ready. The shadowy outlines of the shore were just apparent against the slightly paler sky. She must slow down. Bring in the genoa. "Douse the jenny!" Geoffrey used to yell.

She reached over to free the genoa sheet and pulled hard on the smaller furling line. Filled with wind, the sail was hard to roll up. She should come up into the wind, but she didn't dare, with the land so close. She took her gloves off to improve her grip and pulled with all her strength. Gradually the sail rolled up. This time she remembered to cleat the furling line. No more accidents.

Now *Sea Girl* sailed gently, the water almost calm, the wind speed only seven knots . . . fourteen meters on the depth gauge. Must get the anchor out. Still nothing but dark gloom ahead. Leaving the boat to sail itself, she opened the lazarette and put the flashlight on the deck to see in. She dragged out the heavy coil of line and laid it on the cockpit seat, then pulled out the anchor, not as heavy as she had feared but awkward, with its hinged shank flopping away from the flukes. Holding them together, she heaved them onto the transom and picked up the flashlight to find the end of the line. Still had to undo the turns holding the coil. The thick rope was stiff for her frozen fingers. Afraid of the land rapidly approaching, she tore at it, broke a fingernail, but ignored the sharp pain and got it free. She took a turn around the cleat and tied the best knot she could with the unyielding rope.

The mainsail was flapping. She grabbed the wheel and looked ahead. There was a light on the shore. Depth seven meters. Standing on the transom, Francesca lifted the anchor and dropped it over the stern. No dinghy to worry about now. She heard the *ker-ploom* as it hit the water and watched as the coiled line snaked out astern.

She climbed up to the mast and released the main halyard. The sail fell, smothering her in its folds. She would look after it in a minute. The wind was very light. Apprehensive, she stood on the transom and shone her light on the anchor line. Slowly, the boat kept moving. Perhaps she had let out too much line and would run aground before it was taut. The depth gauge showed three meters.

Gently the boat drifted, rising and falling softly. And then the line creaked taut. She was anchored. She was safe! Francesca found herself weeping.

When she wiped her eyes, she noticed the navigation lights still on. She switched everything off. She was safe. She had made it.

Exhausted but elated, all her muscles trembling, she furled the mainsail roughly, then went below. The clock showed a few minutes before midnight. She took the red wine bottle from its rack but her hands were shaking so much that she spilled as she poured a mugful. She lit a cigarette and collapsed in the cockpit to gain strength for the effort with the dinghy. All was quiet on the shore. No sign of life. Only one light from the motel up the hill. She took off the safety harness and cumbersome foul weather jacket, then went below.

She dragged the heavy dinghy bag to the companionway steps and stood it on end. She could just manage to push it up the steps and let it fall into the cockpit. She could see quite well in the gloom. She wrestled the unwieldy rubber mass out of the sack and fitted together the jointed oars. Spreading out the flattened rubber, she attached the nozzle to the first chamber and pumped with the foot pump. When it was hard, she inflated the second, and then the rubber cylinder, which served as a seat. Filled with air, the dinghy was cumbersome but light to carry as she manipulated it over *Sea Girl*'s stern and firmly cleated down the painter. No more mistakes! She let down the stern ladder, then looked at the anchor line pulling gently over the stern. Perhaps she should lead it around so that the bow would face the sea. But there was no wind now, and the sea was almost calm. She was weak in the legs from exhaustion and her arms ached. She couldn't face another heavy task.

Wearily, she climbed down the companionway and shone the flashlight around the cabin, messy with discarded clothes, charts strewn about, unwashed dishes and mugs. She couldn't face it now. In the morning she'd come back and pack her bag. Too tired. She found her purse. Even climbing the few steps to the cockpit made her leg muscles shudder. The rough stow she had done on the mainsail was a mess. It could wait till morning.

She went down the stern ladder and dropped the oars carefully into the rubber dinghy, then climbed down herself. This was the point in her plan where she would have cast off, letting the yacht motor out to sea. How crazy it seemed now, even criminal, like a movie she half-remembered.

Holding on with one hand, she untied the line and sat down in the dinghy. Before letting go, she pulled herself up to the stern where the name *Havsflickan* was painted. She leaned out of the dinghy and kissed the white hull, tasting the dried salt.

"Thank you, *Sea Girl*," she whispered, then pushed off and drifted away. Fitting the oars, she rowed quietly ashore, stepped out, and pulled the dinghy up the sandy beach. In her plan she was to push it under one of the cottages. No need to hide it now.

Then, her legs unsteady on the land, Francesca walked up the little hill to the motel. The one light she had seen came from the office at the other end. There were no cars in the parking lot. She found her room and dug the key out of her bag. Inside, she went immediately to the sliding door and opened it onto the small balcony to look out to sea. She could just make out the white shadow of *Sea Girl*, motionless and secure. Off to the left was the red light of the buoy winking and, beyond the point, the faint flash of the lighthouse.

Closing the door, she went into the warm room. There was the bag she had stashed excitedly, flying over from Helsinki four days before. In the wardrobe were the dress and coat she had hung there. They seemed to belong to someone else's life.

Too tired to do anything else, she removed her clothes and slipped into the delicious bed. For a few seconds she felt her exhausted body still rocking with the movements of the sea. Blissfully happy, she drifted into sleep. She had brought the boat safely to harbor. She and *Sea Girl* were safe.

TWENTY-SEVEN

BRUSSELS

DAVID HAD FALLEN asleep when Jean Luc rang. The digital clock showed 3:03.

"Hello, David. I'm sorry to wake you up, but I thought you should know."

"Know what?"

"The police called me again. In the woman's apartment, they found a bundle of letters—apparently from you."

"Oh, my God."

"Some of them are on official stationery, so they've assumed—not so dumb—that you're with us. They're pressing me to tell them. I've stalled them till Ottawa wakes up, but obviously I've got to call for instructions. Then I guess the shit hits the fan."

"You'll have to tell them?"

"I don't see how we can avoid it. That's what I'll have to tell Dennision, anyway."

"Yeah, I see."

"Any more delay and it's just going to look as though we have something to hide, eh?"

The letters. He had written scores of them—passionate, chatty, free-flowing commentaries on political issues. Wildly indiscreet.

"As a friend, David, are they bad?"

"They're bad."

"God, I'm sorry to hear that."

"Bad, I mean, if they get out."

"Well, maybe they won't."

"Is there any news about—"

"The woman? No. At daylight they were going to send out another plane. It's too early for any news. Oh, yes. They've found out she ran a business here. A dress shop. Very chic. Christine knows it. Did you know that?"

"No, I didn't."

"So apparently she was a successful businesswoman. Well, I'll call back if I hear anything. But I'll have to get on to Ottawa in a couple of hours before they find out some other way."

"You mean the press?"

"Yes. I'm sorry to say it's in the papers here and the television news."

"You mean my name?"

"No, no. Just that the boat was found abandoned and the woman is missing."

"And her name?"

"Not yet. I'll call you if I hear anything."

"Thanks, Jean Luc."

David hung up, got out of bed, and walked around the apartment, turning on lights.

She'd kept the letters. Many diplomats wrote private diaries, but he'd never started that. When the urge came to put down private thoughts, he'd sent them to Francesca, all the unlicensed stuff a man poured onto paper he was certain would never see the light of day. And she had kept them! Well, that would can it for sure. The PM's political instinct would snuff out any idea of making David a political star. And what he didn't kill, External Affairs would.

But it wasn't just his career; it was Marilyn. There were countless things in the letters that would hurt her—and the girls. God, what a mess!

Francesca running a business. He had an image of her in a shop, very chic, quick movements in a skirt taut against her lean thighs. The idea of seeing her was insinuating itself again. She was dead! But if not . . . if the only way to clear this up . . . a quick flight to Helsinki . . . he could find an explanation.

Nonsense!

He needed something but couldn't drink Scotch at three in the morning. He went into the kitchen to make coffee, then, bewildered by the complicated coffeemaker, settled for tea. Even the large stove was unfamiliar. He couldn't find a teapot and used a tea bag in a mug. All the years of having other people do things. He looked around the kitchen, equipped to produce dinners for a dozen or more. This would end all the perks he'd come to take for granted, servants to do everything since he'd reached head-of-mission rank. It was years since he'd taken out garbage or washed dishes.

He drank the tea. There couldn't be a worse time to be running External Affairs. The old sense of important mission had gone, and now it was trade. Fine; trade was probably of more practical benefit than most of the diplomatic games of the past. But the challenges in foreign policy today didn't compare with the struggle at home to hold the country together—Mulroney making Quebec a battle for the life or death of the nation.

David had always known what he represented abroad, the socially progressive democracy, nonbelligerent, internationalist, good world citizen. All still true enough, but the future definition of Canada was much harder to find.

He used to think Canadians were the social democratic opposition to America's reflexive conservatism. Now Canada seemed caught in the same rightist tide, Mulroney & Co. sailing happily along with it, Free Trade making that tide run faster.

You needed a real sense of community, a valid social contract, to make progressive social democracy work. People had to believe in the justice of their deserts to pay the taxes. And Canada's sense of community was deeply threatened now, because everyone suddenly wanted more rights, more power, more sovereignty—not just Quebec, but the west, the east, the north, founding nations, first nations, women, ethnic everything.

It wasn't a time to be in foreign policy . . . even without this personal mess. He should simply hand in his resignation and go quietly at once, this morning, before the storm broke, defuse the scandal and the personal humiliation to Marilyn. He could call the PM . . . I thought you should know before it breaks in the papers . . .

But he'd have to tell Marilyn first . . . call her very early . . . three-thirty now, in a few hours . . . the worst time for her, with her father seriously ill . . .

He must be calm and think this through. He still had a few hours. Beaubien wouldn't wake Dennison in the middle of the night. It wasn't a threat to national security. Diplomatic careers were the sum of such judgments, as many wrecked by pushing the panic button too soon as by failing to push it. He still had a few hours to think it through. But he couldn't stop the other channels interrupting.

As clearly as if she were there, he could hear Marilyn ask, "David, who is Francesca?"

Ten years ago; 1981. He'd been deputy high commissioner in London for two years, firmly back on the fast career track after eighteen months in Ottawa. Trudeau had trounced the Quebec separatists in the referendum and needed an amended constitution to lock the province into Canada. To be amended, the original act of the British Parliament had to be repatriated to Canada. But other provinces were balking, and so were members of Margaret

Thatcher's government in Britain. With other Canadian officials in London, David was lobbying them energetically.

It was early fall. He had come back from Canada House, his driver waiting while he changed and collected Marilyn for a reception. He had expected her to be dressed and waiting, but found her in a skirt and sweater, sitting on their bed, looking pale and strained.

"Are you feeling all right? We've got to leave in fifteen minutes."

She looked at him strangely. "David, who is Francesca?"

At the name on her lips, he froze, the hair rising on the back of his neck, his eyes locked on those of the woman who suddenly seemed a stranger. She was composed and cold, but it was obvious that she had been crying and had wiped her eyes many times. She had a wet handkerchief clenched in her hand.

"I found that." She picked up a letter on which he instantly recognized Francesca's handwriting. "It's getting chillier and I took your raincoat to be cleaned. The letter was in the pocket."

She let it fall on the bed. It must have been the last time he'd worn the coat in the spring. He had still not found anything to say.

Marilyn said, "I can't go anywhere tonight. Go alone if you have to. But you've got to talk to me." She began to cry, just as Peggy, the eleven-year-old, slouched into the room, saying petulantly, "Are you guys going out *again*!" a line she had been saying for weeks, *guys* the in-word from the American school in St. John's Wood. Seeing her mother crying, her eyes widened, and she said, "What's happened? Is everything OK?"

"Leave us alone, sweetie. Mummy and I have to talk about something."

"But are you going *out*?" the girl insisted.

"No, we're staying home."

"Great!" Peggy said sardonically and left.

David dismissed the driver. Jenny was staying the night with a friend. Marilyn washed her face, and they got through supper with Peggy.

And then, in the hours afterwards, it all came out, a conversation that tore him up, pity for Marilyn fighting the realization that this was the moment he had approached many times but had shrunk from provoking.

He actually had a date with Francesca, a weekend long planned. She was doing a fashion show in Brussels and he had contrived a need to visit the European Commission. Now he had to make the break, or tell Marilyn it was all over with Francesca. He was torn. If ever he was to do it, this was the time. But Marilyn had had hours to compose her own speech, and it tumbled out of her, as they sat in the bedroom with the door closed, the sound of Peggy's rock music insulating their misery.

"It's obvious from the letter that you've been deceiving me a very long time."

"Yes."

"I was sitting here all afternoon, after I read it, thinking of how much I've loved you. I have loved you, David. I have loved you from when we were going to school dances. I've never loved anyone else. One little crush on a painter I met at the National Gallery, when I was still at Elmwood. I never told you about him because it was too childish. I've never really looked at anyone else—more fool me. But I've known for a long time that something was going on. Every time you came back from a trip you were different. I didn't need lipstick on your collars—the cheap things wives are supposed to find. I knew. Each time, you came back a slightly different person. I noticed the first time you went away that winter to Guyana, years ago, before we went to Lusaka, but I put it out of my mind because I thought it was some casual flirtation, some brief affair. That hurt but it didn't kill me, and you came back and were very nice to me. But now I know it went on and on—it's still going on—and all the times you've come back and been nice to me, you were seeing this woman. That's the worst thing to realize. Even when you were being nice you were pretending, because you were seeing her."

"I wasn't always pretending."

"Well, what good does it do to say that? If you really loved me you wouldn't have been off—screwing this woman!"

David had never heard Marilyn use that word.

"And you have been, haven't you? Screwing. Meeting in hotels and going to bed with her? Haven't you? It's in the letter. You don't have to lie to me. It's in the letter. Poking, is what she calls it, for God's sake. Poking! Oh, my God!"

And she began weeping again.

"The betrayal! The betrayal. I can't stop thinking of the betrayal. All the times I thought things were good between us, you were betraying me."

"I have been very torn for a long time about what to do."

"Was it because I wasn't good enough for you? I thought we were good together that way. I thought you liked it with me. Oh, all the times—all the times! God, I don't know how I can stand it!

"Sweetheart—"

"Don't you dare call me sweetheart! Don't you dare say those things. They're meaningless! They're empty. They're lies! All along they've been lies!"

"That's not true. I have meant it. I have loved you. I do love you. This other thing—"

"Other thing? It's not a thing. It's a woman, a real woman, who writes to you as if she knows you as well as I do, better than I do."

"Marilyn, please listen for a moment. I am deeply sorry about this. I've been agonizing over it. It kills me that I'm hurting you. But I have not been able to stop myself. It's uncontrollable."

"You're not any different from other men, and other men control it."

"I don't know about other men. I broke off with her once and was totally loyal to you. I thought it was completely over and I was glad. I wanted us to to be together."

"When was that?"

"When we were in Africa."

"Naturally! You couldn't see her then."

"I didn't want to. I had put her out of my mind. But when we got to Helsinki, she reappeared. I couldn't stop myself."

"How often have you seen her?"

"A lot—to be honest."

"And what are you going to do now? Do you expect me to go on as though nothing has happened, while you continue sneaking off to her?"

"No."

"No what?"

"I'm going to see her this weekend in Brussels."

"Then it's all over between us."

David, pacing in the New York living room, could not believe now that he had done this to her; it was inconceivably callous.

Marilyn got off the bed and went into the bathroom. He heard her running water in the washbasin and had to follow her.

"Look, I've got to make a decision. I've got to see her one more time and decide once and for all what to do."

"That's the most selfish thing I've ever heard. *You* have to make a decision? And what do I do? And the girls? Wait here for your decision? Till you call us up and say, 'Sorry, *sweetheart,* but I've decided to go off with Francesca.'" She pronounced it Fran-sessca.

"Fran-chesca."

"I don't care how she says her stupid name! It just makes her more real to me. What am I supposed to do? Go on with my little duties as your wife, going to teas and receptions and being bright and happy? Oh, David? Sorry he can't come. He's off in Brussels for the weekend with his girlfriend. Come on, David! I don't know how you can be so cruel. Just tell me right now."

She turned from the mirror where she had been wiping her eyes with a washcloth.

"Tell me right now. You have decided already. You're just afraid to tell me straight out."

"I haven't decided."

242

"You wouldn't be going to see this woman again if you weren't sure. If you were sure you wanted to stay with me, you wouldn't go."

"I must go."

"Why? You could call her up and say, I'm sorry, it's over."

It went on like this for hours, with quiet moments, then stormier, until, finally exhausted, they had to go to bed. She rolled over as far from David as she could get.

When he thought she was asleep, she said, "What does she do?"

"She's a fashion model."

"A model? How cheap! I'm suprised at you."

He was tempted to say, *She is not cheap in any way*, but held his tongue.

In the morning Marilyn, as haggard-looking as David felt, said decisively, "When you come back . . . I suppose you have to come back whatever you *decide* . . . I'm going away. I have to go away. You can look after the girls. I can't stay in this house."

Sick at heart, but determined, David went to Brussels, his emotions fluctuating during the flight between a terrifying but exhilarating glimpse of freedom, deep misgivings, and anguish at the chaos he'd left behind. There was the anticipation he always felt approaching Francesca—and the anxiety. He hadn't seen her for nearly eight months, since the terrible weekend in Barbados.

In reprisal for the divorce, her husband had taken the children off to Italy. At first she had joked about it in her letters. Now she no longer mentioned it. But recently on the phone she had sounded more demanding and more unstable.

He'd chosen the Brussels Hilton because the fashion show was happening there. Francesca had already checked in, using his name. She was not in the room, but her clothes were strewn about, as though she had flung everything out of her bags until she found what she was looking for. On the dressing table was a bottle of cognac, partly drunk, with a clutter of make-up things and a paperback volume of Anaïs Nin's diaries, the corners of many pages messily folded down. The spectacle gave David instant misgivings. Her movements, her behavior, her letters had become more and more bizarre.

When she appeared, her physical presence was electrifying as always, but she was distressingly thin, with gaunt hollows under her cheekbones,

The shy smile on greeting him after a long separation was the same. She kissed him warmly, holding her body against him, but when he began to respond, she broke away. "Not yet! I've only got a minute to shower and go down for a rehearsal. We can have dinner afterwards."

With no coquetry she threw off her clothes and disappeared into the bathroom, leaving him hungry for her but with the knowledge of Marilyn's pain making him ill at ease in the room Francesca had so messily occupied.

She came out in a towel, reanimated. She pulled on her pantyhose, her pelvic bones making two sharp points, saying, "You should come to the rehearsal. Lots of pretty girls!"

"You're the pretty girl I came to see."

She gave him her broadest smile. "Actually I'd be furious if you looked at them."

She dressed in a few seconds and was brushing out her thick hair in the familiar way, backwards, then down over her cheeks, longer on one side than the other. "You can look all you like, but no evil thoughts, do you hear? I wouldn't trust any of them with the high commissioner in London."

"Deputy high commissioner. Do they know that?"

"Of course. I'm very proud it. Just have to do my face."

David leaned against the edge of the bathroom door, watching in the mirror as she expertly applied eyeshadow, mascara, and lipstick. Then she turned and pirouetted, her hands on her hips, "There you are. Tah-dah! How do I look?"

"Unbelievable." And the sight did warm his spirits, suppressing his doubts, the horrors with Marilyn.

He watched for two hours as Francesca and the other models displayed a succession of outfits, the designer fussing over the order, the drape of a dress, the way the girls carried themselves, hands here or there, in pockets, holding a shawl, opening a coat to show a skirt beneath.

David had never seen Francesca in action. During the rehearsal she lit up with the music and the lights, her movements more graceful than the others', her disdainful professional smile more assured. She came down the ramp, her head held imperiously, but with quick turns of her chin, flicking her dark eyes here and there, coming to rest with particular intensity on him, giving him a smile of such ravishing affection that he felt dazzled anew.

She was clearly a favorite, obviously good for the designer. She combined the conventional haughtiness with a playful, irresistible flirtatiousness that made her stand out; in fact, made David wonder whether she wasn't showing off too much. It was a bravura performance, which the onlookers, designer's assistants, and others applauded enthusiastically.

When it was over she grabbed David and pulled him into the dressing room to introduce girlfriends, who shook hands in the European way, unembarrassed at being in some stage of undress, to the head of the fashion house, the designer, and to a handsome young black male model used as stage dressing for the girls. The atmosphere was frenetic, excited, hot, thick with clashing perfumes.

"Hands off! He's mine and now he's taking me to a wonderful dinner." She left on his arm like a grand actress.

Outside the ballroom, she said, "Let's just eat something quick in the hotel. I'm not hungry and I'm exhausted."

In the restaurant she nibbled at her food but drank several glasses of red wine, smoking nonstop, chattering on about this show, the impossible clothes, a grander show in Paris.

He wanted to tell her that Marilyn knew, that finally this was the moment of decision—but her mood was too brittle. He suspected she was talking to prevent serious conversation.

David gazed at her, hypnotized by her beauty still breathtaking despite her new thinness and her frenetic manner.

She leaned against him in the elevator. "I'm so tired! I need to stop everything for a while and slow down. I've been going and going so much I can't sleep properly."

And when they got into bed, she entwined herself with him and said, "Could you just hold me a little? I just want to feel you close again . . . to remember . . ." and she was asleep.

David awoke some hours later. Light from the open bathroom door half-illuminated the room. She came out in a dressing gown, carrying a glass of water.

"All you all right?"

"I told you I can't sleep these days." She took pills from a phial and washed them down with water.

"Sleeping pills?"

"Tranquillizers," she said matter-of-factly and then disturbed him by pulling the cork from the cognac bottle and taking a swig.

"Want some?"

"No, thanks. I can't drink brandy. It gives me a terrible head."

"Oh, yes, I forgot."

She lit a cigarette and walked up and down the room, stumbling over a shoe, kicking it away.

"What did you think of the show?"

"Very good. You were terrific. I've been trying to imagine you doing this. You're very good at it."

"Was I the best?"

"By a mile."

"Would you make love to me?" She pulled off the dressing gown and stubbed out the cigarette, which continued to smolder. She slid into bed and wrapped a thigh over his. Her mouth tasted of brandy and cigarettes.

"Make love to me *hard*. Make love to me so well I'll want to go to sleep," she whispered between kisses.

Unnerved by her behavior, David wasn't sure he felt like making love but eventually responded. She seemed more frenetic, more violent, and when they were locked together, whimpered in a different way and panted in his ear, *"Viens! Viens! Viens tu, chéri!"* which she had never said to him. He felt he was with a different woman, harder, full of anxiety and hysteria.

When he awoke again, to see a pale light through the curtains, she was out of bed in her dressing gown, smoking, a glass of cognac beside her.

To justify his trip David had to keep appointments at the EEC, and didn't return to the room until nearly six. He found her asleep, looking as youthful and calm as when he had first met her. The room was even more disheveled. She had dropped another layer of clothes. The ashtrays were full, the cognac bottle half empty, a plate of room-service sandwiches untouched. He had trouble waking her. When she came around, she sat up groggily and reached for another bottle of pills.

"What are they?"

"To wake me up."

Then she flew distractedly around the room, saying she'd be late, dashing into the shower, dressing, a repeat of the previous evening.

"You've forgotten your make-up."

"Don't have to. They have a professional to do it downstairs. Here's your ticket. Mind you come!"

"Have you eaten anything today?"

"I'll stuff myself at the party afterwards. Madame has gorgeous food. You're invited. Come and find me after the show."

She gave David a quick kiss and ran. He surveyed the chaos in the room, wondering what he was doing there. Decidedly what he had treasured in her, the indescribable sweetness of her personality, had vanished. And her humor. He felt he was sitting amid the wreckage of Francesca's life and his.

He cleared some of her clothes from a chair and spent an hour trying to read a memorandum he'd been given. It was impossible to concentrate. His eyes kept straying over the discarded clothing, the overflowing ashtrays. Intimacy and indifference. How could she look so impeccably turned-out when she threw her things about like this?

The show was more vigorous than the rehearsal, the audience packed, the models electrified by the applause. Again Francesca was more energetic than the others, more extreme in her skirt-flaring turns, far more rhythmic and supple in her movements to the music, almost breaking into the dance David remembered from the Caribbean. When she spotted him in the seat reserved near the ramp, she flashed her extraordinary smile, again making him feel caught in a beam of high energy.

He worried that she was performing too close to the edge, like an acrobat playing on the fear that she will fall. She was the same girl who had captivated him ten years earlier, but with every gauge of her personality tuned to a higher pitch. Once in a letter she had mentioned models on drugs. Could she be? Were her pills more than tranquilizers and stimulants? David didn't know enough to recognize the signs.

She came out in the dazzling evening gown and coat she had modeled at the end of the show.

"Madame said I could borrow them for the evening. But see that I don't get drunk and lose the coat, do you hear?"

Her eyes were brilliant with make-up and a gleam of excitement from the applause. Yet under a bright light as they waited for a taxi David noticed through her make-up that there were small lines around her eyes. At only thirty-one she was showing signs of very hard living.

The party became a nightmare to him. The expensive house was so jammed with animated people in evening clothes that he could barely squeeze through. Francesca repeatedly introduced him, but David lost the names in the din of French conversation and loud music. He took her to a buffet table and tried to get her to eat, but she put down the plate he had filled to kiss a woman, in the French manner, three times on the cheeks, caught another eye, and slipped into the crowd. Hungry, he stood still and ate. When he finished, he went looking for Francesca, picking up two glasses of champagne from a tray and carrying them aloft until someone jostled his elbow and one spilled. He found her and gave her the glass that was still full. She took it, dancing with a short man with flashy studs in his evening shirt, emptied it at a gulp, and let the glass stem slither through her fingers until the last drops fell on the man's head. He laughed but continued to dance, excited by the proximity of Francesca's bare shoulders and low bodice. She gave David a mischievous smile and danced away.

Left on his own, he went to the bar and ordered a whiskey, which he drank watching the crowd, hating the blaring music, which hurt his ears, until a man he vaguely recognized began talking, having to shout in David's ear to be heard.

"*Monsieur l'ambassadeur. Quelle plaisir de vous revoir! Gaston Foure.*"

Embarrassed to be accosted by someone from his other life, David remembered the official from the Belgian Foreign Ministry at the Geneva negotiations. The natty little man continued to hold him in conversation. "I could not help noticing the young woman whom you accompany this evening. *Ravissante!* I saw her at the *défilé.* What elegance. What charm." His little mustache moved sensually with his lips, as though they could taste Francesca's beauty.

David extricated himself, disturbed that this encounter would become part of the buzz in the inveterately gossipy world of European diplomacy. He shouldn't have come to the party, and it added to his uneasiness about Francesca's exaggerated, impetuous behavior.

His discomfort mounted when he found her on a sofa curled up affectionately with the young black model. David was sure she saw him standing there awkwardly, and deliberately put her arm around the diffident young man and kissed his ear. She must he drunk, David thought, or high on the pills she had taken to rouse herself before the show.

He stood his ground. "Francesca, I think it's time to go."

She turned to him dreamily, her eyes with the long false lashes half-closed, and said indifferently, *"Fais comme tu veux. Moi, je suis tellement content ici."*

"I really think we should go now," David repeated more firmly in English.

"Peut-être, je ne rentrai pas. Peut-être je m'occuperai ailleurs," and began stroking her companion with passionate interest.

He'd had enough. In a quick flare-up of anger, David said, "Suit yourself!" and rapidly left the house, thinking, as a servant opened the street door, that he had not said good night to the hosts and that he had never spoken to Francesca so sharply.

"Well, that's it," he told himself as he walked, looking for a taxi. "That's it. That's the end."

And yet he lay in the hotel bed half-hoping, in fact expecting, that in a few minutes she would burst in, sweetly contrite. She had done it just to taunt him. She would quickly feel ashamed and come back. He slept in fits, awakening at later and later hours to find himself still alone.

The telephone rang at seven A.M., and he assumed it was Francesca. But it was only the hotel operator telling David the time. He had a sudden resolution and called home in London.

Marilyn's voice turned instantly cold when she recognized his.

"Marilyn. I have been making a ghastly mistake. I realize now that I love you more than I knew. You are the one I want to be with, to make my life with. I want to come back. I'll do everything I can to erase this—this nightmare. I have never been as sure of anything. If you can find a way to forgive me . . ."

She was silent.

"Marilyn?"

"I don't want to talk to you."

"But I've got to talk to you."

"We'll see," she said and hung up.

Now David was feverish to get back to London, to convince her that he was serious. He had another appointment at the European Commission and couldn't cancel without serious awkwardness. He called to book an afternoon flight and dressed quickly. He fretted impatiently through the meeting, only habitual discipline dragging his thoughts from the slovenly hotel room.

When he returned to the Hilton, Francesca had been there and left with her clothes. Going into the bathroom for his shaving things, as in New York years before, he found a lipsticked message on the mirror.

One morning we set off, our brains full of passion,
Hearts swollen with rancor and with bitter desires

He felt disgust, then a fleeting sense of the pathetic, then disquiet that the hotel would find such extravagance in a room registered in his name. With tissues, he tried to wipe out the words, but they smeared. Determined to remove them completely, he used hot water and soap, conscious of how absurd he looked in the mirror, in a dark suit and tie, aware that he was erasing more than the lipstick. It was too much. She had gone too far. She had gone over the edge.

"How do I know you're telling me the truth now?" Marilyn asked. "You've been lying to me for so many years. Why should I trust you now?"

"I want you to learn to trust me again. I want that with the core of my being."

"You sound like a dumb soap opera."

"I don't know what else to say. Real feelings sound trite. I don't know any other words."

"I've decided to go to Canada. If we can't afford it, I'll ask Daddy for the money. This has turned my life completely upside down. I don't know what to think. I think I hate you."

"Don't ask your father. We can pay for it."

"I suppose you'd be ashamed to tell him the reason."

"Yes, to be honest, I would."

"Well, that's something!" she said.

At Heathrow, her eyes filled with tears.

"You have really hurt me, David."

"I know it and I'm sorry. But I will never hurt you again." She looked at him searchingly, then handed her diplomatic passport and ticket to the attendant and walked through the gate.

I will never hurt you again. Sitting at his desk in the study, David looked at his watch. After four. In a few hours . . .

On the empty pad he wrote, *Dear Prime Minister*, and stopped. He needed to get a few words on paper before telephoning; the habit of years to write a draft and study it before committing to any action.

Dear Prime Minister . . .

On the desk was a picture of Marilyn in the gown she had worn to be presented in London.

He couldn't call the PM or Dennison before calling her, and he dreaded that more. In the last ten years they had, he thought, grown as close as two people could be. Once the wounds had healed, the turmoil caused by Francesca had brought deeper affection and trust. He had no secrets from her, once that long-festering secret had exploded into the open and was, so painfully, metabolized.

After the first break in New York it had never been the same with Francesca. He had kept all those strained rendezvous because he yearned for something he imagined they would recapture if only they kept writing and meeting and making love, because it was too easy with Marilyn, too unchallenging, too untesting. Sporadic yet compulsive sex with Francesca never satisfied the yearning but fed it.

Francesca had her own wistful sense of unfulfillment, of waiting for the ultimate experience, the bigger wave. And despite all her talk about sex, her avidity, her aggressiveness, her apparent insatiability, she gave the impression of diffidence, as though she were

252

reaching for a level of satisfaction that was only in her mind and always eluded her.

He had kept her, like a child's secret from his mother, something that belonged only to him, his talisman, his hook into a destiny more exciting than that allotted to him in the conventional way. Perhaps many men—urbanized, civilized, tamed—secretly guarded this piece of themselves, the possibility that the gods will reach down and snatch them off for an adventure, that something thrilling can still happen.

Every day during those years in Helsinki, back in Ottawa, then in London, he had carried Francesca like a companion in his head, at breakfast with Marilyn, at dinner, through all the intimacies of married life, a sense of open possibility . . .

Of vast, shifting, unknown pleasures

Marilyn had found the poem in her French studies and thought it fitted David. But he had made it his and Francesca's—another betrayal. He took the Baudelaire from the bookshelf and read "The Voyage":

> *One morning we set off, our brains full of passion,*
> *Hearts swollen with rancor and with bitter desires,*
> *And we go, following the rhythm of the waves,*
> *Rocking our infinity on the finite seas:*
>
> *Some, glad to leave an abhorrent homeland;*
> *Others, the horror of their cradles; and some,*
> *astrologers drowned in the eyes of a woman,*
> *Tyrannical Circe with the dangerous perfumes.*

Again the dreadful image of a thin body floating somewhere off Sweden . . . a boat drifting . . . its sails slatting about . . . and David shuddered.

Could Marilyn absorb this too? See him resign in disgrace?

He went back to his draft.

Dear Prime Minister:

With great regret I feel required by circumstances to submit my resignation as Consul General in New York and from the Department of External Affairs. I do this because indiscretions of mine, years ago, of a personal, not a professional nature, are about to become public. While they in no way affect the security of the country, when published they will reflect badly on me and the Department, and my usefulness as your representative in New York will be severely compromised. Needless to say, I am deeply sorry but I know of no other way to lessen the probable damage than to remove myself quickly.

I deeply appreciate the confidence you have shown in me and regret that I am not able to pursue the course you recently suggested.

With my deep admiration and best wishes . . .

Deep admiration was excessive. No point in surrendering all his dignity. He took it out.

He would call Marilyn, then the PM at home before he left for Parliament Hill, read him the letter, and put it in the pouch to Ottawa for the record. If the PM asked questions, just tell him the truth. No point in being coy now.

Finally he'd call Dennison. It would gall him that he wasn't called first. Too bad.

And he'd have to call the girls. Perhaps he dreaded that the most.

Nearly five o'clock. Two hours before he could decently call anyone.

TWENTY-EIGHT

SWEDEN

SHE DID NOT awaken until after noon. Her whole body was stiff and sore as she stretched in the bed. She had forgotten to close the curtains. Outside was a clear autumn day, with yellow-leafed birches tossing against the intensely blue sky.

Now she had to face the embarrassment of calling the boat yard and asking for help. To get the boat back to Finland someone would have to come and clear the line fouling the propeller. They would probably know a boat yard here on the Swedish coast. She felt like dozing again, but her bladder demanded that she get up. After going to the bathroom she wrapped herself in a towel and rummaged through her purse, but couldn't find the card with the yacht yard number. It must be with the file of papers on the boat. Well, she had to go out to *Sea Girl* anyway to collect her things and tidy up.

She walked over to the window—and the boat was not there. Incredibly, it wasn't in sight! It must have drifted off behind some trees that were blocking her view. She opened the sliding door and leaned over the balcony. She could see past the trees, and there was no boat. The harbor was empty except for two small motorboats pulling hard at their moorings in the strong wind. She looked out to the horizon. No sign of *Sea Girl*! And the dreadful reality closed in. The light anchor must have dragged. The wind had changed. It was blowing hard off the land. That's why the motorboats were turned out to sea, the force of the wind obvious from the way they plunged on their moorings. And there were whitecaps on the water farther out.

Her heart was beating in panic. She had lost the precious boat! After all that effort. Coming through all that danger in the dark. The anchor must not have bitten in deeply enough. "OK for a lunch hook, these things," Geoffrey said. "Never hold in sand anyway." And this bottom was sandy.

Dressed only in the towel, she was freezing in the cold wind. She went back inside and closed the door. What to do? Suppose *Sea Girl* had blown out to sea? Or, worse, had blown ashore on the rocks beyond the harbor? God, God, God. She had lost it! No. Perhaps it was just around the point. Perhaps it wasn't too late. She should go and look to make sure. Get dressed and go out to look. No time to shower and put on the city clothes she had brought. She yanked on the jeans, sweater, and anorak she had worn on the boat and ran out of the hotel to the beach, half-hoping she had been wrong, *Sea Girl* would be there, hidden from her sight.

The dinghy was safe above the high-tide line, but no yacht.

There was a path leading away from the beach to the headland on the left of the bay. She followed it rapidly, stumbling over rocks and tree roots. The anchor could have caught on a rock and she'd find it safe from danger. The wish was so strong, she could picture the white hull jauntily rising and falling on the waves. But she could also picture it lying helplessly, the waves lifting and pounding it harder and harder on the rocks, breaking open the hull, smashing the mast. She rounded each small promontory with dread.

She felt the cold wind even in the anorak. If only she had taken the anchor line to the bow. But she had been too exhausted. And even then the anchor might not have held. The wind had changed so drastically, it would have twisted around in the sand and pulled loose anyway.

Breathless, she reached the point she had cleared so nervously in the dark. There was nothing in sight, only the buoy half a mile away, gleaming red in sunlight so bright it made her tired eyes ache. Off to the left on the larger point was the lighthouse that had guided her in.

Shivering, the wind whipping her hair, she gazed, mesmerized, against the sun at the metallic expanse of vacant sea. Somewhere out there, *Sea Girl* must be drifting, rolling, and pitching drunkenly with the waves. Any passing ship should see that something was wrong. Or the boat might drift around unsighted for days and days, going wherever the winds and tides took it. This wind could blow it back to the Aaland Islands, or past them to the Finnish mainland, or, if the winds changed, back to the Swedish coast to crash on the rocks. Crash on the rocks. The words sounded terrible in her head.

Yet this was just what she had planned. To do this deliberately. And now it had happened by accident. Strange, she had never thought until yesterday how awful it would be to cast an expensive yacht adrift—on purpose—to fend for itself.

Of course, boats were insured. The boat yard man had mentioned it. He had insisted that "her husband" come and sign the papers. He needed the signature of a qualified skipper. Without that was the insurance invalid? If the boat was really lost, she would be legally responsible. All the pride she had felt at her competence and daring now vanished.

It was too cold, and she started walking back to the motel. During all that time it had never come into her mind that, even if she survived the dangers, the plan was utterly reckless—criminal. She had planned deliberately to throw away a fine yacht worth . . . she didn't know how many thousands. Now, if it was lost, they could charge her, take her to court, and make her pay . . . force her to sell the business, all the money she had to live on—her freedom.

Another thought made her stop. Her things were still on board. If someone found *Sea Girl* drifting, they would find her clothes and the envelope addressed to David. Just as she had planned. Even the gold bracelet she had put back for safekeeping while sailing. The whole ghastly scheme was coming true anyway!

She had to warn someone, tell someone the boat was abandoned. She began to run, and ran until she was out of breath, then slowed to a rapid walk.

A sea gull glided by on the air currents near the cliffs, croaking, the sound complaining, disconsolate. In a normal mood Francesca would have laughed at the sulky bird, talked to it, understanding what to say to it. Today she felt cut off, isolated.

In her motel she immediately sat on the bed looking at the telephone. No number for the boat yard. She'd have to call directory inquiries in Helsinki. Long explanations to the manager of the yard, who had treated her so condescendingly.

But there was Matti Koivisto! A strong feeling of relief came with the thought, as though he had already lifted the weight from her shoulders. Full of hope, she dialed the code for Finland and the number of the apartment in Helsinki. It rang many times, but no one answered. Not quite three-thirty. He could still be at the university. He spent more time there since Kaarina's death. Two hours or so until she could reach him at home.

She lay back on the bed. She needed to bathe and change the clothes she had worn for days. She was hungry but felt an overpowering tiredness. In a few minutes she'd get up and shower.

She'd have to tell Matti everything. As phrases to use with him began to form, she realized how strange it was that she would turn to him for help.

It was five or six years since the night he had climbed into her bed and she had pushed him away. The years had softened the incident in her mind, leaving her slightly amused about it, comfortable with him but alert to hints of fresh ardor. He'd been very shy and correct at first but gradually relaxed, and she could read the message in his affectionate social embraces.

She was in Paris when she heard that Kaarina was ill. By the time she got the phone message it was days old, and the fact that *he* had called, not she, was ominous. Kaarina had developed breast cancer; both breasts had been removed and she was in chemotherapy.

Her changed appearance had shocked Francesca. She was thinner, the skin stretched around the fine cheekbones, the blond-silver hair drawn back, making her head look smaller. She was resting when Francesca arrived and sat beside her on the bed.

"You should have called me."

"Oh, you had your work to do."

"I would have dropped everything and come."

"There was no time. They made some tests and I had the operation two weeks later."

"Does it still hurt?"

"No, the pain is gone. But the look is still awful to me. Matti is horrified. He can't look at me."

"Well, that's stupid. *I'm* not horrified."

"One part of me is ashamed, and one part . . . I don't know how to say . . . practical . . . resigned."

"It's nothing to be ashamed of. You can share it with me."

Kaarina pulled open her nightdress and inwardly Francesca winced, feeling the mutilation in her own body.

"Oh, Kaarina, it's so sad. But you're alive . . . and you're still a beautiful woman."

"No . . . I feel so ugly." For the first time since Francesca had known her, Kaarina began to cry.

"Let me hold you."

Francecsa embraced her, aware of her own breasts against that vacant chest, feeling sure that by holding and stroking her she could pour some healing into the wounded woman.

"There, there, my darling." She kissed Kaarina's tear-wet cheeks and smoothed the hair, saying, "You're beautiful and I love you. You're the most wonderful person I know. You can cry with me. You can cry as much as you want."

Kaarina clung to her, and seemed to be releasing all the stored-up sorrows in her life, weeping until she could no more.

There was nothing erotic, as she had sometimes fantasized. She felt only a strong desire to use her body to salve the emotional wounds the surgeon had left.

She continued modeling but chose the jobs more carefully, wanting to be close as Kaarina's condition improved and the chemo-therapy ended. In a few months she felt herself again, and the strain of the illness began to leave her face.

Concern for Kaarina, but also the cleanliness and calmness of Helsinki, finally persuaded Francesca to move there. When a modeling job came up, she flew wherever she was needed, hating the scruffiness of life in hotels, longing to come back to her quiet flat, which Kaarina helped her to furnish with Finnish simplicity. It felt like her first real home.

Matti too gradually began to relax and, with her own apartment to go home to, Francesca could relax with him. They had good times when she was in Helsinki that year and they became deeper friends. They had passed through not just the fright of her illness but an emotional crisis for all of them. And perhaps she had begun to grow up.

Even with the expense of flying to and from Helsinki to work, she began to put some money aside. She was thinking more and more of changing her life. Modeling was for young women, and she began to yearn for something more substantial that she could take pride in. Quite unexpectedly, her father's death provided the push. She had never expected anything from him except gruff complaints that she was wasting her life. But suddenly he was dead and there was the money he had made by selling out to Bookers in Guyana . . . and there was Nigel trying to get her to invest it in Barbados.

She got the idea on the flight from Barbados to London to Helsinki. Something Kaarina and she could do together. For all that she loved Helsinki, she'd always thought the clothes were dowdy. Even the shops that sold fashionable things lacked sparkle, lacked an eye. Finland was becoming more prosperous. With all the contacts she had in the trade in New York, London, and Paris, why couldn't she start a shop with smart ready-to-wear and sports clothes, and with Kaarina? Her manner and her elegance would be perfect. Francesca would be the buyer, and Kaarina would deal with the customers. They would start small, and if it worked, they could bring in some Finnish designers. Even start their own line. The Finns had very refined taste in all other matters of design. They made beautiful fabrics and furs. Why not clothes too?

Matti, living on a professor's income plus royalties from his few books, was very cautious.

"Do you really want to take such a risk with your money, Francesca?"

"I've always taken risks. I was made to take risks."

Kaarina picked up her excitement. In the months it took for her father's estate to be settled and taxes paid, they investigated where to rent shop space. Her trips abroad became more interesting as she started talking business with designers and suppliers, some of them pretty dubious, thinking of her only as a flighty model. Anthony was the most helpful. He'd branched out himself in London and seemed to know everything about the trade—credit lines, delivery and payment schedules, insurance, size ranges. And he wanted to become a partner.

"Why shouldn't I take a flutter and come in with you?"

"You might lose your money."

"I'm always losing it, darling. But somehow I always find it again. Live by my wits and the lolly comes in. Ask old Belinda."

"Are you two still married?"

"Well, she cooks my supper and washes my socks."

With Anthony she always had private visions of shady dealings, imagining bundles of dresses mysteriously falling off lorries and into his hands, but all his advice sounded perfectly straight, and he was willing to find stock and supply on credit. His optimism excited her.

"Other models have started their own lines . . . perfumes, accessories. No reason why you shouldn't. Francesca's a smashing name for it."

When her father's money finally became real, Nigel made one more try to persuade her at least to put it into safe investments in New York or London. She refused, and *A New World* opened on December 1, 1989.

The name was Matti's idea, because the Cold War was ending, everything seemed more hopeful, as it was his idea to repeat the name not only in Finnish and Swedish but English, French, and Russian. They were in the shop arranging stock when he came in breathlessly to say the Berlin Wall had been smashed down. They all ran to the television shop nearby and watched the incredible scenes in Berlin. He was so moved, he bought a bottle of champagne and they stood in the half-finished shop to drink to peace and *A New World*.

It was hard to believe that Kaarina was sixty-one. She seemed like a young girl, rushing here and there, her eyes sparkling, and Francesca had never had such a feeling of fulfillment. People actually came and bought. They loved the clothes. A couple who saw the sign in Russian must have told others, because they began having a surge of people from Leningrad who came by train to shop in Helsinki. Within a week, they were ordering replacement stock on some items.

Christmas Eve was a Sunday, but they stayed open and collapsed with exhaustion in a restaurant nearby, too tired to eat, toasting each other like actors celebrating a hit show.

They all got a little drunk. Matti said, "To Francesca and the *Joulupukki,*" Finnish for Father Christmas. When Kaarina went to the ladies room, he said to Francesca, his eyes misty, "You have done a wonderful thing for Kaarina. I have not seen her so happy for many years. It has taken her mind completely away from that terrible thing. She is a somewhat melancholy person. I suppose we Finns all are. It may be in our nature—some think so—only I like to think there is a knowing melancholy in all sensitive human beings. You too."

"I don't feel very melancholy tonight."

"I cannot tell you how fond of you Kaarina is, more than a sister, more than a child—something more."

"I know, Matti. I feel it for her."

"And I feel just as strongly myself. We both love you, Francesca."

"And I love you both."

In this slightly boozy state, he was leaning closer and she felt his interest becoming obvious, but Kaarina came back and took him home.

The months that followed sobered them up. The Christmas rush evaporated, business slowed, even with prices marked down, and Francesca felt too insecure about the first profits to give up modeling fees entirely. She took the best jobs offered and tried to combine them with buying and checking out new collections. It was exhausting but rewarding.

They really needed a manager but didn't want to hire someone until they were sure the shop could hold its own. Until then, Kaarina refused any salary, because Francesca had put up the starting money. It was different from the days when they had hours to sit and chat, and yet they were as close working together as they ever had been. Kaarina would look up from a customer and catch Francesca's eye in a busy moment and, for a second, give her a look of such pleasure and affection that Francesca felt it physically. She had never felt such a close bond with anyone.

They wanted her to go to the island with them that summer. Matti needed the annual break and so, obviously, did Kaarina, who some days looked very tired. Francesca insisted they go while she looked after the shop.

She felt lonely without them. She had no other close friends in Helsinki, and there was time to examine her feelings in the long evenings alone. The ethereal summer nights, when it hardly got dark, made her feel weightless and floating in time, in a dream.

One night she dreamed of David. She saw him coming into the shop, which was bigger and more impressive than the real shop. She noticed him looking around, but when he saw her he seemed disapproving, and when she turned around again he had left. The following day she felt his presence as though she had actually been with him during the night. When it was time to close she sat for a long time thinking in the empty shop. In the dream she had been seriously disappointed at his reaction. Why should he disapprove of this beautiful shop? It was elegant and stylish and obviously it was going to be a success. If she had married him years ago, she might possibly be no happier nor more satisified with her life. And yet as she sat there in the long twilight, she didn't feel satisfied.

When Kaarina came back in late August she looked tanned and rested. They threw themselves into the fall season, gaining confidence every week. A month before the first anniversary it was clear from the October books that they had nothing to worry about.

Now . . . if they made her pay for the boat she could lose all that.

It was nearly dark. Turning on the bedside lamp, she dialed Matti's number. Still no answer. She could imagine the ringing echoing through the apartment where she had found such serenity. An awful feeling of loss possessed her. She tried to shake it off by undressing and standing a long time in the first hot shower in days, washing her hair and repeatedly soaping herself.

Looking down at the water streaming over her breasts she saw Kaarina's flat chest after the operation, neat but fearsome scars where her breasts had been. How tidily mutilated she looked, flattened skin stretched over her ribs—like the chest of a young boy.

She'd been packing a suitcase for a quick trip to London when

Kaarina called to say she wouldn't be in because she needed to go to the doctor.

"Anything wrong?"

"No, just more tests," she said. "But it means the whole day."

"Right, I'll tell the girls. They can manage."

Ever since her operation she'd been going for check-ups, at first every month, then every few months, but they had been quick visits with a lab report a few days later. Uneasy, Francesca called her back.

"Why does it need to be the whole day?"

"Just tests. The doctor wants some more tests."

"For the whole day?"

She didn't answer, and in that moment of silence Francesca guessed everything.

"Is there something you don't want to tell me?"

"I was going to tell you when he tells me what there is to do. The cancer has come back." Matter-of-factly, as one might say the leak in the roof has come back.

"Oh, Kaarina! I'll come with you."

"No, no, no, no. There is no need—"

"I'll come with you."

She dropped the trip to London and took Kaarina to the hospital. New tests confirmed that the mastectomies had not prevented the spread of cancer cells through the lymph nodes.

They put her back in the hospital and tried more chemotherapy, but she deteriorated quickly.

Francesca had planned to celebrate the first of December with a party in the shop but canceled it. She opened the shop in the mornings, then left it with an assistant and spent the days at Kaarina's bedside. Matti, full of desolation, trying to work at the university, came in the evenings.

At night, alone, Francesca was heartbroken, but being with Kaarina in the daytimes was not sad. It was more like the afternoons they had spent talking in her flat all those years ago, Kaarina quite cheerful . . . resigned, not self-pitying. They talked about everything. Francesca's children—how often did she write to them? What did they reply? When would she see them? Did they know about the shop? What did they think about it?

About David: Kaarina wanted the whole story again, every detail, from the night they met.

"I liked him very much, too," she said. "I liked when he came in the evenings. And of course when he brought you. He was very shy about it, very hesitant to offend us."

She talked again about her father in the Winter War. She asked Francesca to go back to the the cemetery to light a candle by Arno's grave.

"Do it because Matti can never bear to go. Be kind to Matti," she said.

The day she died, her skin like yellowing old linen stretched taut over the bones, her gray eyes huge, Kaarina smiled, and whispered, "Would you do something for me, dear Francesca? Go to the island . . ."

"I will, my dear, I will." Francesca squeezed her hand.

A little later, her eyes opened again. ". . . and Francesca . . . be kind to Matti."

She went to sleep, her body no bigger than a child's in the bed. The moment of death was almost imperceptible, but knowing it, Francesca felt the room suddenly empty—and heard the sounds of her own breathing. She was scared but calm and did not call anyone . . . wanting a moment alone.

Looking at the gaunt, dismayingly still body, Francesca remembered feeling embarrassed to be alone with Kaarina after that afternoon when her own feelings ran away with her. Kaarina had gently pushed her away. Francesca was being pushed away from something she desired as intensely as anything, and yet knew Kaarina was right. Her look as she separated seemed to promise that later, if they knew each other better . . . perhaps . . . but it never came to that, and Francesca was glad . . . she supposed. She imagined what women who loved each other did—of course she had read and heard—but it wasn't the same as doing it. And it might have been empty afterwards, and they might have become strangers. She didn't know . . . she had never really made up her mind about it. She would look at other women, the models, in dressing rooms— they were often mostly undressed—and notice that she felt no attraction to them. Yet with Kaarina, in the few seconds of real contact, she had felt the indescribable pleasure of mutual complicity. But when Kaarina stepped back, that feeling ended.

Francesca reached over and touched the lifeless hand on the bed. It was already cold.

Because she was so wasted, Matti did not want to take the customary photograph in the coffin that Finns put in the family album.

For weeks, Kaarina's departure left Francesca feeling disembodied herself, a sensation that she was floating, suspended, unattached to the earth. She saw Matti outside but could not bear to go to their apartment. He was lost alone, came to the shop quite often, and asked her to have supper with him or a drink. He drank too much and got so morose that she tried to avoid him, but in the end still went because she was as lost as he.

She got out of the shower and dried herself. Apart from bruises from the buffeting on the boat, her body, for a forty-year-old woman's, was gratifyingly lean and trim. It was the condition of her mind and spirit that dismayed her. If only she could have had Kaarina's calm, balanced spirit in her own body. Kaarina never abused her body. She drank very little; she never smoked. She kept fit, skiing and swimming, not fanatically but in the same measured and reasonable way she approached everything in life. Francesca had treated her own body with contempt, yet here she was in perfect health—and Kaarina was dead.

Francesca combed out her wet hair and filed her ragged fingernails, then put on the dress she had brought to look unlike a woman just off a boat.

She dialed Helsinki again. No answer. If Matti was away or out for the evening . . . Her head was aching. She had to eat something.

In the restaurant three Swedish men were drinking. They assessed her appreciatively as she walked to a table and kept glancing at her as they laughed and smoked and clinked their glasses. Finally one of them came unsteadily to her table and asked she if would join them for a drink.

She said sharply and loudly in English, "Go away!" and the the other men laughed. She wished she were still wearing the jeans and sweater.

The man bowed elaborately—"I am so sorry"—and stumbled back his table, where his friends raised a derisive cheer. She quickly ate an omelette and drank a glass of wine.

This time when she rang, Matti answered.

"Oh, Matti"—she was almost weeping from relief—"it's Francesca."

"Francesca, my dear. Francesca, my love." He sounded strange, but it took her a few moments to grasp how drunk he was.

"Francesca, beautiful . . . bellissima Francesca . . . I have missed you so much . . . please come to see me . . . come to see me tonight . . ."

"Matti, I'm in Sweden."

"It would be so beautiful if you come to see me . . ." he rambled off in Finnish.

Hopeless to try to tell him her bizarre story.

"Go to sleep, Matti. You're drunk."

He couldn't help her. She'd have to call the boat yard and do all the explaining herself. And the evening was gone. Tomorrow. Then take the bus to Stockholm.

Poor old Matti . . . lonely and drunk. He had brought the chart . . . of course! That's what started this. He'd been making ineffectual efforts to tidy up the apartment . . . which he really didn't want to touch. He'd mention things, she imagined him picking something up, experiencing a painful memory, putting it down. But he was very pleased to bring her the chart he had lent to David to guide them to the island. It gave him more contact with her.

"I thought you might like to have it."

She thanked him and put it aside. It was too big to unfold in the restaurant. They had a drink, and she saw people looking as them, imagining father and daughter . . . or God knows what. She was always a little on her guard, expecting that Matti's loneliness would revive the old interest. Remembering Kaarina's "Be nice to Matti," she put up with him but didn't think it meant she had to be nice to him in that way. Sometimes when he dropped her off at her apartment building, she could see good manners struggling with the temptation to ask himself up. It was plain that night, but she did not bite.

In her flat she pushed fabric samples off the work table to unfold the chart. There was Matti's bearing line into the cove, and David's penciled notes. She had not seen his handwriting for a long time. It looked precise and something . . . smug. Damn him! she thought. And in an instant it was like fireworks bursting inside her head. Damn him. She knew just how to make him pay attention. Kaarina had said go to the island. She would go to the island, all right . . . on her fortieth birthday—just as they'd planned! The whole plan popped into her head and she felt full of life for the first time in many months. She went to bed and kept thinking up new details. And there she got the idea of the mystery yacht, drifting abandoned . . . the only clue an envelope addressed to him—not in New York but here—in Helsinki. She was so excited by her brilliant scheme, she couldn't go to sleep. She was thrilled . . .

I must have been crazy, Matti. Kaarina's death must have unhinged me. It's the only way I can explain it.

Tired, restless, uneasy, she slid open the balcony door and went out. The night was clear and the wind had dropped. On an impulse she went back into the room, slipped the anorak over her dress, and walked down to the beach.

In the dim light, it felt like the night before, when she had arrived and anchored so proudly. Tonight the sea seemed closer to the rubber dinghy. Perhaps someone had moved it. She sat on it and watched the phosphoresence of the small waves approaching her feet, withdrawing, advancing, retreating. The sand above the waves was wet. The tide was going out.

Elbows on her knees, chin in her hands, she gazed at the sea. She should call the police . . . she dreaded that. But she must call someone. Call the boat yard in the morning. Call Matti when he'd sobered up. Take the bus to Stockholm and the ferry to Hanko on the Finnish coast, then a bus to the boat yard, where she'd left her car. Or bus to Stockholm, fly to Helsinki, and deal with the car later.

Matti, isolated in his own grief, depressed her, because she was just as forlorn and alone in her own feelings for Kaarina.

The waves were lapping quietly at her feet. If she nudged the dinghy a few feet into the water and sat in it, she could drift away on the tide . . . pretend she had lost *Sea Girl* . . .

She could walk into the sea and float away. The tide would carry her out. It was like the feeling she had had in Kaarina's house . . . if she died it wouldn't matter to anyone. She could feel herself doing it . . . sliding off her shoes . . . dropping the anorak on the sand . . . slipping out of her dress . . .

And freeze in that paralyzing water! She felt chilled enough just sitting in this thin dress.

"Don't be stupid," she said aloud and stood up, shuddering. She dragged the dinghy well clear of the water and ran back to her room.

TWENTY-NINE

NEW YORK

A FEW MINUTES after six David heard the thump of the newspaper and outside the front door he picked up the *New York Times*. He scanned it quickly, picturing the words YACHT ABANDONED OFF SWEDEN, overlaid with the vision that hours of anxiety had burned into his mind . . . Francesca's golden body floating like a sodden doll, limbs lolling with the movements of the sea. Obsessively he searched every page, feeling a rising desire to explain.

If he could have seen her briefly, he might have explained that he had just not understood what he was doing. He had kept her like a fantasy—the unattainable movie star fantasy—that he could summon into living flesh when convenient, by rubbing the magic lamp, to avoid having to resign himself to the ordinary, to the extreme propriety of his profession, of his background. But a fantasy was not supposed to be a real human being with her own emotional needs. How hard it was to break out of the prison of one's self-absorption.

That he could have been so deeply in love with her, slept with her, eaten with her, talked with her so often, yet seen her only as a creature of his needs? Then, when she embarrassed him too much, he had pushed her off—and forgotten her.

It was devastating to realize how unaware he had been, a man who considered himself, and was considered, liberal, compassionate, and principled in his dealings with the world.

Still, there was another way of looking at it. He felt tender now towards Francesca because she was dead, because she had died in a tragic way that might be, very indirectly, due to him. But at the time he'd had more than adequate provocation and felt perfectly justified in leaving her.

Well, they each held responsibility in the affair. They were both adults, each with others dependent on them. Each contributed to the irresponsibility . . .

This wasn't getting him anywhere. There was no story from Sweden. He closed the *Times*.

The two big front-page stories—Bush vetoes extended unemployment benefits, man kills twenty-two in Texas restaurant. A professional reflex to think: not Canada. Canada looked after her unemployed, and mass killers were very rare. But for how long could Canadians be so smug, in the inexorable Americanization of their lives?

Literal political integration—Canada constitutionally a part of the U.S.—wasn't likely. More likely was gradual *de facto* integration.

Americans would tend not to notice it happen. A few Canadians would notice every dropped comma. For some north of the forty-ninth parallel, like some south of the Mason-Dixon Line, the psychic wound would never heal, because it made some Canadians, like some Southerners, too interesting to themselves.

Already Canada couldn't really pay for the very services that defined its different political culture. It was borrowing from Japanese postal workers to support unemployed Newfoundland fishermen. Something would have to give—though obviously not before the next election.

But what had to give would be the responsiblity of a finance minister, not External Affairs. No change in foreign policy would help matters at home. Pulling out of the Free Trade Agreement would be absurd; however painful the early effects, Canada had to be part of a North American common market. Mulroney was right about that. The only question was how long Canada could preserve its own political and social culture in that pitiless common market of ideas and values—one generation, two, three?

In any case, economics would determine Canadian influence and drive foreign policy.

Well . . . irrelevant now anyway. It was 6:44. In a few minutes Marilyn would be awake. He'd have to tell her everything, even if it hadn't reached the papers yet.

THIRTY

SWEDEN

FRANCESCA FOUND THE story on an inside page of the Wednesday morning paper.

SEGELBÅT FUNNEN
Osthammar den 16 de Oct.

En segelbåt utan vare sig kapten eller besättning upptäcktes igår på drift tre kilometer utanför Alands kust. Den tio meter långa båten var fullt utrustad och in perfekt kondition. Den fanns dock inga tecken på att segelbåten var på väg att förlisa. Spåren tyder dock på att manskapet lämnat båten i all hast. Polisen söker nu ägaren genom segelbåtens registreringsnummer.

Her Swedish was just enough to let her understand that the boat had been found abandoned by its crew and police were trying to trace the owners.

With enormous relief, she thought, The boat is safe. Thank God, the boat is safe. She need not have the loss of a beautiful yacht on her conscience—or the cost to bear.

The pleasure of knowing that transformed her mood. She was very hungry. She hadn't ordered breakfast. She had rushed in and sat down to read the newspaper, and no one had come into the deserted dining room. Francesca had to go into the kitchen to roust out a waitress.

Waiting with a cup of coffee, she thought, They'll wonder what happened to the crew. They'll find my things on the boat . . . probably already have . . . and David's name and the Canadian Embassy address. They'll trace *Havsflickan* back to the boat man in Finland . . . he'll give them my name . . . he'll guess I was alone. By the time it takes them to do all that, I can get back myself . . . and explain. Much better than trying in bits of Finnish and Swedish and English on the phone. As long as the boat is safe . . . by the time they know it's me, I can get back there, explain to him, get my car, and leave. Matti could help me explain. Perhaps I should go Helsinki . . . Maybe I'll have to pay for the anchor—two anchors —and the dinghy. But his boat is safe, anyway. I could go to Turku on the ferry and then get a bus to the boat yard, or fly straight to Helsinki. First . . .

She got up and went into the small lobby to ask about buses.

"Now there are only two to Stockholm. Early morning and late afternoon. You've missed the morning one. The next is at seventeen hundred."

A little deflated, with hours to wait ahead of her, Francesca went back to finish her meal.

THE OUT-OF-season bus meandered towards Stockholm, stopping at every little village and gradually filling with country people. They eyed Francesca curiously, women with a closed glance, men with the little shock she was used to. She ignored them and settled into a reverie, watching the neat villages pass by.

Being forty was no different from being thirty-nine. The tipsy man in the restaurant had noticed, like these men on the bus. Well, she looked good. Tanned; clean hair. Why had she assumed forty was the end of the world? She might live to be eighty, half of her life still to live.

Between the villages were stretches of forest, dark conifers and white birches, farms, Swedish tidiness, healthy animals, very blond children.

The sailing had changed something in Francesca. People still looked at her and thought her beauty explained her. They looked as though they owned her and needed to know nothing more about her than her legs, face, body. But the sailing had freed her from her beauty. She had screwed up at the end, but she knew she could do something tough and dangerous on her own, something that had nothing to do with her looks.

The slow progress of the overheated bus made her drowsy. She awoke when a blond young woman sat down beside her, her pale skin pink from waiting in the crisp air. She pulled a textbook from her haversack and began reading, underlining and making marks in the margin.

"Are you a student?"

The girl looked up, suprised to be addressed in English, and answered politely, "Yes, at Uppsala."

The name of the old university she had once visited stirred Francesca.

"What are you studying?"

"Oh, biology. It's part of becoming a doctor."

They chatted on. The girl asked what Francesca did, and when told, responded enthusiastically, "Oh, I guessed something like that. You are so refined-looking."

"I envy you knowing just what you want to be, so young."

The girl said complacently, "My boyfriend is studying to be a doctor and my father said, 'Are you just going to wait around for him?' So I decided I'll do it too. Then we'll both be doctors, and we can go anywhere in the world and be useful."

She returned to her textbook and Francesca stared out the window at the darkening landscape. Her father had said university was a waste of money for a girl so "boy crazy," who would probably get married any day. He'd had enough expense with her mother's scheme of sending her to Switzerland . . . "and a fat lot of good that did."

Several times Matti had told her, "You could take some courses. You have a quick mind, and languages are no obstacle for you." But she always had to go back to work. As for languages, she did pick up easy conversation, even in Finnish, but she couldn't read or write it —much too difficult, with all the endings she never had the patience to learn.

The windows of the bus had misted up with the warm breath of many passengers. She cleared it with her hand but could see only blackness and an occasional passing light. It felt like the night on the sea, when the only relief from fear was her own determination, the confidence she forced herself to feel. Then the inexpressible joy at the first pale flash from the lighthouse.

The girl beside her read on methodically, underlining, making notes with soft, white hands. Francesca looked at her own, still red and hot from the days of pulling lines on the boat. Hers were more delicate, the fingers longer, but the student's hands, patiently turning pages, manipulating her ballpoint pen, had a calm purposefulness that spoke of harmony between mind and body, of steadiness. In a few years, this girl's hands would be touching patients, feeling for pain, perhaps performing operations, all directed by a mind that knew why it was put on this earth.

Francesca gazed at her own hands and saw her life in them,

thinking of all they had touched and held in forty years—lifting a wine glass, lighting a cigarette, fastening clothes, applying make-up, caressing men, holding Kaarina's dying hand.

Well, she could study . . . spend the money her father wouldn't spend . . . sell the shop . . . immerse herself in education . . . Matti suggesting studies to follow . . .

For a moment the idea consumed her, like flames in a new fire, and the warmth of it ran to her fingertips.

But there was something suspiciously familiar about this excitement . . . just what she'd felt making the ridiculous plan to abandon the boat . . . to send that futile message to David. In fact, she had felt it often . . . all her life overwhelmed by sudden enthusiasms . . . hurling herself impetuously in new directions . . . the little tingle of excitement beginning like this and catching fire . . .

All because a Swedish medical student had sat down beside her. Because she was still annoyed at her father. Pretty stupid. Whatever he thought of her, he had left her enough money to start a businesss, to get her out of the modeling rat race. And it was a very good business.

If she wanted to make friends with Colin and Samantha, be worthy of them, make them proud of her, she had to settle down in life, stop flinging herself into things, like the travelers in David's poem, "not knowing why, they always say: Let's go!" At some time you had to stop leaving for the sake of leaving.

To be more like Kaarina: the wish that had overtaken her in Kaarina's house on the island. Perhaps Matti would sell her the island. He dreaded going there now. She could spend her summers in Kaarina's house.

To buy it, she'd need to work hard at the business. It was doing well now, making money. It amazed her to sit in a corner and watch it hum with customers, particularly at lunchtime and when the offices closed.

That was the way to honor Kaarina. Put her energies fully into the business she had really started *for* Kaarina.

The bus droned on . . . and another thought arrived: Drop the silly Francesca! It was childish, her teenage badge of sophistication because Frances had sounded so dowdy. But if Frances, why not Williams? Drop the D'Anielli too! Another affectation, a name secretly admired because it sounded glamorous and foreign.

She was Frances Williams. She would *be* Frances Williams.

Her excitement at this hugely liberating idea made her want to blurt it out to the girl beside her, but just when the temptation was irresistible, another piece of new thinking came to her.

She was Francesca before David. He knew her only as that. To call herself Frances was to go back to who she was before all that began, before all the years tied to him, wrestling to get away from him, yet always coming back. This entire crazy scheme with the boat —the envelope, the bracelet, the visit to the island—was all because, however tenuously, she was tied to David. The person she had been striving to be was dependent on him.

Her mind was bursting with these thoughts, as though a symphony orchestra were playing the climax of the Sibelius Fifth Symphony in her head and only she could hear it.

Of course, forty was still young. Kaarina had lived to sixty-two, even with cancer. The way to honor Kaarina was to be like her, steady, calm, considerate of others, including Matti, especially poor old Matti.

They were driving through the lighted streets of Stockholm. She had to find whether there was still a plane tonight to Helsinki, or stay at the airport hotel and take the first flight in the morning.

As they got up to leave the bus, the girl said wistfully, "It must be a wonderful, exciting life to be a model. All the beautiful clothes, all those exotic places to visit."

"I thought so too," said Frances Williams.

THIRTY-ONE

NEW YORK

MARILYN'S VOICE, NORMALLY musical and friendly when she answered the telephone, had a strange, disembodied tone.

"Oh, David!" she said and because she used his name only when she was very grave, he thought, She knows!

"It's so weird you called just now. I was just going to call you. David, Daddy died a couple of hours ago." And she began to weep.

"Oh, God, sweetheart. I'm awfully sorry."

It took a huge effort to squeeze this reality into the turmoil in his own mind.

"Mummy and I just got back from the Civic. He's dead! He was fine last night. I mean, there was no sign of him getting worse. Then we heard a noise in the middle of the night. We both rushed in there and found him lying on the floor. We think he tried to get out of bed and must have had another stroke and just fell down. We called the ambulance, but they said it was too late."

She started to weep again, the quiet, keening sound David heard only when she was utterly bereft.

God, not now! She sounded as desolate as a child crying, and the sound opened David's heart to her.

"Oh, that's terrible. Awful for you to have it happen like that." He had an image of Wallace Farquhar's imperious face lying on the floor. Well, the old man wouldn't know about this scandal.

"It's so hard to believe!" Her voice was beginning to sound normal. "In the taxi coming back from the hospital, Mummy said maybe he was trying to tell us something last night. I told you he was trying so hard to talk. Well, perhaps he had something terribly important to say. Perhaps he could feel some new pain coming." And she was crying again.

"Sweetheart, there wasn't anything you could have done."

"I know, but Mummy says—"

"How is she?"

"She's all right. Right now, she's making some tea. I mean, we're both all right—but it's such a shock. We came in a few minutes ago and we just stood in the kitchen and looked at each other, saying, I can't believe it. You see all the little things. Just now in the hall, the Chinese thing with his walking sticks and umbrellas; I looked at it and I . . ."

He'd have to let her talk for a few minutes. He couldn't put this on her right away. But all the words in his mind were phrases he'd been preparing: This is going to be a little hard for you . . .

"I had to go to the john and I passed the guest bedroom where he's been and the bedclothes all are still mussed up, kind of dragged down to the floor when he fell . . ."

But he had to tell her. It was 7:13. If he was going to reach the PM . . .

"We're both only half-dressed. We just threw on anything and got into the ambulance . . ."

And something in that image made him yearn for her . . . a picture of her suddenly startled out of sleep . . . running in her nightgown across the hall from her old room . . . her body still warm from bed . . . made David feel how much he loved this woman and longed to put his arms around her and let her cry.

"I wish I were there with you, just to give you a hug."

"I know," she said sweetly and intimately. "But, sweetie, it's so good just to talk to you. It's making me feel better. Would you speak to Mummy for a moment?"

Oh, God.

"Yes, sure."

"Mummy, it's David. He wants to talk to you. She's coming."

He liked Margaret Farquhar, often wondering how she had accommodated her self-centered husband.

"Hello, David," she said warmly. "Isn't it sad?"

"I'm really awfully sorry to hear it. It must have been terrible, having it happen suddenly in the middle of the night."

"It was 4:04. I looked at the clock. Wallie hated it because it's one of the new ones that tells the exact numbers."

"I know. They're so damn precise. But things are frightening when they happen when you're asleep. You feel defenseless."

"That's exactly right. I was frightened out of my wits. Well—I'm just trying to get used to the idea that he's gone, David. I've been thinking how long it's been."

"You just had your forty-fifth—"

"No, forty-sixth."

"Of course, I'd forgotten. Marilyn told me."

"We were married in 1935 just after Wallie joined External . . ."

How long could he go on with this—so necessary to comfort her and Marilyn—so frighteningly irrelevant to his anxieties? It was 7:19. If he missed the moment . . .

". . . and you know he was so proud when Marilyn married someone in the foreign service. He admired you a lot, David—"

"Well, thanks."

"No, I know what you mean. He could be difficult. He argued a lot and he liked to lay down the law on everything . . ."

She sounded less distraught than Marilyn . . . fathers and daughters . . . the poignant bond . . .

". . . but he was as pleased as I am that your career is going so brilliantly."

"You're very generous."

"No, I mean it, David. He thought you could be the minister one day . . ."

He couldn't listen to any more of this. The minutes were slipping by.

"Do you think you'll be able to come to Ottawa for the funeral? It'll be all the people you know."

How could he go after resigning in disgrace? How could he not go? The entire senior staff of the department would go; all the diplomatic corps would turn out—

"Did Marilyn tell you that the prime minister phoned yesterday . . . ?"

Everything was coming together in a monstrous way. He must find some comforting words and end this.

"Well, I still can't believe it. My heart goes out to you both."

"You're a sweet man, David. It's a comfort to talk to you. I'll give you back to Marilyn. Bye for now."

Bye for now. Marilyn said that. It sounded so cozily Canadian, coming in her distinctive Ottawa accent to David's ears now accustomed to American speech.

"Bye, bye."

It was 7:24. Now he'd have to tell her. But how could he throw this at her? It would need a long explanation. But he must.

Marilyn was back, sounding fully herself, affectionate and intimate.

"Thanks, sweetie. You made her feel a lot better." In the few words she seemed to express all that bound them together now—

her trust, loyalty, playfulness, quiet sexiness, the healed wounds. He could feel it all—all the decency of the woman he was fortunate to have as his wife.

"I heard Mummy mention the funeral. We haven't done anything about it yet. Let's see, it's Thursday. It's usually two days, isn't it? That would be Saturday. Is that going to be difficult for you?"

That was an opening. But before he could take it—

"Look, I know you've got a lot on, but couldn't you come up for the whole weekend? It would make such a difference, having you here . . ."

Full of trust.

"Sweetheart, I've got to—"

But she was rattling on, not wanting to disconnect the security of having him on the line.

"Tony will be coming from Toronto, but you know what he's like. His life is so messed up with Diana at the moment . . . I don't know whether she'll even show up. You know what I think about that! There's going to be so much to do. If you could make it tonight or tomorrow morning, it'd be neat."

Neat. The fifty-one-year-old woman still used expressions she had as a teenager. Once they had irritated David. He'd thought they made her sound naïve and provincial. But that was when he didn't have her truly in focus. Or himself. Now words like *neat* sounded sweet and true to him. They were the Marilyn he cherished.

But 7:36. It couldn't wait. He was growing more nervous.

"Sweetheart, I've got to tell you something."

"Oh, what?" Her voice bright, comradely.

He couldn't go on. He couldn't tell her now.

"Well?" she said.

"It can wait."

"What time do you think you'll be able to get away?"

"I'll have to figure that out. I'll call you from the office."

"Bye for now. David?"

"Yes?"

"I feel so much better, talking to you."

Feeling numbed after hanging up, David looked at his note to the prime minister. He took another puff on the cigarette and stubbed it out, then searched his briefcase for the small notebook of private phone numbers. He was reaching for the receiver when the phone startled him by ringing.

"David, Michael Dennison. Sorry to call so early, but I thought you would want to know the news."

"Yes, Wallace Farquhar died. Marilyn just called."

"My goodness, I didn't know that. Well, well. Fine old chap . . . great man . . . last of the golden age . . . all that. Please tell Marilyn and Margaret how sorry I am. I'll call a bit later. But look, you'll want to know this. Beaubien just called me. The woman on the boat, Francesca D'Anielli, is not dead after all."

"Oh, my God," David said.

"The police called Jean Luc. Apparently she simply turned up at her apartment . . . as right as rain. They've called off the search and the investigation. So, no problem, eh?"

"I see. No more explanation?"

"No more explanation. An accident, perhaps."

"I see."

"I don't know what that means to you. None of my business . . . unless you care to tell me the story sometime." He gave a little chuckle. "But it means no problems for the department, no messy stuff with the minister. Just as well, with the way things are going. So-oh, sorry if I gave you a scare yesterday but nothing to worry about now. We can forget it and go about our business."

David did not hear the usual sarcasm in the voice of his old rival. Dennison sounded positively friendly. But it took all David's professional self-control to say casually, "Well, thanks, Michael. I'm glad to hear it. Thanks for letting me know."

"Just part of the service. Oh, now that I think of it, I suppose you'll be coming up for Farquhar's funeral. Bound to be one of those events. See you there!"

"Goodbye." David hung up.

He could go to the funeral with no worries. He sat at the desk looking over the New York skyline to the west, a dazzling October morning making the buildings glow optimistically. His hands were shaking. All night he had felt his world crashing about him, and suddenly—it wasn't true. Everything was in its proper place, and the sun was shining.

He didn't have to drag Marilyn through it again. He looked at his letter to the PM on the desk. He didn't have to resign. Francesca was not dead! It was too much to think, all at once. He went back to the box in the living room for one more cigarette. He'd have to stop before the habit dug in again. Just one more.

So it was all a mistake, or an accident—or an elaborate joke.

Whichever it was, once again she had brought his life, his marriage, his career close to the precipice.

She would still have his letters. He could call Jean Luc to get them back. And he knew, before it came quite to the front of his thoughts, a part of him was urging, Go there yourself! At once! Call the airline. Go. See her. Talk to her. It's the only way to put a civilized end to the affair. Little whispers of justification, like the unwilled compulsion to light this cigarette. David stubbed it out.

Don't be stupid! He could hear Francesca say that.

His eyes fell again on his letter to the prime minister. So abject it seemed. There was no need to resign. In fact, he could still accept the offer to make him a minister. Or he could refuse.

Obviously if he refused so personal an invitation, Mulroney would do nothing more to advance his career. And Dennison would always know of his close brush with public scandal.

He could just wait it out. Despite all the bravado, Mulroney might decide it was wiser to retire than face an electorate that so reviled him. Or he could say yes to Mulroney and see what happened.

And Marilyn? Beyond the negatives he'd already considered, saying yes to Mulroney meant years of social and political drudgery

for Marilyn, more self-abnegation. She couldn't hold a serious cura-
tor's job and be a cabinet minister's wife in Ottawa. She deserved
better. She deserved her turn.

Almost eight o'clock. He could still make the Americas Society
breakfast a few blocks up Park Avenue. But he had good reason not
to. He needed to be with Marilyn . . . to go to Ottawa . . . where
he would see the PM . . . who'd be expecting an answer.

And David suddenly realized, with a surge of lightheartedness,
that he didn't care what Brian Mulroney thought! Or Michael Dennison! Or External Affairs! The rush of understanding gave him an
intoxicating sense of freedom. He actually did not care!

All these years his mind had been like a branch terminal of a
government computer, the government's program patterning his
thoughts, the government's data dictating the content. He had sold
government policies, making himself believe, eager to move advan-
tageously on External's chessboard, without developing any other
aim in life.

The man from the National Gallery had reminded him how
little he'd thought about anything but policy. He had to get something else in his head. He'd spent his career analyzing the behavior
of nations, but never analyzing his own; never challenging the un-
seen and subversive hand that guided his behavior with Francesca.
He'd felt an urge to explain to her, but it was he who needed to
understand. From the Greeks to the Bible to Freud, all of Western
civilization urged man to examine his life, to know himself. If he
remained healthy, he might have twenty, even thirty years to live.

In the department, they considered him the best writer. Why
shouldn't he write for himself? Even if he quit now, his pension
would support them. But there was no need to quit right away. Let
Marilyn finish her degree. She had her heart set on it; it was her way
of surviving the trauma of Francesca. And if she found a job, they
could live near her work instead of his.

David tore up his letter to the PM. This time he didn't need to
make a rough draft. Putting the legal pad aside, he pulled out a

sheet of writing paper embossed in red with the arms of Canada, and picked up his pen.

> *Dear Prime Minister:*
> *I have thought very carefully about your generous offer*
> *and have decided to decline. After a long career in the*
> *foreign service, I do not think temperamentally I would be*
> *suited to a career in politics. I am grateful for the*
> *confidence you have expressed in me, but I am convinced*
> *this is the best decision for your government and for me.*

His thoughts went back to Francesca. Why had she done this? Obviously it was deliberate. It couldn't have been an accident. But why?

He could call Jean Luc and get her phone number. Better still, he could call Helsinki information himself.

David considered that for a moment. Why did he have to know? In fact, he didn't have to. Really . . . it was better that he did not know.

For twenty years, ROBERT MACNEIL has been the co-anchor of the award-winning PBS nightly newscast "The MacNeil/ Lehrer NewsHour." Born in Montreal, Mr. MacNeil began his journalism career with Reuters in London and subsequently worked for NBC News and the British Broadcasting Corporation. He is the author or co-author of five previous books, including, with Robert McCrum and William Cran, *The Story of English,* the companion volume to the PBS series of which Mr. MacNeil was host; and two volumes of memoirs, *The Right Place at the Right Time* and *Word-struck.* Mr. MacNeil fulfilled a lifelong ambition in 1992 with the publication of his first novel, *Burden of Desire.* With his retirement from "The MacNeil/Lehrer NewsHour" in October 1995, Mr. MacNeil plans to devote himself full-time to writing, especially fiction. He lives in New York City.